AN

TRIAL

An utterly gripping page-turner

FAITH MARTIN

writing as

MAXINE BARRY

Originally published as *River Deep*

JOFFE BOOKS

Revised edition published 2020
Joffe Books, London
www.joffebooks.com

First published in Great Britain 2009
as *River Deep*

ISBN 978-1-78931-666-7

CHAPTER ONE

Melisande Ray walked to the half-length mirror set on top of her dressing-table and reached for her hairbrush. It was barely seven o'clock in the morning, but already she could hear some of her early-rising guests beginning their morning ablutions.

She quickly ran the brush through her tangle of curling auburn hair. It was the rich colour of ripe chestnuts with the occasional natural tawny highlight, and it hung to the middle of her back. This wasn't always convenient, of course, but every time she thought about getting it cut, various members of her family and friends — mostly male, it had to be said — set off a chorus of disapproval. So, over the years, she'd had to learn various ways to keep it looking both neatly under control but still attractive. This morning she reached for a dark green velvet scrunchy and pulled her hair up in a high ponytail, letting small tendrils cling to her forehead and cheeks.

Then she slid on to the padded stool in front of the dresser and began to apply her make-up. With naturally high cheekbones and a good complexion, she only had to apply a mere hint of blusher and a single stroke of smoky green-grey eye shadow, which made the most of her large slate-grey eyes.

She selected and donned a pair of dangling jade earrings, and quickly stepped into a dark green elegant pencil skirt with a strategic split to enable her to walk unhampered. She teamed it with a lacy cream-coloured, high-necked blouse. The outfit was both businesslike and feminine, and showed off her slender curves to perfection — a combination that went down well with the Ray of Sunshine Hotel guests.

As the owner, she had a large suite of rooms in the converted attic, and when she left she walked lightly past the other doors, lest she disturb sleeping guests, then went quickly downstairs into the cool, pleasant lobby.

Here a grandfather clock ticked ponderously, and original tiny tiles in white, green and terracotta formed a pleasing pattern on the floor. She stopped to check the flower arrangement that was set to one side on the reception desk, but the blooms that she'd picked from the garden yesterday still looked flawless, and she decided to leave them until tomorrow. That was the good thing about not having to depend on shop-bought flowers, she mused happily. She got to choose exactly the combination she wanted, and could opt for flowers that lasted. This arrangement, given that it was mid-May, was a pastel mass of pinks, love-in-a-mist and moon daisies, within a spray of frothing green leaves.

Leaving the lobby, she went down a narrow corridor, clearly marked *STAFF ONLY*, and into the large, well-equipped kitchen.

Mary and Bridget Stokes looked up at her and smiled as she entered. Sisters, they shared the same dark hair and small button-brown eyes. Neither had married, and both lived in the village still, sharing a small stone cottage. Although neither of them had had any formal training, they were locally acknowledged as being the best cooks in five counties, and Melisande's father had been lucky, over twenty years ago, in snaring them for the Ray of Sunshine.

'Don't worry, we've already seen to the Bennetts,' Mary said to her cheerfully, referring to the couple in number 8. They'd been coming to the hotel regularly every spring and autumn for the rambling, and were notorious for rising well before six.

'Bless you,' Melisande said, sincerely.

'Oh, they're no bother,' Bridget said. 'They only ever want porridge and toast. And I'm always awake by five anyway, so I might as well be up and doing.'

Melisande looked around as a large, shambling man crossed in front of the window outside. Dressed in a frayed plaid shirt and dirty trousers, and sporting long grey hair and a white-whiskered chin, some might have mistaken him for a tramp. But Brian Gould had been the head gardener since before Melisande and her twin brother Melvin had been born. An intensely shy man, he had an almost miraculous way with vegetables and fruit, and was another of Gareth Ray's inspirations.

Melisande's late father, on inheriting the large shambling house that had been in his family for generations, had quickly seen its potential as a country house hotel, and had accepted the challenge with typical relish. Aged only twenty-two, he'd taken out a massive loan to refurbish and convert the residence, but he'd been both canny and far-sighted, and didn't spend wildly. He'd kept all of the house's original features in situ, preserving the old woodwork and even — where possible — the original flock-velvet wallpaper. Cornices and ornate light fittings and plasterwork had been lovingly cleaned and restored and fireplaces meticulously cleaned.

Forty years ago, when new and bold had been all the rage, he'd insisted on keeping all of the old brass rails and curtain rods, even converting the old wall gas lamps to tasteful electric lights. He'd raided the attics and made use of every item he could — and since his Victorian forebears had never thrown anything away, it was quite a haul. Dusty curtains were aired and ironed and hung up in the public-access areas, and the old-fashioned but beautiful tableware had been dispatched to the dining room.

Most of his contemporaries had called him mad, but Gareth had stuck to his plan, and was careful to advertise the

Ray of Sunshine Hotel as an authentic olde-worlde indulgence for those who liked their nostalgia to be coupled with elegant but traditional living. The brochures had proudly proclaimed that staying at the hotel was like stepping out of the modern hurly-burly of the present day and taking a stroll in gentler times.

And part of that experience, of course, was eating organically grown fruit and vegetables straight from an old-fashioned, almost Victorian-style kitchen garden. The man he'd chosen to oversee this enterprise, far from being an educated professional, was a painfully shy local lad who kept the best chain of allotments in the village, and was a perpetual winner at the local flower show.

Again, most of his friends had called it madness, but Brian Gould had not let him down. The result was that today, in an age when organically grown food had become so popular, the dining room at the Ray of Sunshine was perpetually booked solid.

'We thought we'd put Oxford herb soup on the menu again today,' Bridget said, crossing to the large, scrubbed oak kitchen table and opening the menu folder. 'It's always so popular at lunchtime. With Scottish morning rolls to go with it of course, and the parsley butter. That and the farmhouse pâté can do for the starters, yes?'

Melisande nodded at once. Although, as the owner, she was technically in charge of the menu choices, she deferred to the sisters as a matter of course. Their menus were never extensive, but were always delicious and innovative, and Bridget, she was sure, only kept her informed as a matter of courtesy.

'Then for the main courses, we thought a stuffed marrow dish with rice and wild mushrooms for the vegetarians, and then a choice of crayfish salad, venison, or chicken-and-ham pie. Brian says the watercress down by the weir is perfect. With walnuts and extra-virgin olive oil, it would make a good side dish.'

Again, Melisande nodded. As well as enjoying cultivated food picked fresh from the gardens, the Ray of Sunshine guests were also treated to wildly grown and locally gathered ingredients according to the season. The venison she assumed would come courtesy of Jack Regis, a wild-game specialist who lived in the nearby village of Aston. His father had been a notorious poacher in days gone by, and it was considered impolite by amused locals to enquire too closely where Jack came by his rabbits, pheasants and deer.

'It all sounds wonderful, as usual,' Melisande said. She went to the fridge and poured herself a glass of freshly squeezed orange juice. This she sipped carefully as she went through to the dining room. Here the girls were busy laying out the tables for the breakfast rush.

The Ray of Sunshine always employed locals from the village, Royston-on-Thames, where it stood in pride of place next to the river and opposite the small church. These were usually young men and women who were waiting to go to university, and sometimes more mature women with children in school and the need to earn some cash to pay off the mortgage. Melisande made a point of knowing all of their names. Now she called out a cheerful greeting to them as she went by, but she didn't stay to hover over them, knowing she could trust them to do their jobs properly.

Instead, she stepped out through the open French doors on to the patio outside and stood in the early-morning sunshine sipping her juice.

She'd been born in this house twenty-eight years ago, when it was already a thriving hotel. She had never known, or wanted, any other life. As a little girl, she'd solemnly helped out in the kitchen, served food, weeded the gardens with her mother, and dressed smartly to welcome and charm the guests. As an adult, she'd taken a degree in hotel management and for her father and herself there had never been any question that she would take over the Ray of Sunshine when he retired.

Luckily perhaps for both of them, her brother, Vin, had never had the slightest interest in the family business. Since a lot of people called Melisande by the diminutive Mel, and probably would have done the same for her brother, Melvin had always been called Vin simply to prevent confusion. As a youngster, his passion had always been photography, and nobody had been surprised when he'd made it his life's work by becoming a professional wildlife photographer.

Their mother, who'd died when they were only sixteen, had sometimes seemed rather anxious over the preordained path her husband and daughter took so much for granted, and would often speak smilingly of a husband and children. It made Gareth Ray laugh and tease, but Melisande had only sighed elaborately.

Somehow, men had always come a poor second to the Ray of Sunshine. It was her home and her career, her biggest challenge and greatest delight. Oh, there had been men, of course. At university, her beautiful Titian looks had attracted them like wasps around a jam pot. And there was still — and probably always would be — Rupert.

But none of them had ever been able to woo her away from the Ray.

She sometimes wondered, with a pang, what her mother would have said about things if she'd been alive today. For here she was with the big three-o looming on the horizon, and the sound of wedding bells was as elusive as ever. Sometimes, Melisande wondered why that thought never seemed to worry her, as it did most of her still-single friends. She was even beginning to wonder whether love was simply not for her. After all, nowadays lots of career women never bothered to get married and have children. It simply wasn't an issue.

But there was another side to her nature, too. A side that loved to read Austen and sigh over Mr Darcy. A side that smiled wistfully at Hollywood romantic comedies, where the heroine always got her man — even if in rather devious and outrageous ways. And that side sometimes looked back at her from her reflection in the mirror and gave a little tweak to her heart.

A pair of grey wagtails swooped past her, twittering excitedly as they headed for the river, and brought her sharply out of her bittersweet thoughts. She shrugged off her contemplation of the sorry state of her love life and breathed deeply, a slow smile gradually returning to her face.

This time of morning had always been her favourite. Before long, the guests would descend for their breakfast, and the dining room would be full of cheerful chatter and clinking cutlery. The waitresses would be rushed off their feet and the scent of toast and bacon would waft across the terrace. Then there would come a lull as most of the guests left for their morning's activities. Some would sightsee in the nearby towns of Henley-on-Thames or Windsor. Some of them might hire a day boat at nearby Hambleden Mill Marina and spend the day messing about on the water. Others might ramble across the glorious countryside, while some might simply stay at the hotel, walking around the extensive and beautiful grounds, and perhaps sunbathe by the river.

Finishing her juice, Melisande returned to the kitchen with her glass, then went through into her office. This was a small, somewhat dark room, but had lovely old diamond-paned leaded windows that overlooked a small part of the garden dedicated to roses. From her functional plain desk she took a set of keys and stepped back out into the hall.

There she noticed an American couple walking down the stairs, newcomers who had booked in yesterday. She smiled brightly. 'Mr Blomfeld, Mrs Blomfeld, how are you today? Fully recovered from the dreaded jetlag, I hope.'

Mrs Blomfeld, a large, well-maintained lady wearing newly bought country tweeds with a rather uncertain bravado, beamed right back at her. 'We certainly have. And I can't wait to get outside on the river. The Thames has so much history, so I'm always saying to Ollie. Right, Ollie?'

Mr Blomfeld rolled his eyes indulgently. 'I can vouch for that,' he agreed with a mock long-suffering sigh, and his wife nudged him ostentatiously in the ribs with her elbow. Melisande got the feeling it was a well-rehearsed act that the couple used to cover their basic shyness. 'I'll have to telephone and thank Mira and George for recommending this place. It's lovely, my dear, you must be so proud of it.'

Melisande smiled. 'I like it,' she said simply. 'Would that be Mira and George Roper you're talking about?' The Ropers from Minnesota had been coming to the hotel ever since the late seventies. George, a retired motor manufacturer, called his month-long stay at the hotel his rejuvenation therapy.

'Yes, they said to say hello.'

Melisande chatted with the friendly Americans for a while, then excused herself, leaving them to go on to the dining room in cheery anticipation of trying out the much-vaunted full English breakfast.

She went out through a discreet side door that led on to a paved pathway. This skirted the main gardens and took her directly across a vast area of well-mown lawn, and thence to steps set into the bank which led down to the river itself, and a small, newly built wooden jetty.

Here Melisande paused to look at the three brand spanking new narrowboats that were berthed there.

These represented her first new venture. It was all her own and she had mixed feelings of apprehension and proud excitement as she viewed them. Since her father's death five years ago, she'd carried on running the hotel strictly on his tried-and-true methods, only slowly adding her own improvements as she found her feet and gained confidence.

And the fact that these improvements had proved so successful surprised no one but herself. Thus finding herself with an excess of capital for the first time since inheriting the business, she'd cast about for a way of putting that money to good use. And after some thought, she'd decided that the one thing Gareth Ray had never fully exploited to its full potential was the hotel's site right on the riverside.

So, last winter, she'd had the jetty built, and with practically all of her spare capital she'd purchased three narrowboats. These had been mere shells at the time, and she'd hired her own choice of designer to fit them out. And the pleasure she'd taken in planning everything from their names and colour schemes, right down to the quality and nature of their fittings, had been immense.

When they'd arrived just two days ago, her excitement had reached fever pitch. Now she walked down the steps and on to the wooden pier. She gazed at them happily.

The *Dancing Grebe,* the *Patient Heron,* and the *Stillwater Swan* swayed barely perceptibly on the river's gentle current. Each boat had a depiction of their eponymous water bird painted on the forward panel of each side of the boat, and inside, a matching colour scheme.

As she went to the *Patient Heron,* she reached for her keys and carefully stepped on to the back deck. This boat was painted an overall soft blue-grey, with smart black and pale gold trim. When she opened the padlock on the double metal doors and went inside, a flood of light greeted her. Everywhere in the main salon, pale blond woodwork created a sharp contrast to the comfortable slate-grey leather seating. There were small porthole windows in the master bedroom, but elsewhere, large, gold-trimmed picture windows sparkled.

As she walked the length of her latest acquisition, she became very much aware that she was on the water; she had to look upwards through the windows, for instance, in order to see the towpath and jetty. And whenever she walked, there was always just the faintest, but pleasant sensation of shifting movement beneath her.

First she went into the galley and checked that the hot and cold running water was working properly, then she made sure that the gas oven and electrical kitchen gadgets were all as they should be. The cupboards beside the bathroom were full of freshly laundered bed linen of the finest quality and large, fluffy towels.

Although the purists in the boating world scorned modern boats with their electric toilets and power showers, Melisande had insisted on the most luxurious of everything for her small flotilla, knowing that her clientele would demand the best.

She was not, after all, going to lease out her boats to people who wanted to live permanently on the water, or even to those particularly interested in the history of the Thames or canal boating. What she offered was a luxury boating experience; a gentle four mph ride through beautiful countryside in a narrowboat that offered all the comforts of a convenient home away from home.

With all the paperwork and licences now settled, all she had to do was set up a website for her new Ray of Sunshine marina. Vin had promised to come by tomorrow to take flattering photographs of the boats, inside and out, and she was fairly confident that, even charging top rates, all three boats would soon be snapped up and booked for the whole of the season.

With a smile, she locked up the *Patient Heron* and went back to her hotel. Breakfast would now be under way, and the guests liked to see her strolling between the tables, checking that everything was satisfactory and that there were no problems.

But as she stepped into the lobby and heard the cheerful sounds of her guests, she had no idea that a human whirlwind was heading her way, intent on bringing tempestuous change to her well-ordered business life, and a passionate challenge to her untouched heart.

* * *

In the town of High Wycombe, Gisela Ashley walked slowly towards the courthouse, her footsteps dragging. It had started to drizzle, and the sudden damp coolness took many people by surprise. But the change in weather suited her mood, and she sighed heavily as she crossed the street and looked up at the building.

She'd been dreading this day for months now, but at least soon it would all be over.

Or so she hoped.

She straightened her shoulders and climbed the stone steps. One old man stopped to watch her with interest. Such a pretty little thing, he thought, but she looked as though she had the weight of the world on her shoulders. Then he shrugged and walked on.

Inside, Gisela headed straight for the ladies, where she used the hand-dryer to tease out the moisture from her hair. Like most people, she hadn't brought an umbrella with her when she stepped out into the wide world this Thursday morning.

She went over to the wall of mirrors above the washbasins, reached into her bag and pulled out a small hairbrush.

She had a short, neatly geometrical cut of blonde hair so pale that it was almost white. As she looked at her reflection she had to acknowledge wryly that she had a face to match! Tension had made her look like a ghost. With a sigh, she applied a little more blusher, then stood back, her heart beginning to pound.

At only five feet two inches tall, she was wearing her usual elegant black high heels. And, for the ordeal she faced today, she had donned a severe, almost mannish two-piece trouser suit in charcoal grey, with just the barest hint of a blue stripe that matched perfectly her large, pale blue eyes. With this, she wore a simple white blouse underneath the jacket, and a Wedgwood blue-and-white cameo brooch. She wore no other jewellery, and hoped she looked suitably business-like. Although, with her heart-shaped pretty face, coupled with her small stature, she knew that most people tended to see her as a cute little doll.

She could only hope that the jury would take her seriously.

At the thought of testifying, her heart rate thumped sickeningly in her breast. Her hands shook just a little as she gave the jacket a last-minute, unnecessary tug downwards, then she retrieved her bag and headed back out into the hall.

There she saw Alice Smythe, the prosecutor's assistant, looking around and glancing at her watch. She was, Gisela knew, looking for her. As Alice spotted her and gave a relieved smile, Gisela took a deep, calming breath. A few more hours and it'll all be over, she told herself, yet again.

It was something she'd been telling herself all last night, when she'd tossed and turned restlessly, trying not to make too much noise and disturb Andrea asleep in the next room. She wasn't altogether sure that she'd succeeded, however, for this morning her flatmate had given her a wry look the moment she'd emerged for her usual breakfast of grapefruit and toast.

'Hello, what awful weather,' Alice said briskly. She was a tall, lean, grey-haired woman who'd worked in the law for many years, and was probably used to dealing with nervous witnesses. 'I don't think you'll be kept waiting for long, you'll be relieved to hear,' and she led the way up the stairs to court 2, where the case was being heard.

Gisela managed a weak smile, but supposed Alice was right. The worst part of any ordeal was usually waiting for it to start, wasn't it? But as she sat on the hard wooden bench in the corridor, joined by Alice, she wasn't so sure.

'The defence will try to shake you on your identification, as we discussed yesterday. Simply take your time, don't rush into any answers, and think carefully before you speak. Don't let the defence lawyers rattle you. Remember, the jury will be on your side, and the judge won't let the defence actually eat you.'

Gisela knew that was supposed to be a joke, and managed another weak smile. But her hands were still shaking, and they felt cold in her lap. Silently, Alice Smythe reached out and briefly clasped one hand. 'I have to go now,' she said gently. 'But I'll be in court the whole time. If you get panicky, just look for me, and I'll give you a wink. I've got a magic wink, so I've been told. It has healing properties.'

'I'll be fine,' Gisela said firmly. But not altogether truthfully.

Alice nodded and left her. As she pushed open the door to the courtroom she heard a voice demanding that 'all rise for Her Honour Judge Cordover'.

So it's a female judge, Gisela thought with some surprise, and then instantly felt ashamed of herself for her unexpected sexism. But the fact that it was a woman in charge of the proceedings gave her spirits a distinct lift, and some of her dread left her.

She looked up as a young man took a seat opposite her and reached nervously for a magazine. A moment later, a middle-aged woman with a teenage daughter came and sat next to him, and Gisela wondered what their stories were. Of course, nobody spoke. The quiet but ponderous weight of the building seemed to quash any desire for light conversation.

Gisela tried to distract herself by wondering what the people at the office would be doing now. She'd worked as a secretary in a large private medical clinic in the centre of town for nearly five years now. Converted from a Victorian mansion, the Webster Clinic catered mostly to older people, and Gisela was grateful to her boss for letting her take her three weeks' holiday all at once, and at short notice.

She'd known the date of the court case for some time in advance of course, and the thought of returning to work after appearing in court hadn't been something she had looked forward to. But it was typical of her employers to be so understanding.

She glanced at her watch and saw that it was nearly ten. That would mean that Jenny and Vera, the two receptionists, would be making coffee, while the junior consultants—

'Calling Miss Gisela Ashley. Miss Gisela Ashley please!' A man calling from the open doorway of the court let his eyes roam over those waiting outside.

Gisela, her heart in her throat, got to her feet and walked towards him. It was a good thing that she was a veteran of high heels, for her knees were distinctly shaking as she passed him and entered into the courtroom.

The room was surprisingly light and modern. Like many people who got their ideas of courtrooms from watching dramas on the television, she had expected a lot of dark wood and a raised area for the judge and defendant. But everything was on ground level, and there wasn't a wooden panel in sight. Large windows let the light pour in, and Gisela noticed that the drizzle had stopped and the sun was trying to come out.

Lines of benches faced the judge, who watched her approach, and she was aware of Alice Smythe and her senior, Keith Wheeler, sitting to her right as she passed. She was careful not to look to her left, where she assumed the defendant would be sitting.

An usher opened a small wooden wicket-fence type gate for her walk to a chair placed to the judge's right, then followed her through to swear her in.

Again, she'd expected to have to recite the famous, rather ominous 'I swear by Almighty God' speech, but no; a modern and painless oath was all that was needed. As she repeated the words, she heard her voice, sounding calm and surprisingly confident, fill the silent room.

She briefly glanced across at the jury and saw only a line of strangers' faces. Middle-aged men and women, a younger woman wearing a headscarf, and a young man who could only be a student. Two older people were almost certainly pensioners. Just normal, everyday people you could pass in the street and not even think about.

Again, Gisela felt some of the tension leave her.

Then Keith Wheeler rose and approached her chair. He was wearing a short black gown and a traditional wig, and she felt herself tense.

'You are Miss Gisela Ashley?' he asked affably.

As he'd promised yesterday, in their final briefing together, the prosecutor began with simple questions, and she answered easily.

'Yes.'

'You work as a secretary for a doctor's practice here in town, I believe?'

'Yes.'

'Can you tell the jury what happened on the morning of the eighth of December last year?'

And there it was. For the last few months, ever since that shocking morning on a dark December day, her life seemed to have been leading up to this moment.

She took a slow breath and nodded. 'Yes. I was going to work, as usual.' She was careful to keep her eyes focused on Keith, as he'd told her to do. He was a short, rounded man, with bright twinkling eyes and a surprisingly bushy beard.

'I always walk to work, seeing that I share a flat only five minutes away from the office. Normally I keep to the main roads, but that morning it was pouring with rain, so I took the shortcut through the back alley that runs past the row of shops on Cardour Street.'

Out of the corner of her eye she saw some of the jury members nod, obviously recognizing the spot she meant. But for the benefit of those who weren't so conversant with the byways of High Wycombe, Keith stopped her there and went to a map, set up on an easel.

She listened, with a growing sense of calm, as the barrister went through the legalese needed to submit the map into evidence, and listened as he used a ruler to show her route that morning to the jury.

'Please, go on,' he said, coming back to her and smiling reassuringly.

'Well, I was about halfway down the alley when I heard a door crashing open. It really made a banging noise and made me jump. I looked behind me to where the sound had come from, and I saw three men coming out of a back door. They were all dressed in dark blue overalls — the kind you often see garage mechanics wearing. And they all had black hoods on. The knitted kind, with eye-holes. Ski masks, I think they're called.'

For a moment she was back in time, reliving that heart-stopping moment. She'd never been so scared or shocked in her life. She simply stood rooted to the spot, too scared to move but dreading the moment when one of the men spotted her.

But they never did notice her. Possibly because of the rain, or maybe because her small stature and grey raincoat helped her blend into the background.

This reassuring reminder brought her back to the courtroom, and the man standing in front of her, waiting for her to continue, and she gave herself a sharp reminder to keep her mind on the job at hand.

'The door had hit the wall and bounced back, and I was just in time to see the last man push it open again,' she continued, hoping that nobody had noticed her momentary lapse of concentration.

Keith Wheeler nodded and interrupted smoothly, 'And what time would you say this was?'

'Well, I start work at nine, so it must have been about half past eight or maybe twenty-five to nine.'

Keith Wheeler smiled and glanced at the jury. 'You like to be at the office in plenty of time, I see,' he commented, and Gisela understood at once that he was highlighting to them what a conscientious worker she was. She supposed it was to reinforce her image as a trustworthy witness.

'Yes. Sometimes patients are early. They're anxious about appointments, and either myself or the receptionist makes them a cup of tea and has a chat.'

It was true enough but, even as she said it, she heard the defence barrister give an elaborate sigh.

She shot a quick look at Keith Wheeler. Had she just made a mistake of some kind? But the rotund barrister gave an almost imperceptible smile and a shake of his head.

'So, what happened then?' he prompted.

'Well, I heard an engine revving hard, and I saw a van backing up fast into the alley. I was surprised — the alley is really narrow, and there's a sharp dogleg turn about halfway down, and traffic never goes down there — even the smallest of cars would get stuck. But the van stopped just before it reached the men, and its back door swung open.'

Wheeler nodded. 'Can you describe the van?'

Gisela smiled wryly. 'I'm sorry. I suppose it sounds a bit girly, but I'm not really sure. It was white, and had two back doors that opened out. They each had a window in the top. And the whole body of the van went in straight lines to the cab. It wasn't like a postman's van, or something that looked like a car in the front.' She gave a small shrug, but that was honestly the best that she could do.

'A transit van, in fact?' Wheeler said, and before she could speak, the defence barrister was on his feet.

He was an older man, with silver hair showing at the sides of his wig, and a lean, rather imperious-looking face. His voice sounded well educated and slightly bored. His name, Keith Wheeler had already informed her, was Malcolm Betteridge.

'Objection, your honour. Leading the witness.'

'Sustained,' the judge agreed. 'Your witness has already stated she is no expert on vans, Mr Wheeler,' she said calmly.

Keith Wheeler, not looking a bit put out, bowed his head briefly in apology and turned back to Gisela.

'So it was a big white van. The rear doors opened. Was it just one of the doors, or both?'

'Both,' Gisela said, after pausing just a moment. 'Yes, I'm sure it was both, because of what happened next.'

'Which was?'

She was aware that the members of the jury were hanging on her every word now, and she swallowed hard, feeling her mouth go dry. She glanced at the jug of water and empty glass on the ledge in front of the little alcove where she was sitting, but merely licked her lips instead. She didn't trust herself to pour a glass without spilling any.

'One of the men climbed into the back of the van, and the next one followed. But the third man, waiting for them to go in, pulled off his mask and shoved it into one of his pockets.'

'But he would have had his back to you, yes?' Wheeler said smoothly. They'd been through all of this before, of course, and the barrister had worked out as carefully and thoroughly as he could all the ways to spike the defence's guns even before they had a chance to cross-examine her. 'You said you had to turn around to see where the noise had come from?'

'Yes. I'd gone past the door to the jewellery shop by then.'

'The jewellery shop?' Wheeler enquired. 'Did you know that was the door to the jewellery shop at the time?'

Gisela felt herself blush. She shook her head in apology. 'Sorry. No, I didn't know that until afterwards. When the police came and the newspapers printed the story. I'm terribly sorry. To me the alleyway was just a row of doors.'

'That's all right,' Wheeler said, spreading his hands in a comforting gesture. 'It's just that we have to be careful and get everything right when it comes to a court of law. So, you'd gone past the door from where the three masked men had emerged.'

'Yes.'

'So the men climbing into the back of the white van had their backs to you?'

'Yes.'

'So when the third man took off his mask, what exactly did you see?'

'At first, just the back of his head,' Gisela said honestly. 'He was about five feet ten, and had a full head of just slightly curly dark brown hair.'

'But you were later able to give the police a full description,' Wheeler said, letting his voice take on just a tinge of puzzlement. It was all theatre of course, Gisela realized, with the barrister playing to the jury, because he already knew the answer. But she was happy to follow his lead.

'That's because the left-hand side door of the van began to swing back, and I saw the man's face in the reflection of the window.'

'Ah, I see. And you saw him clearly?'

'Oh yes.'

'What happened then?'

'The man climbed in, and even before he'd shut the door behind him, the van was pulling away.'

'Did he see you?'

'I don't think so. I was so scared that the van was going to come to a screeching stop, and I was getting ready to run if any of the men jumped out to chase me, but the van just pulled out on to the main road and was gone. It only seemed to take a second or two.'

'Did you see the number plate?'

Again Gisela felt herself blush. 'No. I'm sorry, I felt such a fool. Especially later, when the police asked me that. But I just didn't think. It all happened so fast. I couldn't really believe what I was seeing. I mean, it was just a normal Tuesday morning. You read about robberies and things, but you never think you're going to see it actually happening. And not in High Wycombe, somehow.' Gisela glanced briefly at the jury, but saw only nodding, understanding faces.

'All right, Miss Ashley. What did you do next?'

'Well, I wasn't sure for a minute what I should do,' Gisela said, her voice now unknowingly echoing the helplessness and shock that she'd felt back then. 'I didn't really want to stay in the alley, in case those men had seen me and came back for me. So I walked back towards the main road and carefully looked out. But the van was gone. Then I realized I should be calling the police, and I used my mobile phone. The dispatcher told me to stay where I was, and took my name, and then the police came.'

Wheeler nodded encouragingly. There followed a detailed question and answer session between them, where Gisela went over her police interview with Inspector Matthew Greenslade, the senior investigating officer.

At last Wheeler, with one eye on the clock, said calmly, 'So, after you'd finished with the police sketch artist, the police showed you a folder of photographs, is this correct?'

'Yes.'

'And these photographs were all of men, with dark hair, between the ages of twenty to fifty?'

'I think so. Yes.'

'And did you recognize the man you saw in the alley that morning in these photographs?'

'Yes I did.'

'Did you point him out to Inspector Greenslade?'

'Yes I did.'

'And did he ask you to take part in a police identification parade?'

'Yes.'

'And did you pick out a man from that parade as being the man you saw in the alley?'

'Yes.'

'And can you see that man in court today?' Gisela swallowed hard.

'Yes. He's sitting there.' And she pointed to the man sitting beside Malcolm Betteridge.

'Let the record show the witness has indicated Mr Robert Pride, the defendant,' Keith Wheeler said portentously.

After that, there were just a few more questions, then Keith Wheeler returned to his seat. 'The prosecution has no more questions for this witness, Your Honour.'

The judge nodded, and glanced across to her left. 'Your witness, Mr Betteridge.'

Gisela felt herself quail as the imperious-faced Malcolm Betteridge got to his feet, and she shot a quick look towards Alice Smythe, who winked at her supportively.

And suddenly, Gisela felt the last residue of her fear slip away, as she knew it was going to be all right.

Alice really did have a magic wink after all.

* * *

And that was it, really,' Gisela said, seven hours later, as Andrea Gormley sneezed over her pasta. 'The defence lawyer took me through it all over again, and tried to trip me up. He asked me, seeing as how it had been raining at the time and the light was dim, and presumably the rain was running down the window of the van, how I could possibly be sure of my identification.'

She paused to wrap a few strings of spaghetti around her fork while Andrea sprinkled some more Parmesan cheese over her own dish.

'What did you say?' Andrea asked, her brown eyes wide with awe.

Gisela shrugged. 'There was not a lot I could say. I simply said I saw his face clearly and was able to recognize it later.' She waved her fork in the air and shrugged. 'After a while, when he kept on trying to get me to make mistakes and trip me up, Keith Wheeler began to object more and more, and suddenly Betteridge seemed to realize he was alienating the jury or something, and that was it. I was dismissed.'

Andrea grinned. 'I'll bet you were relieved.'

'You can say that again!' Gisela said wryly. 'I shot out of the courtroom like a cork from a bottle.'

As she spoke, her face darkened, and Andrea, always sensitive to mood, looked up sharply. 'What?'

Gisela shrugged. 'Nothing.'

'Come on, what?' Andrea asked, then began to cough. 'Damn, I've had a runny nose all day. I hope I haven't caught the dreaded lurgy.'

'Is that a medical term?' Gisela teased, knowing her friend was a nursing student, but Andrea wasn't to be sidetracked.

'No, come on, what's wrong? Did something else happen?'

'No. Well, it was nothing really,' Gisela said hesitantly. But her appetite had suddenly disappeared, and she pushed her half-full plate away. 'It's just that as I was going down the steps outside, this woman came up to me and, well, threatened me.'

Andrea's eyes widened. 'No!' she hissed, scandalized. 'Who was she?'

'Mrs Pride, I think. The mother of the man I identified.'

'I was reading in the papers about the Pride family,' Andrea said darkly. 'They're no-goods from way back. Their father died in Wormwood Scrubs, and I think most of the uncles and sons and what have you are doing time. Hardly an apt name for them is it, the Prides?'

Gisela shrugged. 'Oh well, I dare say it didn't really mean anything. She was probably just upset and letting off steam.'

'What did she say, Gisela?' Andrea asked soberly, then gave an almighty sneeze. 'Damn.'

Laughing, Gisela reached across to the window ledge where a box of tissues resided. 'Here, take the box,' she said, gathering her plate and some of the other things together. 'I think you're going to need it.'

She'd shared the small two-bed flat with Andrea for nearly three years now, and as she washed up and made a pot of tea, she wondered, sadly, whether her friend would stay on in the flat after she got her final degree.

An hour later they were settled down in front of the television, but neither of them was really watching the soap that was on.

'So, you've got three weeks off now, you lucky thing. Are you going away somewhere?' Andrea asked.

'I'm not sure. Alice Smythe wants me to stay around up to the weekend, just in case I have to go back in court. But she thinks it'll be all right after that, so long as I don't leave the country and can be reached on my mobile. That way I can always get back in case I'm needed. But I haven't booked anywhere yet.'

'Google!' Andrea shouted with glee, and reached for her laptop. Gisela watched her and laughed.

'I swear you're addicted to that thing like some people are to cigarettes.'

'Don't you just know it,' Andrea agreed. 'Right, holidays.' Her nimble fingers flew over the keys. 'Now, not abroad, you said. Hmm, it's still early in the season so the prices are low, that's one advantage. What do you feel like? The English Riviera? Or are you a lakes and mountains kind of girl?'

Gisela shrugged, looking without much enthusiasm at what was on offer. 'I'm not really sure,' she said weakly. 'The thought of mixing with a bunch of strangers doesn't really appeal.'

'Oh come on, after all you've been through you need a break,' Andrea admonished. 'You look pale and washed-out, and I know you haven't been sleeping well recently. You know I don't have any exams for the next two weeks. If you like, I could come with you,' she added craftily.

Gisela laughed. 'Oh yes. Going to go halves, are you?' she asked, knowing that her permanently poverty-stricken flatmate was suggesting no such thing. But she didn't mind. She knew Andrea was only offering to go with her at all because she suspected that Gisela would end up moping around the flat for all of her annual holiday leave if she didn't.

'I wish! Come on, there's a whole world out there. Well, the UK at any rate. You must fancy something?'

Gisela rolled her eyes, but joined Andrea in looking at what was on offer as it scrolled across the screen.

Suddenly, something leapt out at her. 'Wait, go back to that other website.'

'The rock-climbing in Wales!' Andrea squeaked.

'No, you muffin. The one with the beautiful boats.'

'I didn't know you sailed.'

'I don't!' Gisela laughed. 'I mean the narrowboats. What was it? River Holidays, wasn't it?'

Andrea quickly found the website, and the two women read avidly. 'Hmm, three weeks on the Thames. Or do you want the canals?'

'Let's start with the Thames. It's such an iconic river, and yet I don't think I've ever been on it,' Gisela replied.

'Me neither, come to think of it,' Andrea agreed. 'A bit tame, though, isn't it? I mean a narrowboat. Don't they go ever so slow?'

'Actually, a slower pace of life is just what I could do with right now,' Gisela said with feeling. 'And isn't there supposed to be something really soothing about messing about on the river?'

Andrea grinned. 'Girl, you've convinced me. Besides, there are bound to be some hunky lock-keeper types and athletic rowers and whatnot on the river, right?'

Gisela rolled her eyes, but within the hour the two girls had decided on their choice. It was a small company with only three narrowboats for hire, but the photographs of both the exterior and interior of the boats made their mouths water.

'No slumming it for us,' Andrea said, as they read out all the various mod cons on offer, then sneezed mightily.

Gisela agreed. But she blanched a little at the price. The boats could each sleep six, and if six of them had been going, each paying their own share, it wouldn't have been so expensive.

But on the other hand, it *had* been over three years since she'd taken a proper holiday, and she'd been industriously saving her pennies for a rainy day.

And if her situation now didn't qualify as being a rainy day, she didn't know what did.

'OK, Andrea, go for it,' she agreed impulsively.

And ten minutes later, with her bank account looking much the worse for wear, Gisela Ashley became the proud owner — for the next three weeks at least — of a beautiful boat called the *Stillwater Swan*.

And Old Father Thames beckoned!

CHAPTER TWO

Keefe Ashleigh strolled through the park, breathing in the cool dawn air. At just gone five o'clock in the morning he had the usually crowded green space to himself. Only a lone, hardy jogger at the other side of the park caught his eye. It was the movement, of course, and the colour of his jogging suit.

Old habits died hard.

The grass was wet with dew, but he was wearing his old army boots, another habit he was trying to wean himself from, now that he was no longer enlisted. But the boots were waterproof and comfortable, and supported his heels, ankles and instep to perfection. If he should ever need to run for his life, he knew he could do so with confidence.

Not that he foresaw that particular possibility while walking in a small market town in deepest rural England.

Overhead, the newly arrived swallows were busy darting about, gathering mud from the riverbank and taking it back to their nesting spots under the eaves of the older buildings in Ledgefield.

Keefe, at just over six feet tall, was a wiry, energy-packed man who could lope along for hours without needing much rest. In the deserts of the Middle East that trait had once proved useful. Now he felt restless and edgy. He decided, after his morning walk, to go to the gym and work out for an hour or so. His doctors had told him to rest and recuperate, but had agreed that healthy exercise, taken in moderation, was more than acceptable.

A good thing too, or Keefe thought he would go mad, cooped up in his rented flat.

The thought of the flat made him sigh. When he'd been given his honourable discharge and had finally emerged from hospital, he'd come back to the town of his birth, simply because he couldn't think of anywhere else to go. But both his parents were now dead, he had no other family in the area, and the six-month lease that he'd taken on a flat was due for renewal shortly. This meant that he needed to make some hard decisions on his future, and soon.

Perhaps it was just as well, since it would force him from the lethargy that plagued him.

He'd joined the army straight after college, and had trained originally in the Engineering Corps. For ten years, he'd helped the army build roads in the face of rebel opposition and construct bridges over wide brown rivers that regularly flooded (and more often than not were filled with things that wanted to eat him) and which made working conditions so horrendous.

Then, when he was twenty-eight, he'd been spotted and recruited by an intelligence officer, who'd decided that he could put his brains and hard-won wiry brawn to other, far more covert uses. And so for the next nine years he'd worked in the shadowy, dangerous area of special ops. Sometimes with the SAS, sometimes with the navy, and sometimes, chillingly, all alone. He'd long since added other skills to his engineering prowess along the way, of course; he was now an expert in communications, and although he'd taken no university degrees in the subject, was knowledgeable on both tactics and logistics. But a small antipersonnel landmine and a very near miss had put an end to all of that.

But the experiences of his past life, he knew, had left him in an ideal position to start up his own business, and many ex-soldiers had gone down that route — usually creating companies that specialized in security. This could range from something as simple as providing well-trained bodyguards to celebrities and people who suspected they needed looking after, to companies that advised banks or other industries — mainly airlines and airports — on their security systems.

Keefe already knew of several men, both ex-officers and rank and file, who would be ready and willing to come and work for him. And since Gretchen had died so devastatingly young, and after only two years of marriage when they'd both been only twenty-three, he'd saved all his pennies and could probably persuade any number of banks to set him up with a business loan.

And, with forty looming on the near horizon, and with his life in the army well and truly over, now was the time to stop drifting and make some sweeping changes.

His scars were mainly healed, and he now walked without a limp; he fully expected his next check-up to be his last. There was nothing to stop him from leaving this small town and setting up anywhere in the UK — or the world, come to that. He could head for Canada or New Zealand, places he'd often wanted to see but had never visited.

But that was probably not practical. If he wanted to start a business, his contacts were mainly UK based. So London, or maybe Edinburgh, made more sense.

Keefe ran a hand through his short brown hair and sighed. His crew cut had now well and truly grown out, but he knew that tomorrow would probably see him going to the barber's for a trim, and he smiled wryly at himself.

He passed through the entrance to the park and loped into an easy jog across the road, totally free of pain. And for the six months that he'd spent in a military hospital, enduring four major operations, that goal alone had seemed an impossible dream.

He walked along the empty streets and turned into the uninspiring block containing his flat. Unlocking the door to the minimalist beige interior, he felt a vague sense of depression waft over him, and knew he had made a decision: he would definitely not renew the lease.

In fact, before he knuckled under and started to make decisions that would affect the rest of his life, he felt that an immediate change of scene was on the agenda. How long was it since he'd had a holiday? He literally couldn't remember.

He walked to the kitchen and put on the kettle, making himself a mug of tea and taking it to a small Formica-topped table. There he turned on his laptop and set a search engine in pursuit of something that took his fancy. Something active, but not too strenuous. He'd done his share of abseiling and white-water kayaking in the army. Nor did he want to test his newly healed body by climbing mountains or bike riding in the desert. On the other hand, he didn't want to sit on a beach in some sunshine spot full of other ex-pats and watch his skin turn brown either. It would drive him insane.

So he concentrated on UK holidays, and, ever practical, decided to kill two birds with one stone.

If he went into business, he'd have to find digs near the capital, within easy commuting distance but far enough away not to drag him into the rat race. Which meant the Home Counties. Not that there were many holiday opportunities listed for this area, the nearest being the coastal regions of Essex and Kent. Then his eye caught the name of the River Thames, and he scrolled down to it, his attention caught by an attractive picture of narrowboats.

Thoughtfully, he began to read. One company had three boats for hire, all modern and luxurious. That didn't really interest him so much as the location of the marina — a small village called Royston-on-Thames, more or less halfway between Windsor and Oxford. Prime commuter country. And what better way to view the surrounding area and check out the real estate on offer than from the water? And if he could find a small pad that would suit his purposes on or near the river, he could also use the water as a training ground for his company's new recruits.

And a narrowboat holiday wasn't exactly an activity holiday, but it would keep him on his toes just enough to be interesting — negotiating the locks and steering the boat, and mooring up at night. It would also be a good test of his ingenuity in finding a way to get a boat, single-handed, under a drawbridge that would ideally need a second crew member. Such a holiday also brought with it the tempting lure of peace and quiet. Just mucking about on the water and taking the break at his own pace, well away from his memories of hospital wards and explosions in a faraway land.

He nodded, made a note of the company name — Ray of Sunshine Marina — and reached for the telephone.

* * *

In Melisande Ray's office, Gina Dix turned away from the computer screen at her desk pushed up against the far wall and reached for the phone.

Gina was nineteen, and fresh from secretarial college that month. Living in Royston, she'd expected to have to go to either Henley or even Maidenhead to earn herself a living, and had been surprised but delighted to see a small advert in the local paper for a secretarial post at the hotel.

Like most locals, Gina knew that Melisande Ray, like her father before her, tried to give jobs to villagers first, so when she'd applied for the job and gone for an interview, she'd done her best to show herself in a good light. Nevertheless, she'd been woefully aware that she had no past work experience, and had been over the moon when Melisande had offered her the position.

She'd been working at the job for only a few weeks, and was in constant fear of making a mistake, which, so far, had not happened. It wasn't that she was particularly afraid that Mel would be horrible to her if she did slip up, so much as the fact that she dreaded letting her down. She knew the hotel owner had been generous in giving her a chance at the job, and was desperate to do it well. So her voice, as she answered the phone, was as cheerful as any real ray of sunshine could be.

'Hello, Ray of Sunshine Hotel and Marina.' It was exciting to be able to add that last bit of the greeting, and she knew how hard Mel had worked in setting up the new enterprise.

'Hello, I'm calling about the narrowboats advertised on the Internet,' a masculine voice spoke into her ear.

'Just a moment please,' Gina said, tapping on the keyboard and pulling up the booking system. A quick glance showed her what she already knew — that all the boats were booked up for the next month. But perhaps the customer wanted to book for later in the year.

'Yes, sir? Do you have a preference for any particular boat?' she asked, since all three boats, although of the same length and standard, had vastly different interiors.

'No. My name's Ashleigh.'

Gina nodded into the phone, and typed A-S-H-L-E-Y into the computer, surprised when the name suddenly jumped up at her as being already there.

'I'd like to book a boat for three weeks, as soon as possible,' Keefe said, glancing out of his flat window and feeling the apathy that had been his constant companion for so long now slowly beginning to lift.

Gina frowned. She'd had her naturally black hair given a bright red fringe and highlights. Underneath this colourful edge her dark brows furrowed. Then it cleared as understanding dawned.

According to her computer, the *Stillwater Swan* had been booked by a Ms Gisela Ashley plus one for three weeks starting tomorrow. She remembered now, it had all been done over the Internet. Obviously the lovely-named Gisela must be this man's wife, she thought with a grin. Talk about lack of communication in a marriage! She saw it all the time with her own mum and dad. More often than not they'd both come in of an evening with an armload of shopping, each thinking it had been their turn.

'Yes, sir, that's been arranged,' Gina said helpfully, trying not to sound either amused or chiding. 'You're booked on to the *Stillwater Swan*. You can come and board her anytime tomorrow after ten in the morning. There's a free one-hour orientation and training session to help familiarize you with the boat's navigation and so forth.'

'That's fine,' Keefe said, slightly surprised at the ease of it all. He'd half expected that all the boats would have been booked for months to come.

'All right, sir. Do you need directions to the village?'

Keefe, who'd negotiated war zones with only a compass and the stars, grinned wolfishly.

'No thanks, I have satnav,' he said, somewhat facetiously. The young-sounding girl on the other end gave a sunny farewell, and he hung up.

It was only as he was replacing the receiver that he realized that she hadn't pestered him for his payment details. He frowned for a moment, then shrugged.

It hardly mattered. He could pay for it when he arrived.

* * *

Wendell James pulled his silver-grey Porsche into the small parking lot and cut off the throaty engine. For a moment he sat behind the leather steering wheel, tapping it gently with one forefinger, before giving a mental shrug and climbing lithely out of the seat.

At nearly six feet two inches tall, he managed this with an easy grace that would have spoken volumes for his leg, thigh and midriff muscle tone, if anybody had been watching him.

But nobody had.

At just gone ten-thirty in the morning, the hotel had a quiet, almost deserted air to it that was familiar to him after so many years in the leisure industry. James Leisure owned nearly twenty hotels, and Wendell, who had in his time overseen them all, knew all about mid-morning lulls.

He retrieved a single case from the car and walked across the pale gravel, glancing around as he did so. The place hadn't changed much since the last and only other time he'd seen it.

Dark brows furrowed over his piercing blue eyes, and he instantly pushed the memory away. It had been a long time ago, when Gareth Ray had still been alive, and the memory was not pleasant. Far from it.

He walked through a freshly painted white gate into the front garden area and looked around appreciatively. The lawns were impeccably mowed, the borders frothing with colour and not a weed in sight. Tasteful white wrought-iron garden furniture was scattered about and totally empty of people, but in the evening, or perhaps for afternoon tea, he could imagine the guests out here, enjoying the fragrance of the roses and sitting under the honeysuckle- and wisteria-clad pergolas.

As he walked up to the front door, recessed in an arched alcove, he cast a quick glance over the facade. Made of local stone, with wide sash windows and host to a now green vine that no doubt turned spectacular shades of red, orange and yellow in the autumn, he had to admit that the Ray of Sunshine put on an attractive, welcoming front.

He walked through the open doors into a traditional, pleasantly cool hall. A large grandfather clock even ticked ponderously in one corner, and the reception desk was made of old, well-darkened timber. He could almost hear the American tourists exclaiming over it, this being their first impression of the interior. Landscapes, nearly all depicting the River Thames, hung on the walls — most of them modern, he guessed, taking a closer look, but all were in traditional deep gilt frames that gave them the impression of age and cosy antiquity.

Clever, he thought. If they ever walked — and sometimes one or two were bound to — they could be easily and inexpensively replaced. Then he managed to find the evidence of discreet wiring, and realized that the security system here was well disguised and unobtrusive.

In his time Wendell had known hotel guests leave with rather more than just soap and bathrobes. In one of his hotels in Torquay, for instance, one guest had tried to leave with a wide-screen HD television by lowering it out of his window into the car park, where his wife was waiting with the car boot open. Luckily, his security manager had been wise to it, spotting them on the car park's CCTV.

As he approached the desk, he saw that it was unmanned. He shook his head, giving a mental tut-tut. One black mark against the management. Although, to be fair, he doubted that the manager would be expecting visitors at this time of the day. It was hours before his official check-in time.

He put his bag down and glanced around. He knew, vaguely, that Gareth Ray had had a son, although he'd never known his name. Had he taken over? And if he had, would he be amenable to selling the place?

The idea of acquiring the Ray of Sunshine was an idle one, but one that he'd be sure to explore during his stay. In reality though, he was sure that this hotel would end up being his biggest rival, and as such, he wanted to thoroughly check it out before he bought the plot of land about a mile upstream. Or was it downstream?

He knew that all trains went 'up' to London (even if, somewhat confusingly, they were coming down from the north), but did that hold true of the river? Seeing as the mighty Thames was flowing downstream towards London and the sea, surely the site of his newest James Imperial Hotel was downstream of here? He'd have to ask a local. It wouldn't do to make a mistake and ruffle feathers!

He was about to ping the old-fashioned brass bell on the reception desk when he heard a familiar whirring sound. It was muffled and for a moment he couldn't place it, then a swinging door that led to a corridor came open, and the noise of a floor-polishing machine filled the air.

He turned to watch, his eyes becoming softer as they eyed the back of the person pulling the machine — a decidedly feminine back. She was tall, perhaps five feet nine or so, and was wearing a navy-blue, well-cut dress that looked somewhat incongruous with a pinafore's strings tied across the waist of it.

As the woman pulled the polishing machine free of the door and began to swing it around, he saw that she had a mane of auburn hair, currently protected under an old-fashioned headscarf, patterned with autumn leaves on a pale blue background.

She was watching the five independently twirling heads going round in front of her, buffing up the small tiles that made up the hall floor. Suddenly, as if aware of his eyes on her, she looked up, and abruptly flushed in consternation.

Instantly, she turned off the machine with her right hand, and pulled off the headscarf with her left. The scarf caught on one of the tortoiseshell hair slides holding up her hair. The woman winced, then sighed, as she fiddled with the clasp, eventually freeing the headscarf but allowing a cascade of long Titian hair to fall over one side of her face.

Wendell felt his breath burst from him, as if someone had just punched him in the solar plexus.

She was, simply, the most beautiful woman he'd ever seen. Graceful dark red brows arched over huge grey eyes the soft colour of a dove's breast. A thin but well-shaped nose led the eye down to soft, luscious lips, coated with just the barest minimum of a soft plum-coloured lipstick that highlighted the severe cut and colour of her dress. Even as he watched, her hands went behind her back to undo the pinafore, which had the counterbalancing effect of thrusting out her breasts to press against the dark material of her dress.

Wendell's mouth went abruptly dry, and he found himself swallowing hard.

With the apron's strings untied, the maid whisked it away under the reception desk as she hurried behind it, and a brief smile lit up her face.

And what a face, Wendell thought, almost groaning out loud. A long oval, creamy and with a flush of embarrassed colour still high on her cheekbones. She had a rounded but strong chin, and a long neck, half-hidden by her hair, which she had now brought back under control.

And for the first time in his life, Wendell James felt himself hating tortoiseshell hair slides. He wanted to reach up and remove both of them from their position above her delicate temples, and let that mass of glorious hair fall free.

Into his mind flashed an image of her in the master bedroom of his manor in Reading. She was kneeling naked on his bed, the black silk sheets open and inviting and providing the perfect foil for her pale skin and that glowing auburn hair.

His eyes went instantly to the ring finger of her left hand, and he felt like thumping the air with his fist. Yes! She was unmarried.

He smiled slowly, and saw her take a deep, sharp breath.

With black hair and a lean, dangerous-looking face, Wendell knew that women found him attractive. It was all down to his Irish charm, or so his grandmother had maintained, although as far as he knew the James clan had never hailed from across the sea. And over the years, he'd done his fair share of exploiting that attraction.

After all, why not? At thirty-five he was still young and in his prime. He'd never married, and had been careful to conduct all his love affairs with due care and attention. He'd never made promises he couldn't keep, for instance, and knew that most of his ex-ladies and other friends would describe him as a 'gentleman'.

But even as he smiled at the stunning maid he could sense her withdrawing from him.

Oh, he could see that she was breathing just a little bit hard, and he didn't think it was from the exertion of wielding the floor cleaner either! And her eyes were having a hard time finding somewhere to settle, which was another clear sign that she was off balance. All signs that he had made a definite impression! Nevertheless, she was mentally, if not actually physically, backing away from him. It was intriguing. And not something that Wendell was used to.

'Can I be of help, sir?' she asked, her voice sounding calm and clear, and he felt like applauding her aplomb.

From the other side of the desk, Melisande watched the stranger and wished her heart would stop jumping about in her chest like a demented rabbit.

What on earth was wrong with her?

Of course, the day had started off badly right from the start, with four of the cleaners coming down with the summer flu that was rampaging across the area. It meant her having to chip in with some of the physical labour herself. But that was hardly new to her. In her time she'd helped unclog the gutters in a downpour and gale-force wind, as well as do mounds of washing-up whenever the dishwasher had broken down. OK, getting caught out in a pinny and headscarf by a guest was somewhat humiliating. But even so!

'Yes, thank you,' the stranger said, and as she forced her gaze to meet his, she could see his blue eyes were twinkling. And no wonder he was so amused. She was acting like a moon-struck calf, she told herself crossly.

But his eyes were so incredibly blue, a voice said loudly in the back of her mind. Just look at them — they're like the colour of bright summer sky. Azure. That was the word her brain was struggling to find.

'I'd like to check in?'

Melisande blinked, then nodded in what she hoped was a calm and businesslike manner. She reached for her mouse and opened the booking details.

That was better. She was feeling in charge again.

When he'd first begun to look at her as if she was on the dessert menu, and her female radar had unmistakably registered his sexual interest, she'd felt one or two moments of real, actual fear.

Luckily, she'd managed to pull herself together, and retreat behind what she'd always thought of as her 'calm face'. It was a trick she'd learned early on, when the sometimes hectic and privacy-starved life as a hotel owner threatened to overwhelm her.

She imagined herself as one of the damsels from the fairy tale books she'd read as a child, safely tucked up high behind a castle wall, protected by strong stone ramparts from dragons and marauding armies.

Or, in this case, from tall, dark and sexy guests who looked at her with dreamy, come-to-bed azure eyes.

'I'm early, I'm afraid. If you're not ready for me, perhaps I can just stow my case somewhere and come back later. I think my booking receipt said two o'clock?'

Melisande shook her head. 'Oh, I'm sure that won't be necessary, sir. Here at the Ray of Sunshine we try not to turn people away if we can help it.'

Wendell managed to hide a wince at the impersonal friendliness of her tone. No doubt about it now, the firebrand had turned into the ice maiden.

Which made the challenge that much more sweet. 'Can I have your name please, sir?'

'James. Wendell James.'

Melisande felt a little finger of pleasure run up her spine. Wendell. An unusual name, strong and somehow suitable. She might have known he wouldn't be called Joe or Harry!

Giving a mental head shake at the silliness of her thoughts, she tapped the keys and nodded.

'Oh yes. You're in the Green Man suite.'

The hotel had several deluxe suites, named after ancient English folklore. The Green Man appeared in many myths and legends, sometimes as a benign influence, but often not. Appearing as a fearsome face in the woods that frightened travellers, he was, in some tales, a terrible foe.

She smiled up at Mr James and reached for a blue leather-bound tome, which was open at today's date. This she swivelled around on the wooden surface of the desk before handing him an elegant black-and-gold fountain pen.

'If you'd like to sign here, sir?' she said. Wendell took the pen and gave it a somewhat ironic glance.

They don't miss a trick, do they? Wendell mused sourly. He knew, when he'd first started researching the Ray of

Sunshine that they advertised themselves as an unashamedly old-fashioned hotel, pandering to nostalgia and 'Little Britain as it used to be'. So far, all he'd seen was the front garden and the hall, and already he felt as though he was stepping back into the past.

As someone in the business himself, he could only admire the clever strategy and marketing. Still, he fully expected that before his stay was over he'd be consoling himself with the beautiful maid.

For a start, he'd lure her away from this place — offer her a better job at one of his top-of-the-range luxury hotels in the city of her choice. And if, as he hoped, their relationship looked like being one of fairly long duration, he could either install her in one of his penthouses, or, if she preferred, rent a pied-à-terre for her in town.

'Thank you, er . . .' He looked in vain for a name tag on her dress, and found none.

'Most people call me Mel, sir,' the maid said, and something in her voice made him look up suspiciously from signing his name.

She'd sounded — what? Amused, maybe a trifle ironic? As if she could almost read his mind and found him more impertinent than audacious. Or was he just imagining things?

Certainly her eyes, those beautiful, calm grey eyes, looked back at him steadily, and her face was composed and blankly polite. Whoever had trained her had done so well. She deserved to be on reception permanently; she was wasted on domestic drudgery.

'Thank you, Mel,' Wendell said. 'Don't worry about a bell boy — I can take my own case up.'

With a non-committal smile, she turned to search for his key, and he noticed a wisp of Titian hair clinging to her neck. And had to fight the urge to lean across and gently pull the strands away.

When she turned back and handed him the key he thought he heard her breathe in sharply, but couldn't be sure.

He smiled at her once more, giving her the full wattage of his black Irish charm, then reached down to pick up his case.

As he walked up the stairs, he fought the urge to look back to see if she was watching him. Mainly because he was sure that she was determined not to do any such thing, and he didn't want to feel the disappointment of finding her gaze firmly fixed to the computer screen or whatever.

And as if in mocking confirmation of his suspicions, before he even reached the landing, he heard the waxing machine start up again, its whirring sounding like ironic laughter.

He found his suite at the end of the corridor and, using an old-fashioned brass key (no modern key cards here!), he felt himself begin to smile as he pushed open the door. And then the smile turned into a rueful chuckle.

'Well, she certainly showed you,' he said softly to himself, walking inside and meeting his reflection in a mirror. 'Mel.' He whispered her name with dissatisfaction. Such a short, unhelpful name — and it didn't suit her at all. Short for Melissa, almost certainly, he mused. Well, Melissa was better, but somehow that didn't seem to quite suit her either. Lissa? No, definitely not. Or perhaps she was a Melanie? He sighed and shook his head. Distracting as the beautiful, intriguing maid was, he was here to work.

He slowly looked around, nodding at the simple beauty of the room. Pale green flock wallpaper with a slightly silver sheen was carefully complemented by lush green velvet curtains and brocaded sofa.

The furniture was old without being antique, and the works of art were pretty and inoffensive. The homely touches of a vase of simple flowers and some gardening magazines on the table were all designed to make him feel right at ease, and succeeded.

The bathroom contained an original claw-foot bath as well as a modern shower cubicle, and the soap and accessories were all lavender and herb, made by a local manufacturer.

The suite was calming, serene and comfortable. The competition, it seemed, was going to be tough to beat. But beat it he would.

Once his new hotel was built, he expected this place to be out of business within the year.

CHAPTER THREE

Gisela Ashley stepped from the taxi and glanced around with a smile of relief and delight. She'd made it!

Once again the sun was shining and getting the weekend off to a blazing start. The jury back in High Wycombe had yesterday come in with a guilty verdict on Robert Pride, and Alice had told her on the telephone that he was probably looking at a ten-year sentence.

While she was relieved to have the whole episode behind her once and for all, it had also, she had to admit, given her yet another sleepless night. She wondered how the Pride family matriarch would feel now that her son faced another long stretch inside. Although her threat to Gisela outside the court had been a vague one, little more than a hissed and malevolent prediction that girls 'wot blabbed got wot was comin' to 'em', Gisela couldn't get the woman's brown hate-filled eyes out of her mind.

Now it was a relief simply to put High Wycombe behind her for three whole weeks and escape on to the river. Here, surely, nobody would bother her. She'd be safe from reporters after her story, and, more important, any thugs Ma Pride might send to scare her.

She only wished Andrea had been able to come. But her flatmate's coughs and sneezes had turned into the full-blown flu bug that seemed to be plaguing the nation this spring, and she'd had to cry off coming on holiday with her. She had promised, however, to go and stay for a while with a nursing friend, who could keep an eye on her while she was unwell. And, much more important to Gisela's way of thinking, it would ensure that Andrea wasn't at the flat on her own. Just in case Ma Pride did send someone around to frighten her, she didn't want Andrea having to cope with it all.

She paid off the taxi driver, who actually got out of the car and pulled her suitcases from the back, his uncharacteristic courtesy a tribute to her feminine charms.

Today, she was wearing a pair of mint-green tapered shorts with matching mint-green-and-white deck shoes and a dark green T-shirt that hugged her figure lovingly — the result, probably, of too many washes at too high a temperature. With the sun gleaming on her short cap of pale hair, the taxi driver watched her figure disappear in his rear-view mirror until she was out of sight, then sighed heavily.

Gisela glanced around, noticing a large hotel off to her right, called the Ray of Sunshine — the same name as the marina. Not sure of her bearings, she left her bags on the gravel car park and walked towards the front door, stepping through into a cool, pleasant hall. A young lad on the reception desk looked up and smiled.

'Yes, madam, can I help you?'

'I'm not sure if I'm in the right place,' Gisela said with a shrug. 'I'm booked on to a narrowboat?'

'Oh yes, you need Gina. Just a moment please,' he said. He picked up the telephone and pressed a number. As he murmured a few words into the receiver, Gisela glanced around. She could smell old-fashioned beeswax and lavender, and the way the sun shone through the high arched windows, picking out dust motes in the silvery rays, had her instantly relaxing. But the hotel, she suspected, was way out of her budget range! Especially since she'd blown so much on renting the boat.

Of course, with Andrea crying off, she'd almost cancelled the holiday altogether, for the thought of handling a boat on her own was daunting. But the thought of staying put in the flat had been even worse — she really needed to get away for a bit. She'd probably end up just taking the boat as far as the first big obstacle on the river — a lock probably — and then moor up and stay in one place. A sort of caravan holiday but on the water, she supposed. It didn't really matter. The change of scenery and the peace of mind would do her more good than anything else.

'Hello, Mrs Ashley?'

Gisela turned and saw a plump, pretty teenager walking towards her. She had black and red hair and a welcoming smile, and before she could correct her on her marital status, she was already speaking. 'Isn't it a lovely day? I'll take you straight down to the *Swan*, shall I?'

Gisela found herself smiling back. The girl had one of those friendly faces that reminded her of a bouncy puppy — all energy and boundless affection.

'Yes, it is nice,' Gisela agreed, and followed her back outside the door. There, the girl insisted on picking up and carrying both her suitcases, making Gisela feel guilty. Then they set off across beautiful gardens towards the river. And as they crossed a vast, well-manicured lawn, Gisela exclaimed in delight, for the River Thames was suddenly stretched out before her, the water a silver-rippled mirror in the sunlight. Willows, both of the weeping kind and the more regular variety, lined the banks, and here and there you could just see a glimpse of the odd house or two. There was a fresh, clean smell in the air, and she smiled as a platoon of swallows swept past her and skimmed out across the water.

'I'm Gina, by the way,' the girl in front of her said, pausing at the top of the bank. Joining her, Gisela could see the wooden steps set into the grassy bank, leading down on to a small jetty. And moored up there was a gleaming white narrowboat.

Real-life swans headed their way, no doubt used to being fed by the hotel guests, but Gisela's eyes stayed on the boat. The name of it — the *Stillwater Swan* — was lettered in black, with gold highlights on the prow, and on the side panel was a painting of a mute swan among bulrushes. The brass frames around the large picture windows that ranged from the middle of the boat to the back, and the small round portholes in the front, gleamed like old gold.

'She's beautiful,' Gisela whispered softly. In fact, for some reason she couldn't quite fathom, the sight of the boat made her feel like crying — but in a good way. From the moment she set eyes on it, she had a rare feeling of almost joyful presentiment. It was as if the boat was calling to her, promising wonderful things to come, and something deep inside her was answering. It was pleasantly spooky, but in a way, Gisela felt as if her whole life had been leading up to this moment.

She shivered slightly. The younger of two daughters, Gisela's life so far had been fairly predictable and unremarkable, she knew. She'd lived in High Wycombe for all her life, going to the local schools, getting good exam results, and going on to take a secretarial course at the local college. She'd moved out of home when she was twenty, dated with varied success, attended her sister's wedding three years ago as a bridesmaid, and had been made an auntie just a year ago. She liked her job, liked her flatmate, had Sunday lunch regularly with her parents, and apart from witnessing the aftermath of a jewellery shop robbery, nothing had ever really happened to her.

And yet here, standing by the River Thames, looking down at the *Stillwater Swan*, she had the extraordinary feeling that she had somehow just become important. And that something amazing and life-altering was going to happen.

It left her feeling a little shaken, and more than a little rueful. Surely she was just imagining things? It was probably no more than the strain of the trial taking its toll.

'Here's your set of keys,' Gina said, handing out a key-ring, which Gisela took with a smile of thanks. 'I expect you'd like to settle in, have a look around and unpack first. I'll give you an hour, shall I? Then I'll come back down and give you a lesson in how to use the boat. I took a crash course in it when I got the job here. Well, not a *crash* course,' Gina gurgled with a giggle. 'I never crashed the boat or anything,' she added unnecessarily, then seemed to sense the other woman's sudden nervousness, for she said impulsively, 'Don't worry, it's easy once you know how.'

Gisela swallowed nervously. The boat looked brand new. What if she ran it ashore or something? Ploughed the pointy end right into the riverbank and got it stuck? Or scraped up against another boat and scarred the immaculate, gleaming white paintwork?

Then she told herself not to be such a ninny. She and the boat were both fully insured, and after all, it was not as if the *Swan* was a powerboat that could get out of control. If she got up to four miles an hour she'd be going at the top speed!

'Thanks, that's great, Gina,' Gisela said, and the young girl grinned at her.

'You'll have a great holiday, you'll see,' the teenager said enthusiastically. She picked up both cases and began to lug them down the steps. Again, Gisela tried to take one from her, and again Gina refused. Mel had gone through the booking-in routine with her plenty of times, and she'd seen the other parties off in the *Patient Heron* and the *Dancing Grebe* without any mishap.

As she gained the pier and put the cases down on the back of the boat she did wonder why Mr Ashley hadn't travelled down with his wife, but didn't ask. Mel had also drilled it into Gina over and over again that the private lives and business of the Ray of Sunshine's guests — be they hotel guests or boating guests — were strictly none of their business.

So she left Gisela searching her keys for the right one to open the padlock on the *Swan*'s metal doors, ran lightly back up the steps and into to the office.

* * *

Keefe Ashleigh stepped off the train and walked to the bus station, surprised to find a bus route that took him to within a mile of Royston-on-Thames.

He paid the fare and took a seat at the back of a small thirty-seat country bus. He put his well-packed holdall on the empty seat next to him. As a soldier, he was used to travelling light, while at the same time managing to pack plenty into a small space. Living on a narrowboat, he suspected, wasn't going to be much different from living in tents or barracks as far as space was concerned.

About twenty minutes later the bus driver pulled on to the side of the road and, as Keefe had asked him to, called out 'Royston'.

When Keefe got off the bus, he found himself in the middle of nowhere. The largely deserted B road stretched north–south beside him, and fields full of grazing sheep and divided by thick hedges went uninterrupted to the skyline for as far as the eye could see. Then he spotted a country lane across the road, and a somewhat dirty white country signpost standing beside it, half-hidden by the leaves of an elder bush.

He slung his holdall over his shoulders and crossed the road. As he'd expected, the signpost promised him that ROYSTON-ON-THAMES — Village Only was only one and a half miles away.

A pleasant hike on a lovely spring morning, Keefe thought with satisfaction. And as if in agreement with him, off in the field to his left a skylark suddenly lifted into the sky, singing its heart out joyously. In the hedges on either side of the road wild honeysuckle and dog roses scented the air, and as he walked, Keefe felt the weight of his past slide away. For the first time since leaving the hospital he felt as if he could contemplate his future with at least a modicum of enthusiasm.

In fact, as he walked, pausing to watch a pair of hares running across the field into a small wood, he felt a rare and almost forgotten sense of peace.

He turned his eyes away from the white rumps of the hares and started walking again, whistling a half-remembered tune as he did so.

* * *

Gisela was delighted with the 'master bedroom' at the front of the boat; the bed, she was surprised to see, was a full-sized double.

It didn't take her long to put her clothes away in the built-in wardrobe and shelves and test the bed. Bouncy and soft, but with enough firmness not to leave her with an aching back when she got up in the morning. Perfect.

The carpeting underneath was a lovely old-gold colour, matched by the coverlet on her bed, and she loved the tiny, almost handkerchief-sized curtains that covered the small portholes. The materials were mainly white, with touches of black and orange, and as she explored the rest of the boat she realized that the *Swan* matched the colour scheme of its wild counterpart. The pure white decor let light flood in, but the touches of orange, black and old gold were striking and added cheerful and dramatic highlights.

It was like living in a mini floating palace, Gisela thought half an hour later, after she'd marvelled over the power shower, the full gas oven, the electric microwave and clever laundry facilities. Everything that could be built in or folded away was, and lots of things had dual purposes — like the ironing board that folded out of the wall and could be used as a breakfast table, simply by pulling down a metal rod fixed to the underside that produced two stabilizing legs.

It was delightful, and gave Gisela the feeling of being a doll living in a miniature replica house. She felt pampered and excited at the newness of it all, and far from feeling afraid of taking to the open water, she now couldn't wait.

Perhaps she'd even have enough confidence to tackle a lock when she came to one!

She was just exploring the galley area again, delighted to find that the fridge was fully stocked with luxury deli items, when she felt the boat move.

Something had rocked it.

A moment later, she felt it move again, and heard the sound of a footstep. It had a hollow, rather metallic ring, and she realized that someone was climbing down the stairs.

Her first thought was that it was probably Gina, coming back to give her her non-crash crash course in piloting the boat. And if she hadn't already been so nervous about Ma Pride and her vague threats, she probably would have simply gone to the rear of the boat and called out to her.

Instead, she froze to the spot, her heartbeat going up a notch, and listened intently.

She was glad that she had. For the tread she heard was heavier, surely, than any that Gina would make. Besides, the teenager had worn fairly high, wedge-heeled shoes, and they'd have made a distinct tap-tap on the metal rungs of the steps.

This tread was flat, and distinctly masculine. Although she had no way of proving it, Gisela simply knew that a lone male had come on board the *Swan*, and panic seized her.

Her first thought was that somehow the Pride clan, or their representative, had tracked her down. Perhaps they'd been camped outside her flat ever since the 'guilty' verdict, and had followed her down here? In any event, she felt suddenly vulnerable. The Ray of Sunshine Hotel now felt a long way away, over the hill of the bank and out of screaming range. And it would surely be another half an hour or so before Gina was due back to give her the orientation lesson.

And here she was, trapped in a narrow space with no way out. Or was there? The stranger had come down the stern steps, but wasn't there a door at the prow of the boat, leading out on to the small front deck?

Gisela heard herself whimper as she realized that she couldn't remember. And although her first instinct was to run, to just get out of there, screaming at the top of her lungs if she had to, another part of her was loath to move, let alone turn her back on whoever was on the *Swan* with her.

In her mind's eye, she saw all those late-night movies where women ran away and were grabbed from behind, usually with a scarf or some kind of strangling device.

With a show of effort she forced herself to stop dithering and took a slow, quiet, calming breath. The stranger was on the floor of the boat now, and she knew from her own tour of the boat that he'd be looking out from the main salon — a lovely, pine-walled vista with comfortable sofas and a panoramic view of the water. From there he would see a small dinette area in a narrower passage, which led to where she was standing now — currently hidden from view.

But he had only to walk across the length of the lounge and come forward, and she'd be discovered.

Then she realized that she was in the galley, with an array of defensive weapons at hand. But even as she glanced at a set of black-handled kitchen knives set in a wooden holder, she knew that she couldn't reach for one. The thought of slicing or stabbing anyone with them made her feel sick. Besides, she knew instinctively that she was incapable of such violence — even in self-defence. She needed something else.

It wasn't hard to make her knees fold, and in a moment she was kneeling on the floor, reaching to open a cupboard where she was sure she'd seen a heavy cast-iron frying pan on her previous exploration. Yes! There it was. Reaching for it carefully, inching it out bit by nerve-racking bit, wincing at every tiny sound it made, Gisela got slowly to her feet again, and pressed herself against the cupboard.

It took all her nerve, but eventually she peered around the wall, and saw a shadow moving across the white wall of the dinette. Someone was coming this way.

She felt her palms become moist, and she hoped she'd be able to keep a good hold on the pan. She'd simply wait until whoever it was had gone by her, and then whack him on the back of the head.

But what if it was another member of the staff here? a little voice fretted in the back of her mind. What if Gina had become busy and had sent someone else down here to show her how to use the *Swan*? But surely, if that was the case, they'd have called out to her by now? Besides, there was such stealthy quietness in the stranger's movements that it raised the hairs on the back of her neck.

The boat was hardly moving now, as if whoever was on board with her was being careful about their weight displacement. And why would he be going to such lengths to make no noise unless he was up to no good, she reasoned grimly.

Swallowing hard, Gisela decided she'd definitely whack first, then run, and ask questions later.

* * *

Keefe Ashleigh stood in the middle of the elegant salon, and knew he wasn't alone.

He'd arrived at the hotel a quarter of an hour after getting off the bus, and had met the colourful Gina a few minutes later. She'd handed him the key, and tried to take his holdall, an attempt that he'd firmly negated, as he had her offer to show him to the boat. After receiving directions, and a brief walk across some charming gardens, he'd found himself looking down at the river.

The boat moored up on the small pier matched the photographs of it, but he'd been surprised to find it unlocked. Perhaps the crime rate was particularly low around here, or maybe the garrulous friendly Gina had been to the boat that morning and had forgotten to lock it up behind her.

But from the moment he'd come down the steps, he knew the boat wasn't deserted. A faint sound, perhaps, or a scent in the air? He didn't question his instincts, knowing they'd served him well in the past, but instead he had quietly shouldered off his holdall and put it beside the steps.

He waited, expecting someone to call out. They must have heard him board, after all.

But no sound came. Worse, nobody moved. If it was a member of the marina staff down here, why were they being so damned shy?

Perhaps, he thought grimly, the crime rate around here wasn't so low after all. There must, he reasoned, be plenty to steal from a high-quality boat like this. And the river made a good getaway route. Someone with a small outboard motor on the other side of the boat could be well away within moments, with little chance of pursuit.

Carefully, he scanned the immediate area. An L-shaped seating arrangement led to a narrower area where a fold-down dining table could be set up. Which meant the galley was probably behind the interior wall facing him. After that would probably come the bedrooms.

As far as he could tell, nothing had been stolen from the salon — the satellite television was still in place, as was the rather swanky stereo system with its compact speakers.

He walked very carefully towards the narrower part and heard the faintest sound. A mere scrape, as if someone was stealthily removing something.

Keefe tensed, moved his back to the outside edge of the corridor, and took two rapid sideways steps, ducking as he sensed a large, flat, dark object heading his way. Like a striking snake, his hand shot out and grabbed a wrist, and he heard a distinctly feminine 'oh' of shock followed by a sob of fear.

It was the fear that galvanized him and told him that he'd got it wrong, somehow. 'It's all right!' He said the words without thinking, and a moment later he was looking down into a pair of enormous blue eyes. The girl looked young and terrified, and not much like a thief or burglar at all. She was dressed in a combination of green, and her pale gamine face was topped with the palest of blonde hair.

'Don't you dare hurt me,' Gisela rasped. 'People know I'm here. You won't get away with it.'

Keefe blinked, then smiled gently and regarded her hand, which was still holding on to a lethal-looking iron frying pan.

'Neither will you,' he warned drily. 'You could bash someone's brains out with that thing, and people know *I'm* here too.' Still holding her wrist he moved her hands up and down, testing the weight of the pan. 'That thing's made out of cast iron! Do you have any idea how dangerous it is?'

He didn't think she did, because her terrified expression quickly gave way to one of horror.

'I only wanted to knock you out and then run and get help,' she said shakily.

Keefe took the pan from her suddenly unresisting fingers, and laid it on the work surface behind her. 'If I let go of your wrist, are you going to behave?' he asked, amusement warring with annoyance. He thought he'd left behind a world where people were constantly trying to kill him!

Wordlessly she nodded, and the moment he let go of her, she scooted back as far as she could go. Which, being on a narrowboat, wasn't very far.

'Good. Now, my name's Keefe Ashleigh. I've rented this boat for the next three weeks. I take it you're not robbing the place?' he asked wryly.

Gisela felt a flood of relief wash over her, and her terror abruptly receded, making her feel light-headed and giddy. Her knees threatened to buckle. As if sensing it, the man in front of her moved to one side.

'Come on, you'd better come and sit down in the salon before you fall down. Is there any brandy on this boat?'

Gisela, further reassured by the way he turned his back on her and went through to the salon, meekly followed and sank into the nearest chair.

'I don't know. I don't think so. Besides, I don't want anything, thank you,' she said, sounding like a prim little schoolmarm. It made her flush.

Keefe eyed her closely. Her colour was coming back, which was good, and her pupils, which had been dilated in shock, were slowly shrinking back to normal size. Her breathing was still a bit ragged, but she was pulling herself together and showing remarkable spirit. He knew he'd frightened the life out of her.

'Do you work for the marina?' he asked curiously. 'Why didn't you call out when you heard me come aboard?'

Gisela shook her head. 'I don't work here. I hired this boat a few days ago. I'm just going off on my holiday.'

Keefe blinked, then smiled wryly. 'Looks like there's been some kind of a mix-up,' he said.

Gisela managed a feeble smile.

The stranger looked as if he was in his mid-thirties, and was dressed casually in old worn jeans and a plain white shirt. But they fitted him like a second skin, hinting at wiry muscle and sinew beneath. He had short-cropped brown hair and chocolate-coloured eyes. A strong jawline and a nose that had been broken more than once gave him a kind of beat-up appeal that she'd never before found attractive in a man.

But something about *this* man broke all her previous rules.

He was watching her intently, quietly, as if trying to read her mind. And something about his gaze made her heartbeat, which had been slowing back down to its normal rate, suddenly start up again.

'I think we'd better go back to the hotel and get this sorted out,' he said softly.

And Gisela nodded without a word.

* * *

'I don't know how it happened!' Gina wailed, looking as if she was about to burst into tears.

Keefe, the spirited little blonde from the boat — whose name, he had learned, was Gisela Ashley — Gina and a beautiful auburn-haired woman who turned out to be the owner of the hotel and the marina were now all gathered together in the hotel's small office.

And Gina's tearful distress was making Keefe feel distinctly uncomfortable — as if he was guilty of being a bully, which he wasn't.

He and Gisela had returned to the reception desk and told their tale to the nonplussed young man behind the desk. He had then led them to the office, where Gina and the hotel owner were working.

Succinctly, Keefe had just explained what had happened, and Gina was obviously appalled.

'I'm sure we can work this out,' the owner said smoothly, rising from her desk with a smile and holding out her hand, first to Keefe. 'I'm Melisande Ray, the owner.'

'Keefe Ashleigh,' Keefe said, with a brisk nod of his head.

Melisande then turned and held out her hand to the little blonde woman, who also introduced herself. 'I'm Gisela Ashley.'

'Ahh,' Melisande said, with a brief smile. 'I think I'm beginning to see the light. You're both Ashleys?'

Keefe spelled out his own name, and as he did so, Melisande pulled up the booking registration on her computer. She looked up. 'Miss Ashley, you booked over the Internet four days ago?'

'Yes.'

'And, Mr Ashleigh — I have no record of you?'

'I telephoned yesterday. I think it was this young lady who confirmed my booking,' he said, careful to smile at Gina and keep any hint of blame out of his voice.

Gina wailed again. 'Oh no. I thought you were a couple! I mean, that Ms Ashley had made the booking — see it says plus one. I thought, when you rang up, that you were the plus one, and simply hadn't realized that your wife had already made the arrangements!'

Her voice threatened to rise even further, and Melisande quickly held out her hand. 'It's all right, Gina,' she said smoothly and calmly, although in reality she was feeling annoyed. Such a silly and basic mistake should never have happened — and on the *Swan*'s maiden voyage too! Once she'd got this sorted out, she'd have to think of a way to make sure it didn't happen again.

Gisela shifted restlessly. Like Keefe, she hated to see Gina so upset. She knew what it was like to be new at a job and terrified of making a mistake. Once, when she'd first started at the surgery, she could have made a bad mistake with one of the patient files, but luckily Margery, another secretary there, had spotted it and put her right. And the last thing she wanted to do was be responsible for getting someone else into trouble.

'It seems an understandable mistake to me,' she said firmly, catching Gina's tearful eye and smiling. 'Ashley's not that common a name, after all.'

'Yes, I agree,' Keefe said instantly, making Gisela give him an appreciative glance. Some men, she knew, could be very impatient and unfeeling. But obviously not this one.

Gina sniffed and cast a hopeful look at her boss.

Melisande smiled and nodded. 'Well, it's regrettable all the same, and of course, the Ray of Sunshine will do all it can to compensate you. Unfortunately, both the other boats are out, but I can offer one of you three weeks at the hotel, free of charge? If that's you, Miss Ashley, I will of course see that you get a full refund for the payment you've already made.'

Gisela caught Keefe's eye questioningly. She didn't really object to staying at the hotel — it was such a lovely hotel, after all. Or perhaps he'd prefer to?

Reading her mind, he smiled briefly. 'Miss Ashley and I will discuss it, I think, and sort something out. Perhaps over a drink?'

'Of course,' Melisande said, grateful that they were both taking it so well. 'The bar is open,' she lied, 'and the drinks are on the house. If you'll follow me?'

She led them through the hall and into a small saloon bar. There she went behind the bar herself and poured them their drinks of choice — a pint of lager for the impressive-looking man, and a simple soda and lime for the little blonde.

Tactfully, she left them alone.

'Well, that's torn it,' Gisela said with a sigh. 'I was looking forward to some time on the river.'

'Yes, me too,' Keefe said. 'I was going to use it as an opportunity to do some house-hunting.'

And Gisela listened as he gave a brief explanation of his past and current circumstances, then sighed. 'Well, that settles it then. You need the boat far more than I do. You've got your whole life to sort out — I just need a break.'

But even as she said it, she wondered. What if Ma Pride really did mean her threats? Wasn't she something of a sitting duck, here at the hotel? Didn't it make more sense to keep on moving? After all, it would be hard to track her down or get to her if she was on a boat.

Not that she really thought she was in any serious danger. But even so, peace of mind was what she craved now. She was still feeling off-balance after her court appearance and three weeks of feeling safe and moving from town to town was vastly appealing.

Perhaps they could share the boat?

But even as she thought it, she wondered whether she was mad. What did she know about this man anyway? And yet she felt a strong compulsion to voice the offer. It was as if Fate was standing behind her giving her a huge nudge, trying to overwhelm her common sense.

But still, it was impossible. She'd be insane to even consider it. And then she had a brainwave.

'I'll just be a minute,' she said sweetly, then picked up her bag and headed for the ladies. The moment she was there she took out her mobile, hoping against hope that Andrea hadn't moved out of the flat yet.

'Gisela? You alright?' her flatmate's cold-induced nasal tone answered after only two rings.

'Oh, Andy, I'm glad you're still there. Look, can you do me a favour? Can you google a name for me? He's an ex-soldier so there should be something on him.'

'Huh? Oh, google! Yeah, even at death's door I can google. I can probably do it in my sleep.' Andrea coughed. 'What's the name?'

Gisela quickly spelled it out, remembering the unusual spelling of his last name.

Over the line she heard Andrea sneeze and cough, then a moment later, she rasped, 'Oh, yeah, here he is. There's not a lot on his work in the army — mostly old newspaper clippings and stuff.'

'Well, I don't suppose the army likes to advertise its personnel,' Gisela mused. 'So what have you got?'

'Medals,' Andrea said, and sneezed. 'There's a photo of him being awarded quite a few. Honourable discharge six months ago. Reading between the lines, I think he must have been injured 'cause there's a newspaper story about him coming out of hospital. Wow, he's a nice-looking brute, isn't he? Lean, mean fighting machine and all that. That broken nose is so sexy, don't you think. Huh, he's married.'

Gisela felt her heart constrict and begin to ache.

'Oh no, wait. He's widowed. His wife died after just a couple of years of marriage, after a short illness, it says. Been in the army all his adult life, not a bad word to say about him — the guy's a regular hero. Hey, what's going on? Why do you want to know about him?' she asked with somewhat belated suspicion.

Gisela laughed lightly. She knew if she told Andrea what she had in mind she'd say she was crazy and try to talk her out of it. So she said simply, 'Oh, nothing much. I just needed to check that someone wasn't having me on about something. So there's nothing fishy about him at all?'

'Nope. Looks like a straight, stand-up guy.'

'Yes, I thought so,' Gisela said. In spite of the nerve-racking way in which they'd met, Gisela instinctively trusted the quiet man with a grip of steel. 'Thanks for the help, Andy. I was glad to catch you before you left.'

'Huh? Oh yeah, right,' Andrea said hastily. She'd told Gisela she'd stay with an old friend simply because Gisela had been so paranoid about leaving Andrea alone. But in reality, the nurse had no intention of moving out of the flat. Who wanted to have the hassle of moving home, even for just a few days, when you were feeling ill? Not to mention the risk of passing it on to some other poor soul. No, she intended to hunker down with a hot water bottle and some paracetamol for a few days, but she knew Gisela would only fret if she told her that. And she didn't want to ruin her holiday.

'Well, feel better soon!' Gisela said cheerfully.

'OK. Have a nice holiday.'

Gisela returned to the deserted bar and studied the stranger called Keefe Ashleigh as she returned. Andrea's description of him as a lean, mean fighting machine wouldn't stop circulating in her mind.

As she sank into her chair opposite him, she smiled brightly. 'Look, I've been thinking. Why don't we share the boat?'

Keefe, who'd been raising his glass to his lips, paused. He shot her a quick, assessing look. 'Isn't that a bit rash on your part? I could be a serial killer or something.'

Gisela smiled wryly. 'No, you're not, I've just had you googled.'

Keefe grinned. 'And I never felt a thing.' Then he sobered. 'Are you serious? About boat-sharing, I mean?'

'Why not?' Gisela said, trying to sound super-casual. 'There's certainly room enough. I'll take the forward bedroom and you can have the one just off the galley. There's even two bathrooms, so there needn't be any embarrassing hassle over who gets to use the bathroom first. We can share the cooking and stuff. And, after all, it's not as if we're crossing the Atlantic or anything,' she pointed out reasonably. 'If it turns out that we get on each other's nerves or whatever, one or the other of us can simply just get off and come back and stay here at the hotel.'

Keefe slowly took a sip of his lager. If any other woman had made this proposition to him, he would have instantly thought that she was offering him a holiday romance.

But as he met her wide, innocent and uncertain blue eyes, he was sure that this woman wasn't being promiscuous. In fact, he was almost sure that something else entirely was going on. She was trying so hard to sound carefree and act like a blasé woman of the world, but he wasn't buying it.

This wasn't the sort of woman who normally took such big risks like sharing a boat with a stranger. On that he would have bet money.

Briefly he remembered her very real terror back on the *Swan*. There was still something a bit off about that. Why had she been so quick to think he meant to hurt her?

And suddenly, his old thirst for adventure was rearing its ugly head again. 'OK, why not?' he agreed amiably.

Gisela Ashley was beginning to pique his curiosity.

If nothing else, the next few weeks should prove interesting.

CHAPTER FOUR

Melisande saw Keefe and Gisela enter the dining room that evening, and moved forward quickly, her gaze speculative. The petite blonde was wearing a silky lilac wraparound skirt with a pearl-grey clinging top, and long dangling amethyst earrings. She looked radiant.

Beside her, Keefe was dressed more plainly in black slacks and a cream polo shirt. But they looked, Melisande thought as she approached them, very much like a couple.

'Hello, I'm so glad you could make it.' She greeted them with a smile. When they'd come back to her after their drinks in the bar and told her they were going to share the boat, she'd offered them dinner tonight at the hotel on the house, which, after a mutually questioning look between themselves, they'd accepted.

Now she led them to a small table by a bay window with a beautiful view of the rose gardens. She'd been surprised by their decision to share, but it was, of course, none of her business. Even so, she'd made a particular note to check on Keefe's details and keep them safe. Just in case. She felt rather protective of Gisela Ashley, who had a slightly hollow-eyed look that led Melisande to wonder if she'd been ill recently. Or been through some kind of trauma.

Such things, she knew, could affect your judgement, and she only hoped that Gisela wouldn't regret her decision to leave tomorrow with a virtual stranger. Not that Melisande was particularly worried about Keefe. Years in the hotel business had honed her people-reading skills, and she instinctively trusted the competent, quiet man.

And it was clear that they were getting along famously, she mused, as Keefe perused the wine list and made a few suggestions, which made Gisela laugh, admitting that he'd already mentioned two of her all-time favourites.

Melisande had had to have a few words with a downcast and utterly contrite Gina, but her secretary had quickly rallied when she'd learned that Keefe and Gisela would be leaving together. The irrepressible teenager had been delighted in fact, and certain that she'd just instigated a great romance. So much so that Melisande rather thought Gina expected to be issued with a wedding invitation in a few months' time.

Who knows? she thought with a smile. Perhaps she just might. She murmured a few words of farewell and tactfully drifted away.

Sipping her wine contentedly, Gisela let her eyes roam around the dining room. It was a lovely room, with dark green velvet curtains, discreet lighting and snow-white tablecloths. She ordered a simple melon dish for her starter, then the grilled trout followed by a lime sorbet. Keefe decided on the farmhouse pâté, with baked hake and then a slice of apple pie with cheese.

'It's a lovely place,' Gisela said appreciatively, looking around at the other patrons — a mix of wealthy American and English, mostly older couples.

'You can always change your mind and stay here,' Keefe said mildly, and smiled when she shot him a quick glance. 'And no, that wasn't a hint that I want to have the boat to myself,' he said, reading her mind easily. 'I just want to make sure that you're absolutely certain what you want. Remember, it's a lady's prerogative to change her mind.'

Gisela felt herself relax, and gave a light laugh. 'Oh, I don't think this particular lady is for turning.'

In fact, she was looking forward to heading out on the river. The long-term weather forecast promised a week of almost unbroken sunshine, and the last of her fears had finally melted away. After all, she had no concerns that the Pride clan might have hired Keefe to hurt her. To begin with, she suspected that anybody they might send after her would be of the low-level criminal type, thugs they knew from their own murky profession. And where would a professional soldier who'd spent most of his life abroad ever have run into the likes of the Prides?

Even more important, she was sure that anybody who wanted to harm her would hardly allow himself to be seen in her company, let alone be observed to leave with her on a boat. After all, if she turned up missing or injured, he would be the first person the police would want to talk to!

And she was sure that an ex-soldier could take care of himself, just in case the worst happened. Then she sighed wearily. The only thing that troubled her about him was her conscience. In her heart of hearts she knew she was using him to ensure her peace of mind. She'd only known him for a matter of a few hours, but already she felt safe in his presence. He had a formidable confidence in everything he did which made her certain that this man could handle anything and everything that might come their way.

Just the way he handled his cutlery when eating, for instance. The way his eyes roamed the room, seeing everything and missing nothing. If he'd been a wolf, Gisela had no doubts at all that he'd be the alpha male! But did she really have any right to expect him to look after her? And was she really such a wilting maiden that she needed looking after?

'So, any idea where you want to go?' Keefe asked, interrupting her thoughts. 'Up towards London, or the other way, past Henley?'

Gisela shrugged. 'I don't really want to head towards the capital,' she said slowly. She was sure the Prides would have had dealings there. And although she didn't really take Ma Pride's threats all that seriously, it was foolish to tempt fate.

Keefe nodded. 'No, nor me either. We could always head towards Oxford — get on the Oxford canal and see something of the university. I don't think I've ever been there. It must be something worth seeing.'

Gisela smiled. She'd been to the city once or twice, but she'd never seen it from the water. And never with this man. 'I think that sounds ideal,' she murmured dreamily.

She was already walking across Christ Church meadow, arm in arm with Keefe on a misty dawn morning, where the deer watched them with benign interest and the college swifts screamed their approval high overhead.

Keefe saw a soft look cross her expressive face, and felt his breath catch. He'd have to be careful. The intriguing Gisela Ashley was turning out to be quite the captivating Gisela Ashley as well.

And he was not at all sure that he wanted to be 'caught'.

* * *

Sitting at the bar and morosely sipping Pimms, Rupert Rice-Jones waited patiently for Melisande to come back from her tour of the dining room and join him for a drink.

Rupert lived in a large house on the outskirts of the village, and had done so for most of his life. It was not quite the manor house, seeing that it was less than a hundred years old, but it was the closest thing Royston had to it. His grandfather had bought it on retiring from his job in the city, and his father had taken to buying up land whenever possible, settling down to the life of a gentleman farmer.

Rupert had gone to Harrow, then Cambridge, but although he'd taken a degree in agriculture, he'd rarely spent much time on the estate his father had built up, opting instead to jump on the property bandwagon that had begun in the 1980s, just after he'd finished his studies.

When his father had died a few years ago, he'd returned to what he laughingly called 'the ancestral pile'. He'd installed an estate manager, and continued to build Rice & Farrow into a major property developer, buying out his partner Roger Farrow just before the millennium.

At the time he'd been gleeful, thinking that he'd pulled off a major coup. But now he was wondering whether Roger hadn't seen the writing on the wall and had craftily got out at the top of the game, while the going was good.

Because now, what with the economic downturn and house prices tumbling, Rupert's future was beginning to look decidedly bleak.

In fact, with mortgages getting harder and harder for the average buyer to come by, he'd seen his profit margins tumble in a way he'd never have believed possible just a year ago.

Grimly he ordered another drink and tried to ignore the beginnings of a headache. He was drinking far too much just lately. But he was under serious pressure, with a massive loan due for repayment soon. Even the ancestral pile was in jeopardy, as he'd used it as collateral. Under the circumstances, surely any man was entitled to a drink or two?

The bartender, a graduate student from Oxford who was working for the summer to earn some much-needed cash, served his drink. He knew that the rapidly ageing forty-something was a close friend of the owner, but he was beginning to worry about his alcohol intake. He only hoped there wouldn't have to be a scene over car keys. But perhaps, the bartender thought hopefully, Rice-Jones had walked here, since it was only a ten-minute stroll from one end of the village to the other.

'Any sign of the lovely Mel yet, Clive?' Rupert asked breezily.

The bartender, whose name was Colin, craned his head to look through the open door and into the dining room. 'Can't see her, sir,' he said neutrally.

Like most members of the Ray of Sunshine's staff, he wasn't quite sure of the relationship between Melisande Ray and Rupert Rice-Jones. The maids gossiped that he'd asked her to marry him on more than one occasion, but the two cooks, who seemed to know everything, said that that was just a habit of his. And that Melisande Ray just as habitually turned him down, with no hard feelings on either side.

One of the older men who sometimes worked the desk had told him that Rice-Jones often acted as an escort for Melisande when she needed to be seen out and about at public functions. But everybody seemed to be in agreement that there was little likelihood of Melisande Ray actually becoming the local bigwig's wife.

Which, Colin thought, was just as well, for there was an air of seediness about him that he distrusted. Though he still had the build of the ex-rugby player he'd been at university, Rupert was running just slightly to fat. His hairline showed imminent signs of receding. But it wasn't his physical qualities so much as the man's manner that gave Colin hives. He had a typical rich man's aura of superiority, mixed with a sense of desperation, and the combination sat oddly together.

Tonight, for instance, he seemed anxious for Melisande to show, and he wondered, somewhat uneasily, whether another marriage proposal was due.

If it was, the Oxford student could only hope Mel had the good sense to turn him down. Again.

* * *

Wendell James strolled into the bar and glanced across at the barman. Damn, he was hoping that Mel would be on duty tonight. He knew that hotel staff often rotated their duties, just in order to be able to cover for one another if someone had to cry off sick at the last moment. Thus it wasn't unusual for a maid to know how to mix a cocktail, or for a receptionist to know how to swing a floor-waxing machine.

With a mental shrug he stood at the bar and ordered a still mineral water, casting a professional eye around the room. The sandy-haired man sitting at the bar was well on his way to getting drunk, but most of the clientele were sitting at tables with cocktails, champagne or wine, and were relaxing after their evening meal. The average age must be approaching sixty, but there were a few younger and middle-aged couples as well. All looked affluent, healthy and happy.

He had to hand it to the management: they'd targeted their niche well.

He turned, then did a double take at the vision that walked through the door.

Melisande was wearing a full-length dress of amber-coloured velvet that glowed gorgeously under the muted lighting. Her long Titian locks had been piled on her head in an artful messy heap of loops and ringlets that must have taken an age to perfect. She wore simple, almost flat sandals in sparkling gold, and a plain gold chain hung around her neck.

She looked absolutely stunning.

For a moment, he couldn't think what a maid was doing, dressed like that and circulating in the hotel, then he realized that she must be acting as hostess tonight. Perhaps she was even the manager? He knew that some of the more old-fashioned hotels still liked to maintain that 'personal touch' among hotel guests. It would never work with big-city chains, of course, where the turnover was too fast for it to be worthwhile. But in an out-of-the-way, specialist place like this, he supposed it could pay dividends.

He watched her with admiration as she schmoozed her way professionally around the room, even catching the odd snippet of conversation as she did so. And he had to admit, she was good at talking to people like old friends, and putting them at ease.

In fact, the more he overheard, the more he realized that she seemed to genuinely know a lot of the people there, and from what they talked about, remembered them from past years.

He wondered idly what the returns rate was for a place like the Ray of Sunshine. Returns being those rare customers who liked to come back to the same hotel, year after year. Regulars, if you got enough of them, could be a reliable source of income, he knew. It was yet another profitable gambit on the part of the management, and it made him uneasy.

Perhaps the Ray of Sunshine Hotel wasn't going to be as much of a pushover as he'd hoped.

'Hello, Sylvia, how are the grandchildren? Didn't you say last year that your daughter was expecting another?' Her voice sounded genuinely interested, Wendell noted, and he nodded to himself.

Once he'd either driven this place out of business, or taken it over, he'd definitely find her a job in his company.

'Oh, they're just great. She had another boy, you know. Orrin John, they called him. They wanted another girl, but perhaps next time.' The woman who answered had a loud nasal twang, and Wendell guessed she was probably Texan.

Melisande bent over to look at the inevitable photographs, and made the appropriate noises, then moved on to the next table. Her glance swept the bar, and halted with a slight frown on the sandy-haired drunk. Then she swept on and her eyes alighted on Wendell. As her sombre grey eyes widened, he smiled slowly, a sexy challenge that had the heat flooding up into her face.

She turned, and went to the next table, where she sat down between two rather aged men, English this time, with whom she flirted outrageously, until they were claimed by their amused wives.

'We're just off to Windsor to see a play,' one of the grey-haired matrons said, and Wendell wasn't surprised that Mel could guess not only the name of the play, but offer them sterling advice on where best to park.

Eventually, she could put it off no longer. Slowly she made her way towards the bar.

'Mr James, isn't it?' she said sweetly, and Wendell grinned hugely.

The minx. She knew damned well what his name was.

'I see you've exchanged the pinny for a — what is it? Versace?' He looked at the dress, letting his eyes caress it where it clung to her slender curves.

'Yves St Laurent,' Melisande corrected him coolly. He was much too sure of himself for her liking. She glanced down the bar and gave a small wave of her fingers to Rupert.

'I'll be with you later, darling,' she said, much more warmly than she'd meant to.

Rupert, surprised by her unusually public display of affection, tipped his glass in acknowledgement. The bartender turned away carefully, and when Melisande turned back to Wendell James it was to find him glaring at Rupert.

Who was this clown? Wendell thought grimly. And did the management know that their lovely maid/hostess was in the habit of consorting with drunks?

'Mr Rice-Jones lives in the village,' she said, almost as if reading his mind. 'He's a regular and very valued customer here. And a personal friend,' she added, with an even sweeter smile. 'Now, I must go and see about the coffee,' she added. With just a slight toss of her head she turned and walked away.

Wendell James grinned ruefully to himself. Once again she'd shown him who was boss.

But that wouldn't last for long. With another long, level look at the happily slurping Rice-Jones, Wendell slipped off the stool and followed her into the dining room.

He felt in the need for a good cup of coffee. He also wanted to check out the food. Rumour had it that it was very good.

* * *

Gisela watched a tall, extremely handsome dark-haired man saunter into the dining room and glance around. Under normal circumstances, she'd have found him distinctly watchable, but with Keefe seated opposite her, she didn't even check to see where he went.

'So, where do you work?' Keefe asked casually, then smiled briefly as a waitress took their plates away. 'We're in no hurry for dessert,' he said softly, and she gave a slow nod of acknowledgement.

'Oh, nowhere very exciting,' Gisela said. 'I trained as a secretary, and now I work in a doctor's practice.'

'National Health?'

'No, private,' Gisela said. 'It was the first job I was offered after being made redundant from the last job I had. I was desperate for anything, really, but I like it where I am now. All the doctors are wonderful and my boss has been really good to me, letting me have time off on such short notice.'

'Oh?' he asked blandly, and was sure she looked somewhat furtive as she avoided his gentle probing for more information.

'I come from High Wycombe.' She said the first thing that came into her head, but was desperate to turn the conversation away from why she'd needed to take sudden leave from her job. 'Not very exciting either, I'm afraid. I'm sure to somebody like you, all this must sound very mundane.'

She fiddled with the petals of a white rose, part of the pretty centrepiece, and Keefe sipped from his glass of wine, watching her speculatively. She was definitely trying to keep something from him, but he wasn't in any particular hurry to find out what.

'No, I wouldn't say that,' he said, in response to her assumption. 'A lot of what I used to do would probably bore you to tears as well,' he lied easily.

'Do you miss the army?' she asked softly. If Keefe had been intent on drawing her out about her past life, she could just as surely do the same.

'Yes. But that's over now,' he said flatly. His injuries, while not permanently debilitating, had been serious enough to make going back to his old job impossible. Besides, the army was a young man's game, and he had to face it. With forty staring him in the face, it was time to think about settling down.

'Are you married?' Gisela asked boldly. 'Only, with you taking a holiday alone, I sort of figured that you weren't. Not that it's any of my business . . . Oh hell!' She laughed. 'My dad always said if you find yourself in a hole, stop digging. So I'll shut up.' She reached for her own wineglass, relieved to hear Keefe Ashleigh chuckle softly.

'No, I'm not married,' he said, not taking offence. 'I was, but my wife died. Leukaemia.'

'Oh, Keefe, I'm so sorry. I can be so clumsy sometimes.' Even though she'd known that he was a widower, something inside her needed to have him confirm it, but now she felt guilty.

'It's all right,' he said softly. 'It was a long time ago. She was a German girl I met while based in Frankfurt. We hadn't been married long when she became ill. It was difficult, trying to look after her when I could get shipped off at a moment's notice. Her mother moved in, and, well . . .' He shrugged helplessly.

'What about you?' He turned the tables on her neatly. 'No significant other?'

'No,' Gisela said simply. 'Oh, I haven't had my heart broken or anything romantic and interesting like that. I've just never found anyone that stuck.'

Until now, a little voice added, somewhere deep inside her, but she repressed it ruthlessly.

'Do you want a husband and family one day?' he asked curiously, and Gisela blinked, and drained her glass.

'I haven't really thought about it much. Especially lately,' she said truthfully, then could have bitten her tongue.

'Oh?' Again he probed delicately.

Gisela, unable to think of a lie in time, after a moment shrugged. 'Things are a bit hectic for me at the moment. But I think that's all over now,' she said firmly, with the clear intention of closing the subject. She glanced up as Melisande Ray passed the table.

'Everything all right?' Melisande asked, and they both assured her that it was.

* * *

Melisande left what she thought of as the 'boat couple' to their dessert, and frowned briefly as she saw Wendell James being served seafood linguine, a speciality of the house.

He caught her eye and half rose, leaving her no choice but to walk over.

'Please, won't you join me for a few moments?' he asked smoothly. 'I do so hate to eat alone.'

Melisande smiled and slipped into the seat opposite him. No doubt he knew that she couldn't refuse a paying guest a simple request, but she knew she was being manipulated, and she didn't like it.

Oh, as a woman, she knew he was pursuing her, and she was only human. It was flattering, after all, to have such a potently sexy and attractive man flirting with her. And exciting too! But her instincts were warning her that there was far more going on here than met the eye.

'Is this your first visit to the hotel?' she asked, firmly expecting him to say yes. So she nearly fell off her chair when he shook his head.

'No. I was here once before.'

'No you weren't,' Melisande said before she could stop herself, then forced a smile as he shot her a questioning look.

'It's not good form to disagree with the customer you know,' he rebuked mildly, and she bowed her head in acknowledgement.

'Forgive me. I simply meant that I've worked here for a very long time, and I don't remember you. And, naturally, I feel sure I would, had we ever met.'

Wendell grinned. 'Both flattering and well-saved.' He put down his knife and fork and applauded softly.

Melisande flushed.

'But much as it pains me to disagree with a lady — and especially one as lovely as yourself — I have been here. It would have been, let me see . . . yes, nearly ten years ago now.'

'Ah,' Melisande said in understanding. He must have come when she'd been away at college. 'You'd have met my . . . I mean Gareth Ray then?'

Wendell's eyes narrowed ominously. 'Oh yes,' he said softly. 'I remember Gareth Ray well.'

Very well indeed, he thought savagely.

Then his eyes sharpened on her. He hadn't missed her little slip, even though she'd covered it up well. She'd been about to say 'my' something or other. But what?

My boss? My lover, perhaps? Yes, that was probably more likely, he thought bitterly, and his eyes ran over her assessingly. He put her somewhere in her late twenties now, so she'd have been in her early twenties when Gareth Ray was still alive.

Yes. He liked them young. And a maid as beautiful as this one working in his hotel would have been bound to catch his eye.

He felt a pang as another, unpleasant thought intruded. Had she started out as a mere humble chambermaid and only worked her way up to her obviously elevated current position with the help of the hotel's owner?

He wouldn't put it past Gareth Ray.

But he was disappointed in her.

Melisande felt a slight ripple of unease along her spine. There was something about his tone of voice, something darker in his eyes, when he talked of her father that made her almost afraid.

'Is the linguine good?' she asked lightly.

'This is one of the best meals I've had for a long time,' he said, and again there was something in his tone of voice that puzzled her. Surely he should be sounding pleased? That was most people's reactions to the divine Stokes sisters' cuisine. Instead he sounded almost rueful.

'Well, I can recommend the baked semolina and apricot pudding,' she said cheerily as she rose from the table.

'I'll be sure to try it,' Wendell said blandly.

But she felt his eyes boring into her back as she walked away, and she was glad to leave the dining room behind.

There was something unnerving about Wendell James. He was up to something, but she was damned if she could figure out what. And even though he obviously took much pleasure in baiting and flirting with her, the man had more on his mind than idle sexual conquest.

Then she spied Rupert at the bar, and realized from the growing volume of his tone that he'd had too much to drink. She'd have to deal with him and get him out of there before he started to disturb the guests.

With a sigh, she headed towards the bar.

* * *

Six hours later, in the small hours of the morning, a man paused in a deserted street. All around him, High Wycombe slumbered. He checked the address once more to make sure there was no mistake, and ran his eyes up the front of the building.

It was a typical Victorian terraced house, converted now into flats, like so many of its kind. And the one he wanted was on the second floor: number 5.

He approached the front door boldly, knowing that to skulk about was a sure way to attract attention. Not that he thought anybody was watching. He'd been here for ten minutes now, and the only thing stirring were a few hunting cats.

He wasn't a tall man at five feet eight, but neither was he short. He was lean, dark-haired and could be any age from thirty to fifty. He was, above all, unremarkable. Dressed in jeans and brown leather jacket, he blended into the night, and when he stepped into the shadow of the porch, his dark clothing all but made him disappear.

His name was Leonard Keating. And as he bent down, he extracted a set of lockpicks from his pocket, and inspected the lock with a quick, professional eye.

It was a simple affair, and barely took him a minute to penetrate. Anybody who did happen to look out and notice him would have assumed him to be a drunk fumbling for his key and taking an inordinately long time to find the keyhole.

Once inside, Leonard glanced around, listening intently, but the flats were quiet. Not even a toilet flushed. Satisfied, he climbed the stairs, and with a small pocket torch found Flat 5. Again he paused and listened, ear to the door, and again there was nothing.

Once more he got to work with the lockpick and within a few moments he was standing inside the flat. His heartbeat picked up just a little, for if he was caught now, it would mean a long stretch inside, simply for breaking and entering. With a record like his, any judge would throw the book at him for that alone.

But Leonard Keating had something much more serious in mind than mere theft.

Although he'd started his criminal career as a teenaged pickpocket, he had progressed rapidly to burglary, auto theft and eventually armed robbery. But then, three years ago, he had gone freelance and branched out.

He had been given his first contract to kill. The mark had been a police informer, and Leonard had simply broken his neck and laid the corpse at the bottom of some stairs.

Since then, he'd never looked back. The work was, oddly enough, less taxing than his previous career, and it meant, perversely, that he ran less risk of getting caught by the law. After all, banks had alarm systems and guards. Not so individuals. He usually spent a week or so checking out his mark and choosing his options carefully. So far, he'd never been caught, and most of his jobs even passed for accidental.

And Leonard didn't think his latest commission would present any problems either. The mark was a woman, and he had a very long, very sharp knife in his pocket. With any luck, she would be asleep in bed, and one quick thrust would do it. No mess, no screaming, and not too much blood.

He looked around the darkened flat, getting his bearings. A streetlamp across the way illuminated the room enough for him to see that he was in a small living/dining area.

He walked stealthily to one door and opened it carefully, but it opened out into a small bathroom and was deserted.

He went to the next door and opened it. At once he heard rather heavy breathing. With the streetlight outside once again providing useful illumination, he approached the bed carefully, then frowned down at the sleeping girl.

This wasn't right. This girl was black. And his mark was a white girl. He retreated, freezing when the girl on the bed suddenly coughed and turned over. When he was sure he could hear her snoring, he tiptoed out.

That left only one more door.

He walked to it, taking the carefully sharpened knife from his pocket and unrolling it from the piece of chamois leather that he used to protect the blade. He let the handle settle into his hand.

It felt familiar and reassuring.

He opened the door and saw at once that the bed was empty. What the hell? He'd been assured by that harridan, Ma Pride, that she'd be here. He stood in the centre of the room for a moment, wondering what to do next. Then he began to search the place carefully. There was nothing helpful in the bedroom, so he retreated back to the lounge. It didn't take him long to find the desk, and he stared at the computer for a while, thinking furiously.

But he didn't really want to turn the machine on, in case it made a noise that woke the sleeping girl. After all, he wasn't being paid to kill *her*.

Instead, he checked the desk drawers, but found nothing worthwhile. Then he saw the wastepaper bin. Carefully he lifted it up and took it over to the window, where the orange light from the streetlamp allowed him to see more clearly.

After searching and discarding the usual rubbish, he was rewarded for his efforts by a printout from a holiday boat-rental company.

Bingo!

The mark had taken to the river for a holiday.

Leonard Keating smiled widely. A nice little jaunt on the river while he spied on his mark would make for a very nice break indeed.

CHAPTER FIVE

Sunday morning dawned cold and bright, but by ten o'clock it was getting seriously warm with just a slight breeze coming off the river. Keefe turned the key on the motor and heard the quiet, almost inaudible hum of the *Swan*'s engine. Beside him, Gisela smiled brightly.

At last, we're off!'

They'd spent the night on the boat still tied up to the Ray of Sunshine pier, Gisela very conscious of the sounds of Keefe as he moved around the boat. Lying in her very comfortable and surprisingly spacious bed, she'd felt the boat rock beneath her, very gently, a number of times before he'd settled down, and the movement soothed her. For the first time in a long time, she'd slept deeply and well.

Now, after preparing a light breakfast for the both of them of scrambled eggs and toast, the time had come for them to start their holiday in earnest.

Gisela felt a little thrill of excitement as Keefe carefully steered the *Stillwater Swan* out on to the open river for her maiden voyage.

'Do you want to take the tiller?' he asked, since they'd both been given a lesson on handling her, but Gisela was content to just sit back and watch. She shook her head with a smile, unaware of the way the sun turned her short cap of pale gold hair into a silver nimbus. Keefe had to command his eyes to look away from her.

She watched him handle the boat, mindful that at some point it would be her turn. But the lessons on handling the boat hadn't been nearly as difficult as she'd expected. A long-handled tiller that required very little physical effort to manoeuvre controlled the rudder and the main thing to remember, she knew, was the contrary steering. If you wanted the boat to go left, you turned the tiller right, and vice versa.

Gisela watched anxiously as a flotilla of ducks — mostly mallards, but with a few pure white Aylesburys mixed in — drifted by in front of the boat.

'Don't worry — I won't run them over,' Keefe said, reading her mind easily. 'River and canal ducks become old hands around boats. You'll see, they'll bob up on the other side, none the worse for wear.'

He was right of course, and Gisela went quickly into the galley for a slice of bread. She came back on the rear deck and began tossing it to the birds. They flocked around the boat like greedy river pirates. She could see she was going to have to spend a small fortune on sliced loaves!

'Weeping willow alert,' Keefe's voice distracted her a little while later. She looked up and laughed as a lacy curtain of green leaves swept across the top of the boat and brushed gently over them. She playfully batted a few strands out of the way.

'I'd better take her a bit further out into the middle of the river,' Keefe said, looking over his shoulder to eye the passing water traffic thoughtfully. Most of the boats on the river, he noticed, were of the sportier white-hulled, cab-in-cruiser type, which went at a much faster rate than the slow, elegant pace of the *Stillwater Swan.*

'Oh no, don't,' Gisela said, brushing the fronds of greenery from her face. 'I quite like it close to the shore. You can see more. Look, rabbits!' she suddenly cried, and pointed off to her left.

Sure enough, a group of small young rabbits bounded up the bank and into the field, their white tails disappearing into the tall meadow grass. 'And just smell that air,' Gisela said, spreading her arms wide and turning her face up to catch the sun. 'I can smell flowers.'

Keefe smiled indulgently. 'That's not surprising. There's a whole field of spring flowers out there.'

Gisela turned to look. 'Isn't it lovely? I recognize the clover, of course. And the big white daisies. Buttercups, and some vetch. And that lovely purple flower is a wild geranium. What are they called now? Purple cranesbill?'

Keefe cast a quick glance at the field and smiled wryly. 'Beats me. I probably wouldn't know a dandelion if I trod on one.'

Gisela laughed. 'Too much time spent abroad, that's your trouble. Now you're back in England to stay, you'll have to get reacquainted with your homeland.'

'True,' he said, glancing across at her thoughtfully. She was wearing a pair of white shorts that showed off her exquisitely shaped, if still pale legs to perfection. With it she was wearing a pale blue and peach blouse, with the sleeves rolled up and the ends tied into a knot across her stomach, showing off her bare midriff. If the sun continued to shine, Keefe mused with softening eyes, she'd soon be as brown as a berry.

They turned a bend, and the hotel finally disappeared from view. 'Wasn't Melisande Ray really nice and helpful about everything,' Gisela said.

'Yes, she was,' he agreed mildly.

Gisela looked at him out of the corner of her eye. 'She's very beautiful, isn't she? All that long Titian hair and everything.'

Keefe looked over his shoulder then steered the *Swan* just a little further out into the river. 'Was she? I didn't notice.' He had, of course, but hadn't really thought much about it. Now he turned his head quickly and caught a delighted smile on her face, and he turned away before she could see him grin in response.

Gisela blushed. 'I think I'll climb on top and get some sunbathing in,' she said, a shade defensively.

'All right. Be careful. Do you want a hand?'

But Gisela was small and lithe, and it took her only a few moments to grab a towel and then clamber on to the top of the flat-roofed boat. There she lay face down on the towel, her head turned to one side to watch the beautiful countryside slide by.

The *Swan* was almost completely silent as she glided along. Once or twice she thought she felt Keefe's eyes upon her. Which was nice.

She smiled gently and, with a sigh of pure contentment, closed her eyes.

* * *

Wendell James looked out of the window and watched Windsor drowsily coming to life below him. He opened the window to let the welcome spring sunshine inside, and heard the peal of the Sunday morning church bells.

His office building was, of course, completely silent. Only workaholics such as himself would have forsaken such a lovely day to don a suit and tie and keep the old grindstone turning. For some reason, the thought made his lips twist into a bitter smile. For some time now, he'd been feeling almost restless. James Leisure was going from strength to strength, but somehow, just lately, that didn't seem to be enough.

Shrugging off the nagging feeling that he was missing out on life, he settled himself behind his desk and was about to go through the projected figures on the new hotel, when the telephone rang.

He frowned. One of the perks of working on a Sunday was being able to go about his business without constant interruption.

He grabbed the receiver. 'Hello?' he said brusquely.

'I thought I'd find you in the office,' a familiar female voice said, openly disapproving. 'When are you going to get married and give me some grandchildren?'

'And good morning to you too, Mother,' Wendell said drily. His mother, Janet James, had begun asking him that question about five years ago, and now it had become something of a standing joke between them. Although sometimes Wendell got the uncomfortable feeling that she didn't find it all that amusing anymore.

'I'm working on it,' he lied. 'What can I do for you?'

'I wondered whether you wanted to have lunch. We could meet at the Cadogan Arms. Or, if you really want to live dangerously, I'll cook us something.'

'No you won't,' Wendell shot back quickly. Janet, although a wonderful mother and a source of never-ending good advice and comfort, had never been able to cook. 'And although I'd love to, I can't.' He checked his watch and saw it was nearly eleven. 'I have to be somewhere in an hour. I'm meeting a man about a plot of land.'

'Aren't you always? I've been trying to get in touch with you for days. There's no answer at the penthouse.' Her voice was more curious than reproving.

Wendell mostly lived on the whole of the top floor of the James Windsor Hotel, not far from the famous castle.

'No. I've, er, been staying somewhere else the last couple of days,' he admitted reluctantly.

'Oh? I didn't know you were going out of town.'

'Well, I haven't, not really. I mean, it's not far away. Just down the road, twenty miles or so.'

'What on earth is that all in aid of?' his mother asked, obviously puzzled, and Wendell bit his lip. He was hoping she wouldn't get to hear about his latest venture for some time yet. He knew fireworks were bound to start the moment she did.

'If you must know, I've been checking out the competition. The land I want to buy is less than two miles from an established hotel.'

'Oh, Wendell!' his mother sing-songed in obvious disapproval. 'I know I'm only a humble artist, and as your father was always saying, bless him, what I know about business could be fitted on the back of a postage stamp. But do you have to be so ruthless? Think of the poor man who owns that hotel — and his staff. They'll all be out of a job. Can't you add to your empire somewhere else?'

Wendell sighed. 'The land is right on the river. It maximizes the asset.'

'Wait a minute,' Janet said sharply. 'Twenty miles down the road from us? In which direction?'

Wendell sat a little straighter in his chair. 'What does that matter?' he stalled, but his mother, who knew him well, was already on to him. There was a moment of appalled silence, and then she spoke again. This time there was no hint of maternal indulgence in her tone.

'Wendell, where are you staying exactly?' she demanded sharply.

'You can always get hold of me, you know,' he temporised. 'You have my mobile phone number. I always carry it on me.'

'You're staying in the Ray of Sunshine, aren't you! *Aren't you?*' And, when he didn't answer, carried on grimly, 'Wendell, the man is dead. Gareth Ray has been dead for five years or more. Can't you let it go?'

'Mother, that's got nothing to do with it,' Wendell said shortly, and then took a calming breath. He knew that whenever he got angry with his mother, it was invariably because she'd managed to catch him on the raw. And in this case, she was making him feel guilty as well. 'This is strictly business. I told you — some land has become available right on the river. It's ideally situated for a hotel. We have Oxford, Henley and Windsor right on the doorstep. Foreign tourists will flock to the place.'

'It already has a hotel,' his mother pointed out in a quiet, ominously even tone. 'And don't try and tell me that you think the area can support two. You want to run the Ray of Sunshine out of business. Don't you?' she accused.

Wendell glanced out of the window. The church bells had stopped ringing now, and from the street he could hear the faint gabble of early tourist chatter.

'I haven't really given it that much thought,' Wendell said at last. 'But if the Ray of Sunshine goes down, I certainly won't shed any tears over it. Will you?' he challenged.

He heard his mother sigh heavily, then she hung up. Wendell pulled the receiver away from his ear and stared at it for a moment, feeling disconcerted that she hadn't even said goodbye. It was so unlike her.

Slowly he hung up.

Then he frowned.

His mother simply didn't understand. He built and ran hotels, tour operators, sports and leisure facilities. Along with the proposed new hotel to be built near Henley, he was also in the process of buying up a speedboat franchise in the Lake District. Furthermore, he was playing with the idea of buying a conference centre in Devon and turning it into one of those paintballing, hiking and therapy centres so beloved of businessmen keen to build up team spirit. And, on top of that, he had just bought a beautiful but near-derelict Victorian pool and lido complex in Brighton.

He was positive that, craftily restored, it would be a Mecca for the discerning holidaymaker.

It was all just business as usual for him.

Except you're not staying in the Lake District, or in Devon, or in Brighton, a jeering little voice popped up in the back of his mind. Instead he was staying in a hotel within spitting distance of his own home. And his new hotel hadn't even broken ground yet. Was he really in danger of becoming obsessed, as his mother so obviously thought?

He certainly, for the moment at least, had no desire to be anywhere else. But there was an obvious reason for that — and into his mind flitted the flaming-haired vision of Mel, the siren of the Sunshine. The thought should have amused him, but somehow it didn't. No woman had yet succeeded in getting under the skin of Wendell James. Now he was beginning to wonder.

Then he glanced at his watch and cursed softly. While he'd been contemplating his navel, time had sneaked by. He'd be late for his appointment.

He shrugged quickly into the dark charcoal jacket of his suit, grabbed his car keys and sprinted for the door.

* * *

Gisela cast her eye over the dining table and nodded. The salad, simple though it was, looked delicious.

'Keefe, lunch!' she called down the boat to the open doorway. She heard him call back in response, and a moment later felt the *Swan* begin to turn and head for the bank. Within a few minutes it had slowed to a stop. Through the window she saw Keefe leap lightly on to the bank with a mallet, so he could hammer in some pegs and tie off the boat.

She was just cutting into the bread rolls, which had been cooling on a wire tray, when he joined her.

He sat down and reached for the pat of butter, then made a brief exclamation as an early wasp landed on the dish. 'Damn things,' he muttered. He reached across to the settee, picked up the Sunday papers and began to roll one up.

'Don't you dare!' Gisela warned. 'I'll get it.'

She reached for an empty glass. Very smartly she caught the insect under it, then wiggled her fingers at him for the paper. He handed it over and watched her with gentle eyes as she inched the paper under the glass, then he got up and opened the window for her to let the wasp go free.

'I hate to see things killed,' Gisela said, once she had sat back down in her chair; then she wondered.

Keefe had been a professional soldier for many years. Had he killed?

He saw the colour flow then ebb from her expressive face, and knew exactly what she was thinking.

He hoped she wouldn't ask him.

Gisela swallowed hard, then smiled brightly. 'Do you want juice with lunch?'

He could have done with a cold beer, but shrugged lightly. 'Have you got any apple please? Or cranberry?'

* * *

Wendell James stood on the edge of the riverbank and looked out across the Thames. The spot wasn't as good as that occupied by the Ray of Sunshine, he saw that at once. The aspect wasn't as pleasing, and the atmosphere felt dank and just a little hostile.

The ground underfoot was also slightly boggy, and he understood why the present owner, a farmer, was willing to sell it. Bulrushes and reeds clogged the bank; a veritable haven for wildlife, but not much use to tourists, who'd expect a cultivated, more picturesque scene.

It would require a lot of work to bring it right, but that had never worried Wendell. 'I'm definitely interested,' he said now. 'You say the site has planning permission for building on?'

He turned to look at Walter Jenks, who nodded curtly. He was a short, squat individual with a dark visage and a morose air about him. Not for the first time, Wendell got the distinct impression that he didn't really want to sell. He supposed that, like most farmers, he was having a hard time of it and needed to realize some assets. But he was keeping a short strip of land to allow his cattle access to the river, so he hadn't lost all his business sense.

'Yes. There's permission for four detached residences,' Walter said reluctantly.

Wendell nodded. That was a major hurdle already overcome. It wouldn't, he was sure, take much to persuade the planning commissioners to accede to his request for a hotel on this site. After all, he wouldn't be taking up any more building space than four houses. And a hotel would bring employment and tourist money to the area as well.

'So, we just need to talk price.'

Walter, who was leaning against a rather old and knotted willow, shrugged. He didn't much like this man in his sharp business suit, although he had to admit that the man did exude a competent air. He didn't like selling his land, either. And worse, he felt guilty about it. A friend of his had warned him that this Wendell James fellow was in the hotel-building business, and not in construction, as Walter had previously thought.

Walter regularly drank in the Ray of Sunshine, since Royston had no pub, which made it his local. And Gareth Ray had been a friend of long standing. What would he say if he knew that Walter was going to sell land to one of his daughter's business rivals?

Perhaps he would talk to Melisande about it first. She might be able to give him a counter-offer. Feeling a little cheered by this thought, Walter now shrugged and muttered vaguely about having second thoughts. He was careful not to meet the other man's astute eyes as he went on to say that he'd been advised that the land would be worth more, should he hang on to it a bit longer.

Wendell listened without comment, and without surprise. The farmer wanted more money. That was only to be expected. It would take a few days of wrangling, but he was sure he could persuade the old man to sell.

He was used to being both patient and canny when it was necessary. As he walked back to his car, he nodded across at the farmer, told him he'd call him in a couple of days, and then got behind the wheel.

Walter Jenks watched him go and sighed heavily.

He needed the cash, there were no two ways about it. That latest bluetongue scare of last year had damned near bankrupted him. He hadn't been able to move his cattle for nearly six months.

Now he climbed into his battered Land Rover and sat staring out at the lumpy, unattractive field. As he did so, a rare marsh harrier swooped across in front of him, and brought a smile to his face.

He hoped Melisande Ray would be able to buy the land from him instead. Just as soon as he'd worked up the courage to tell her about it.

* * *

Leonard Keating drove into the car park of the Ray of Sunshine hotel and looked around carefully.

Being Sunday, there were a lot of guests around, most of them sitting in the sunny garden and awaiting the traditional Sunday roast.

Oblivious to the thought of food, however, he wandered towards the entrance and paused in the front doorway, looking around cautiously. He could see no signs indicating the marina or a booking office. He didn't really want to bring himself to the attention of the hotel staff, and when he saw a young man step out of the corridor and move behind the desk, he swore softly under his breath.

But there was nothing else for it. He knew that what he needed to do couldn't be done over the telephone. Nobody gave out confidential information without being charmed and persuaded in person.

'Hello. I was wondering if I could see someone about booking a boat. Or am I in the wrong place?' He spoke from the doorway, careful not to get any closer. He was wearing a cap and sunglasses, but he'd found it always paid to be ultra-careful. Especially in his profession.

'I'm sorry, sir, but the secretary who deals with that isn't here today.'

Of course not, Leonard thought. It was Sunday after all. 'Oh, that's a shame. I'm driving back to Scotland today and I wanted to get something sorted out for this August before I go.'

Colin, taking a break from the bar, looked at the stranger thoughtfully. His first thought was simply to hand him one of the brochures that Mel had had printed up and tell him to telephone on Monday. But he knew Mel was anxious that the boats should pay for themselves, and he knew how capricious and fickle tourists could be. And what were the chances that this customer would forget to ring, or go with someone else, once he was back in Scotland? Probably pretty high.

And a bird in the hand was worth two in the bush, and all that, Colin mused. Besides, he knew that Gina wouldn't mind; she only lived a few minutes' walk down the road and had said she'd be at home today.

'If you'd like to take a seat, sir, I'll have someone come and help you.'

Leonard smiled. 'Thank you. That's very helpful. I'll be in the garden then.'

'The bar's open, sir,' Colin said cannily. Leonard smiled, but had no intention of drawing any more attention to himself than necessary.

Colin watched him go and reached for the telephone. As he suspected, Gina was only too happy to take a few minutes and come in. She still felt as if she was in disgrace after the double-booking incident, and was anxious to make amends.

So when Leonard was approached ten minutes later by a very talkative, very helpful teenager, it didn't take him long to make a fictitious booking. And, being the kind of man who could turn on the charm, it didn't take him very long, either, to get Gina talking about herself, the new marina, and the awful gaffe she'd made. Gina was even so obliging as to mention which way the *Stillwater Swan* was headed, having overheard the occupants talking about it last evening.

When Leonard pulled out of the car park twenty minutes later, his mind was already planning ahead.

He could easily arrange for an accident in Oxford — always supposing Gisela Ashley and her unexpected boat-mate got that far. Oxford was a busy tourist town, after all. A quick shove in the back on a crowded pavement and she'd be under a bus.

But first things first.

He pulled on to the side of the road and got out a map, looking for the nearest marina. He needed to hire a boat

— just a small, single-cabin cruiser with a bit more speed and manoeuvrability than a narrowboat so that he could catch them up. A craft, for instance, that could easily and quickly run over somebody who was already in the water — a boat that was just heavy enough to make such a procedure fatal.

* * *

Gisela tensed as she spotted the bend in the river ahead then told herself not to be such a wuss. She'd been handling the *Swan* ever since they'd finished lunch, and hadn't run them aground or into the bank yet.

Now she carefully turned the tiller in the opposite direction to where she wanted to go, and just in case, powered the engine down a fraction. At a stately two miles an hour, she guided the narrowboat through the bend, and breathed a sigh of relief.

Then she nearly jumped out of her skin as she heard a hoarse shout coming from below. It was a mournful sound, something that made the gooseflesh rise on her forearms.

'Keefe, is that you? Are you all right?' She half-stooped to call down the steps and into the body of the boat.

After lunch, she'd said she'd take a turn at the tiller, and Keefe had retired to the main seating area with the papers and a wedge of cold apple pie. And she hadn't heard a peep from him since.

'Keefe?' Now she called softly again, but still only silence greeted her.

She was about to shrug it off. After all, there was no knowing what had made the sound. The man who'd shown them how to handle the boat had told her that herons sometimes made a strange sound, and if they heard anything odd at night, they could probably put it down to vixens or even hunting owls.

But this was the middle of the day. She looked around, but could only see peacefully grazing sheep in the fields and a pair of moorhens, who were building a nest in the reeds off to her left.

Then she heard it again, and this time, she had no doubts. It was definitely a human cry — and, moreover, the cry of someone in deep trouble.

Anxiously she steered the boat to the side and cut off the engine. She knew she should moor up properly, but first she needed to check on what was going on below.

She quickly went down the metal stairs, her bare feet making only a light slap-slapping sound as she descended. She saw Keefe at once. He was half-lying, half-sitting on the sofa, the open broadsheet lying forgotten on his lap. He was sound asleep, but as she approached him, she could see his eyelids moving restlessly. He was obviously dreaming.

And then he gave a sudden agonized cry that made her jump. She ran across to him and put her hand on his shoulder. His flesh felt warm but damp under his T-shirt, and her fingers tingled at the contact.

'Keefe, wake up,' she said quietly but firmly. She didn't want to wake him too precipitously from his nightmare, but she was determined to help him. 'Keefe, it's all right. You just need to wake up.'

Keefe's eyes suddenly shot open, their usual dark chocolate colour looking almost black. Sweat beaded his bony but attractive face, and his hands shot out to grab her. Suddenly she was half-sprawled across him, and she gave a brief cry of surprise.

'What? Are you crazy? What are you doing?' he blazed, then slowly the awareness came back into his eyes, the tension left his body and he collapsed back against the settee. 'I'm sorry. I was dreaming, wasn't I? Are you all right?' His voice sharpened. 'I didn't hurt you, did I?' he demanded hoarsely.

Gisela, her heart thumping, laughed with false gaiety. 'Good grief, no, of course not. You just scared me, that's all,' she said breathlessly. 'One minute I was trying to wake you up, and the next . . . I was in your lap.' Her voice became husky as she suddenly became aware of the intimacy of their position.

She was half-lying against him, one of her bare feet on the floor of the boat, her other thigh pressed against his stomach. She could feel the washboard ridges of his stomach muscles against her flesh.

He was superbly fit.

Her left arm was half-looped around his neck, her fingers holding on to the back of the settee for dear life, her left breast pressed against his shoulder. Her nipples began to harden, and she dragged in a deep breath. This close she could see the tiny pores in his chin, darkening with his need for a shave, and she could smell the faint tang of masculine sweat and coal tar soap. Her stomach fluttered wildly.

Keefe stared up into her large, startled blue eyes and saw the sexual awareness slowly creep on to her delightful, elfin-shaped face.

His own lips parted just a little and he saw her swallow hard. He could smell her perfume — something light and floral — and he moved his hand to brush a lock of bright, silver-blonde hair out of her eyes. He moved his head up, watching her closely, alert for any sign of withdrawal, but saw none.

Gisela lowered her face, and their lips met slowly, almost questioningly at first and then more hungrily. She made a small sound in her throat — half purr, half growl — and wondered who on earth was making such a provocative noise. Her eyes feathered closed with a flutter of lashes.

Keefe drew in a sharp breath through his nose, and felt almost giddy with desire.

And then he felt it. That first, almost imperceptible stirring of unease as she tensed in his arms, and he slowly lifted his lips from hers.

Gisela opened her eyes, confusion rampant in her expression. One part of her wanted the kiss to go on and on. But another part of her was far more cautious.

Was a holiday romance really what she wanted? Or what *he* wanted? Was it such a good idea to become intimate when they'd be sharing such a small space for three weeks? And, more important, was she mistaking gratitude for something more? Worse, was some part of her so anxious for them to become lovers simply because it would make her feel more secure? After all, Keefe would be more inclined to protect her if they were in a relationship.

She hated to think she could be so cowardly.

Or was she only using that as an excuse, a reason for her to pull away, because in reality this man scared her? She'd only known him a day, but already it felt as if he'd been in her life for ever. It was all happening much too fast.

'I'm sorry,' she blurted, then began to scramble off him. Keefe immediately opened his arms and let her go.

'Sorry for what?' he asked mildly, determined to play it cool. The last thing he wanted to do now was scare her.

Gisela looked at him, and opened her mouth to tell him about the Prides, the court case, the threat to her life. But something stopped her.

It was ridiculous, after all. She was making a mountain out of a molehill.

Besides, she didn't want anything to spoil the next few weeks. There was an enchantment here on the *Stillwater Swan* — she'd felt it the moment she'd seen the boat, and the feeling had only grown. The river, the sunshine, this man and her fey feeling of kismet were combining to make this time something special. There was a once-in-a-lifetime feel to this whole situation that she wanted to guard fiercely.

She wouldn't let anything spoil it. She just wouldn't. When she was old and grey, this was the time that she would look back on and cherish. She could just feel it.

'Nothing. Sorry, just forget it ever happened.' She tried for light and breezy but wasn't sure she quite pulled it off. 'I'm sorry about your nightmare. I hope it doesn't come back,' she added sincerely.

Keefe sat up straighter on the settee and ran a hand through his short dark hair. The nightmare had been a familiar one — a rerun of those moments before he triggered off the mine. He knew what was coming, but in the dream he could do nothing to stop himself from playing out the scene to the ultimate conclusion. His feet kept walking, no matter how much his brain screamed at him to stop, and then there was the noise that filled his head, the flash of light and the sensation of flying through burning air, the awful smell of singeing and then the pain.

But as he sat on the gently rocking boat, he suddenly had the thought — bizarre but undeniable — that he would never have that nightmare again. It was as if this woman, waking him from it before he'd had a chance to set off the explosive, had set him free for ever.

Gisela saw a strange look cross his face, but couldn't read it. She only hoped he wasn't regretting coming on the boat with her. If he said he was going to get off at the next lock and go back to the hotel, she was sure her heart would break.

'I'd better get back to the tiller. I didn't tie the boat up, and we might be drifting into the middle of the river for all I know,' she babbled nervously, then turned and fled.

Back on deck, she saw that they had drifted, but only a little, and she turned the engine back on. The *Stillwater Swan* came to life with a gentle hum, as if trying to soothe her. It was as if the boat understood her turmoil.

With hands that shook slightly, Gisela began to steer them all towards the town of Henley-on-Thames.

As they moved slowly forward, she felt paradoxically calm and yet fraught. What was going on with her? Why was she suddenly feeling so giddy with happiness?

And where would it all end?

CHAPTER SIX

Vin Ray watched his sister cross the lawn, a large glass jug of homemade lemonade in one hand and a cluster of glasses in the other. Even from where he was sitting under a gaily striped awning on the front lawn terrace he could hear the ice jingle enticingly as she moved. He watched her approach two old couples sitting on the furthest side of the lawn, who were vaguely regarding the river in the distance and chatting animatedly.

Americans, he thought, then nodded to himself as Melisande put the tray down in front of them. It wasn't her job to act as a waitress, of course, and he suspected that the couples were old and valued customers. But then, Mel had never seemed to mind the minutiae of running a hotel — whether it was being charming to customers who made you want to scream, or filling in for staff when they fell ill. He himself, on the other hand, had left the Ray of Sunshine the moment he could — first to go to art college, where he quickly specialized in photography, and from there to travelling the world.

The thought of running a hotel had always filled him with dismay. But for all that, every now and then he liked to touch base with his roots, especially to see how his closest remaining relative was doing. Like most twins, they had a strong bond that time and distance couldn't touch.

Which was just as well.

He'd returned from Guyana just three days ago, and he was off to the Arctic next month to photograph the melting glaciers for an eco-conscious magazine. He also wanted to get some pictures of any wildlife he might encounter there for a regular private customer who had a large collection of contemporary photography concerning the poles.

He saw Mel say a parting word to her guests, then she turned and spotted him and a huge smile lit up her face.

Right now, he was staying with a sort-of girlfriend in Windsor, and he saw Mel look around his feet for his suitcases and come up empty. As she walked towards him he could see the question mark in her eyes. Usually he stayed at the hotel during his brief sojourns in England.

He shrugged at her unspoken question, knowing that she'd be pleased to hear about his sort-of girlfriend, which in turn made him wonder what had been happening with her love life for the last six months or so. Or, perhaps it would be more accurate to say, it made him worry about what *hadn't* been happening with her.

For a while, he'd been worried that she might take that ass Rupert Rice-Jones seriously enough to marry him, but over the years, he'd become convinced that that particular threat had definitely receded. But that, in a way, only left another problem in its wake. Without the ever-present, ever-devoted Rupert, his twin's love life seemed to be all but non-existent.

As she got nearer and began to mount the stone steps up on to the terrace, his eye fell to her hands. But, as he'd expected, there was still no ring on her finger. Just then, a man stepped out on to the terrace further down and stood watching her, his hands thrust deeply into his pockets.

For a second, Vin saw him only in profile — the shock of thick black hair, a finely shaped, rather sharp nose, the strong outline of his chin and jaw. Then he turned full-face as

Mel gained the terrace proper, and with a shock of unpleasant foreboding, Vin recognized him.

Wendell James. What the hell was he doing here?

'Hey, long time no see. What happened to the emails? They dried up about a month ago!'

Vin dragged his eyes from the man he'd never wanted to see again, and at the sound of his sister's voice forced a smile on to his face as he greeted her.

'Sorry about that — I took a trek deep into the jungle. You knew better than to be worried about me though, right?'

He rose to his feet as, out of the corner of his eye, he saw Wendell James slowly remove the hands from his pockets. He wasn't sure, but he thought the tycoon stiffened perceptibly.

So he remembers and recognizes me, Vin thought grimly. Damn, what was he doing here?

'Of course I did,' Mel said, stepping up to hug him with her usual enthusiasm. 'Besides, I'd know if anything bad had happened to you,' she said seriously.

And Vin understood instantly what she meant. As children, they'd always known if the other had been in trouble, even if they were far apart. They always had illnesses at the same time, even if Vin had been in boarding school and Mel still at home, and once, when Vin had fallen off his bike and broken his right wrist, Mel hadn't been able to use her own right wrist either for several weeks. As they'd grown older, this somewhat spooky togetherness had dissipated to some degree, but both of them still took it for granted.

He was about to speak when he sensed movement coming up beside him and the hackles rose on the back of his neck. He turned abruptly, meeting a pair of dark blue eyes.

'Oh, Mr James, hello.' It was Melisande who spoke first. 'Is everything satisfactory?'

Vin flicked his eyes briefly to his sister, catching something in her voice that puzzled him. It was almost too polite. Too carefully neutral. Usually his sister treated all her guests like old friends, and he wondered, with a shaft of protective anger, what this man had done or said to her to make her so aloof.

'The service here is excellent, as you well know,' Wendell said, with a definite hint of irony. He'd been at the hotel two days now, and had yet to find a flaw in either its running or its ethos.

Now he turned and looked at Melvin Ray pointedly. He was interested to see how Gareth Ray's son wanted to play things.

When he'd stepped out on to the terrace and seen Mel, he'd noticed at once the pleased animation on her face. And when he saw it was directed at a guest standing further down the terrace, he'd been disconcerted at the sudden sense of possessiveness he'd felt.

Then, a moment later, when he'd recognized Melvin Ray, he'd felt only a cold grim amusement, for the lovely redhead certainly did seem to have a penchant for the hotel family owners. And he wondered if, when her affair with the father had ended, she'd simply transferred her allegiance to the son and heir.

But what Mel said next made him draw in his breath swiftly.

'Oh, Mr James, this is my brother, Melvin. My twin, actually. We all call him Vin, to avoid confusion.'

Vin saw the business tycoon blink once, and saw something move, deep down, in the expression of his eyes. He couldn't be sure what it was, but it made him feel uneasy.

'I see,' Wendell James said flatly, turning to give a somewhat forced smile to Mel. 'So you run the hotel for your brother?'

Melisande gave him a long, level look, her grey eyes looking distinctly stormy. 'No, Mr James, I do not,' she said succinctly. 'And if I may say so, your chauvinism is showing. I own the Ray of Sunshine in my own right. My father, Gareth Ray, left it to me.'

Wendell felt as if someone had just punched him in the solar plexus. To cover it, he raised an eyebrow as if in amusement, and forced his lips to give a little twist.

'Oh, I didn't want it,' Vin said, as Wendell James shot him a quick look. 'Besides, Dad had his head screwed on the right way, and knew Melisande was the offspring to take over the family empire. She was born with the Ray of Sunshine in her blood.'

'Melisande,' Wendell heard himself say, the very word a caress, and when he glanced back at the beautiful redhead who had somehow inserted herself under his skin when he wasn't looking, he saw her cheeks flush, just faintly, with answering colour.

'What a beautiful name. It suits you.'

Melisande inclined her head slightly. 'Thank you.'

'Well, I won't keep you,' Wendell cast Melvin Ray another long, considering glance. 'It seems to be something of a family reunion. I think I'll take a stroll.' So saying, he moved around them and sauntered casually down the steps.

He was dressed in fawn slacks with a white and pale blue polo shirt. The pastel colours seemed to accentuate the blackness of his hair and the slender, powerful build of his body, and Melisande watched him leave, conscious that her heart was pounding loudly in her chest.

Damn the man, why did he always have that effect on her? It was maddening. And exciting.

She tossed her head unknowingly, and tried to dismiss him from her thoughts, to concentrate on her twin instead. But when she turned back to him, Vin was looking at her oddly.

Always happy-go-lucky and laid-back, he was, most unusually for Vin, scowling. 'What's that man doing here? When did he book in?'

Melisande blinked in surprise at the abruptness of the questions. 'Just a few days ago. And I have no idea what he might be "up to". Why do you ask?'

Vin recognized the curiosity in her voice and could have kicked himself. Right from when she was a toddler, Mel had always been as curious as a cat. He'd have to cool it, or she might start asking some awkward questions. Their father had been determined that what had happened when she'd been away studying for her degree be kept a secret from her, and Vin could understand why.

If she'd known, it would have broken her heart.

'Oh, nothing. I just thought he seemed a bit . . . I don't know. Proprietorial. He looked at you as if he wanted to eat you. Didn't you notice?'

Vin was rather pleased at the way he managed to divert her interest, but when Melisande laughed it sounded false, even to her own ears.

'I can't say I did,' she said lightly. 'Besides, you've changed your tune, haven't you? Whenever I see you, you're always on to me about when I'm going to get married and make you an uncle.'

Vin felt himself shiver. 'I know. But, Mel — just not with that guy. OK?' And when he saw her eyes narrow, he added quickly, 'I just get a bad vibe off him, that's all. Trust your twin, OK?'

Melisande nodded, and forced a smile on to her face. 'You needn't worry. He's not my type anyway,' she said casually.

But as they ambled away, arm in arm, into the cool hall of the hotel, Melisande knew that something was wrong. Although neither Vin nor Wendell James had said so, she was sure that the two men knew each other. Oh, not well, perhaps. And maybe they had only met a long time ago. But she sensed that their association was not a happy one.

What was more, she'd sensed that learning that she was the owner of the hotel had come as a distinct, not to say, nasty surprise to Wendell James. On a lesser man, she might have put that down to embarrassment on his part. After all, she knew full well that he'd mistaken her first for a maid, and then for a manager. But she knew instinctively that that little gaffe wouldn't have fazed him at all.

No, there was something else going on. She could just feel it.

Melisande had always been able to twist her twin around her little finger, so she was confident that it wouldn't take her long to worm out of Vin what it was all about.

* * *

Leonard Keating steered the *Skylark II* into the side of the river and somewhat ineptly moored up. The boat was a medium-sized one-bedroom cabin cruiser, which he'd hired for the week. White with blue trim, it had a reasonably fast engine and good panoramic views from the forward cabin, and it was ideal for his purposes.

Several hundred yards ahead, setting up a barbecue on the towpath, a couple worked busily.

Leonard casually got out his binoculars and trained it on the predominately white narrowboat that was tied up beside them. It looked brand new and sparkled pure white with an attractive orange and black trim that ran along the length of the flat roofline.

He trained the binoculars on to the lettering on the stern of the boat, and mentally nodded.

STILLWATER SWAN.

Yes, it was the name of the boat that Gisela Ashley had rented. He put the binoculars down for a moment, and reached into his shirt pocket to withdraw a folded piece of paper. It was a photocopy of a newspaper photograph, perhaps not of the highest quality, but it gave a good enough representation of a small blonde woman to make her features recognizable.

Leonard studied the image then raised the binoculars once more, turning the little wheel to bring them into sharper focus, and got the couple in his eyeline again.

Yes, it was the same woman, he was sure of it. That was Gisela Ashley all right.

He knew why his client wanted her dead, of course. Mrs Pride was well known for her over-protective maternal instinct when it came to her precious crooked children. In fact, in some circles of modern gangland London, the more moderate members of several factions considered Ma Pride to be a bit of a nutcase.

Leonard gave a small mental shrug as he briefly considered this. But then, what did it really matter? Her money was the same colour as anyone else's, and she'd given him plenty of it.

Under the pretence of birdwatching, he managed to observe Gisela Ashley for a fair while, all the time making mental calculations. He doubted that she was much above eight stone, and was small and slender-boned. Overpowering her would be easy. Hell, he could just pick her up and toss her into the canal, if it came to it.

The man she'd picked up had far more potential for causing trouble. He knew from the talkative girl at the marina all about the double booking, but he knew nothing else about the man with the same surname as his mark.

Thoughtfully, he changed the focus of his surveillance to her companion. They both had their backs to him, and the man was crouched down, trying to light the barbecue. His movements seemed to be just a little stiff, but at the same time lithe. It was a bit of a puzzle. Then he rose to his full height, which the assassin guessed to be about six feet, and Leonard swore softly under his breath. This wasn't good. He preferred the odds to be more in his favour. At only five eight himself, the man's size ruled out any hand-to-hand stuff. Although he was lean, from what Leonard could see of him, he was also wiry. And in his experience, many men of this build could be surprisingly strong. Besides, the man had an aura about him of quiet competence that Leonard really didn't like. Not one little bit.

The more he watched them, the man beginning to barbecue what looked like pork chops, the girl scraping some new potatoes and carrots, the more he realized that he'd either have to get the mark on her own before making a move, or else take the man out first.

Settling down on his boat, Leonard Keating began to mull over his options.

* * *

Walter Jenks stepped into the cool hall of the Ray of Sunshine Hotel and rubbed a hand across his damp forehead. It had been another long hot day, but, thanks be, now that the very last of his late lambs had been born, he could relax. He also had a small dairy herd, but that hardly paid the way, so he was setting aside some land next year to try and grow some of these new bio-fuels everyone was going on about.

But for that he needed capital.

And that was what had brought him here so early this fine spring evening. That, and the prospect of a long cold beer of course.

But tonight, he didn't feel so much like a regular customer of the bar of long standing, but more like a naughty dog, creeping in with his tail between his legs.

He was thankful to see that the bar was almost deserted. At just gone six, most of the hotel guests were probably upstairs, getting changed ready for dinner, or were still out and about sightseeing.

The young barman recognized him at once, and smiled across the empty room. 'Usual?' he called cheerfully.

Walter nodded and shuffled forward gratefully to take the pint of locally brewed ale. 'Is Mel around?' he asked reluctantly, after taking the first long, blissful swallow.

The young student looked a little surprised. Walter was usually the type who liked to come in, find a quiet spot, sink a few pints in peace, and then amble off.

'I think she's in the dining room, doing the usual pre-dinner check,' he said helpfully.

'Oh. Right,' Walter said with a sigh. He picked up his pint and walked gingerly to the connecting French doors. For all the years that he'd drunk in the bar, he'd never eaten a meal at the hotel, and he felt like an intruder as he stood in the doorway looking around.

It was certainly a fancy restaurant, Walter thought with appreciation. Lovely tablecloths set with highly gleaming silver and glass, with vases of flowers in the centre. When his wife had been alive, she'd liked to have flowers on the table too. Although his old scrubbed oak table in the kitchen of his farmhouse was a far cry from this genteel, elegant setting.

'Hello, Walter, you look a little lost,' Mel said, spotting him and walking over at once. 'Is everything all right? The beer's not off is it?'

'Oh no, nothing like that, hen,' Walter said with a bright smile. 'That'd be a disaster!'

Melisande laughed gaily. 'It certainly would!' Without quite realizing it, Walter found himself steered gently back into the bar, and settled on a comfortable banquette in a quiet corner.

Always a competent reader of people, Mel sensed that the quiet, normally reticent farmer was troubled, and wouldn't want to have an audience. Since Royston-on-Thames had no pub, the hotel played regular host to the locals, and Walter had been coming to the bar ever since Mel could remember. Originally from near Glasgow, Walter's accent had almost disappeared over the years, but it seemed to erupt whenever he was upset. Like now.

'Is there something wrong, Wally?' she asked gently.

The old man looked at her, then grinned. 'You know, your old dad said you were a mind-reader. He said that if you'd been born in the old days you'd have had to watch out not to be burnt at the stake as a witch.'

Mel grinned. 'My dad always had a weird sense of humour,' she agreed, not at all put out.

'Yeah. Well, the thing is, Mel, hen, I'm thinking of selling a parcel of land. You know, the one round the bend in the river?'

Melisande blinked. She couldn't see what this had to do with her, but from the way he ducked his head and took a quick, fortifying sip of his favourite ale, she could see that the topic was, for some strange reason, worrying him.

'It's a bit boggy, and too small really to be of much use to me as pasture. Cows don't like it, and you can't trust sheep near water for too long. Stupid things, sheep. And I'm trying to diversify, so I thought I'd sell the land, and just keep a narrow corridor of it for watering, like.'

Melisande nodded. Was the dear old man asking her for business advice? Surely a farmer of his experience didn't need it?

'Sounds ideal,' she said cautiously.

'Ah. Yes. Well, see, I thought I was gonna sell it to developers, you know, those Johnnies who want to put houses up everywhere.'

Mel smiled briefly. 'River-front views would sell well in any market,' she agreed, still puzzled.

'Ah. Yes, I 'spect so. Thing is, I've been having talks with this fellow who, it turns out, wants to put a hotel on it. James Leisure, the company is,' Walter blurted out all at once, and Melisande felt her heart go into freefall.

Another hotel, so close to the Ray of Sunshine! Damn it, someone was trying to poach on her turf!

Walter took a quick look at her, and she forced herself to smile gently. 'I see. Well, that's not very good from my point of view, obviously.'

'No, I know. And I ain't sold it yet. Nothing's been signed like,' Walter said anxiously. 'So I was kind of hoping you might make me an offer for it — the land, I mean. I'd rather see it go to you than some big fancy company.'

Melisande felt her heart sink. 'Oh, Walter, if only you'd come to me a couple of months ago, I probably could have,' she said forlornly. 'But I've just had a massive outlay on buying three new narrowboats.'

'Oh,' Walter said flatly. 'Yes, I heard about them. They're right nice, people say.'

Melisande forced another smile. 'Well, perhaps I can raise the capital some other way,' she said, with more optimism than she felt. 'Can you just give me a few days to see if I can come up with something?'

Walter, vastly relieved, smiled for the first time with genuine warmth. 'Course I can, hen. Any reasonable offer you can come up with and the land's yours.'

He hesitated, then added sadly but firmly, 'But I've got to sell it before winter if I'm to buy in new seed.'

Melisande, realizing how genuinely concerned the old man was, felt tears of gratitude shimmer in her eyes. She reached over to put her hand on his. 'Thank you, Walter. For warning me. And for being so sweet.'

The old man blushed, and Mel smiled. This was why she'd never wanted to venture into the bigger, harsher world of high finance. Here, friendship and loyalty still meant something.

'Ah, well, your father was a good man, he'd have wanted me to look out for you. And this hotel is a grand place,' Walter said, looking around the comfortable bar with a fond eye. 'None of us want to see anything happen to her.'

And for the first time, Melisande felt a sharp lancet of fear ripple through her.

For all the years she'd lived, then worked, in the Ray of Sunshine, the thought that it might one day cease to be had never even occurred to her.

Now, suddenly, it felt as if her whole life had been put in jeopardy.

'Well, I'd better go and see to my guests. I'll be in touch really soon, Walter, all right?' she said softly. She got to her feet and, on legs that felt suddenly numb, walked carefully across the room.

Once out in the hall, however, she went straight to her office. Gina was gone for the day, of course, and she quickly turned on her computer and got online.

What was the name of the company Walter had mentioned? James Leisure. That was it. Of course, Melisande had already heard of it. She even knew that it had headquarters locally, although the company itself had assets that were global.

She quickly found particulars on all sorts of its departments, and what she read impressed her. Customers of James Leisure could have everything from a single night in a James DeLuxe hotel in Budapest, to a two-week, fully comprehensive break in the Bahamas, complete with snorkelling or scuba-diving lessons thrown in. You could skydive in Panama, or learn to bungee jump in Bristol. If you were a student backpacker on a budget there were James Leisure youth hostels in the remotest of places. Alternately, you could enjoy luxury breaks that were available in five-star hotels in nearly every capital city in the world.

James Leisure was, in short, a multi-million giant. So why did it want to build a hotel practically on her humble doorstep?

Feeling more and more chagrined, scared, upset and angry, she tapped a few keys and got on to the website that detailed the board of directors.

And there, right at the top of the page, was a large picture of the owner of the company itself.

One Wendell James.

Melisande heard a sound that was somewhere between a sigh, a moan, a cry of anger and a cry of pain. It took her a moment to realize that it had come from her own mouth.

She drew in a long, ragged breath, and heard herself sob. It was such a shocking sound that she quickly slapped a hand over her mouth, like a guilty child.

After a while, she reached out with a hand that shook, and turned off the computer. The screen hummed, then clicked and fell dark. And for a long while she simply sat there numbly, staring into space.

Slowly, her shocked mind began to function again.

Well, she supposed, it explained why he'd booked into her hotel. He was checking out the competition. And it sort of explained why Vin had got such a bad vibe from him. Had he recognized him as the head of James Leisure, and guessed that his presence at the Ray family hotel couldn't bode well? Somehow, Melisande didn't think so. Vin was hardly interested in the world of hotels and the leisure industry. Besides, the evident antagonism between the two men had seemed more personal than that.

Slowly, Melisande got to her feet and began to pace, and her mind went back to the meeting that afternoon between the three of them on the terrace.

When Wendell James had realized that she was the owner of the hotel, not merely an employee of it, he'd looked more than surprised. He'd seemed shocked. And his eyes, when they'd turned to her, had looked, what exactly? Regretful? Maybe a little melancholy?

She shook her head angrily. Or was she just seeing something that wasn't there? Something that she so desperately wanted to see. For why would the high-flying, ruthless businessman who had, single-handedly, forged James Leisure, care about squashing one little business like her hotel?

Melisande walked to the narrow window and stared out over the roses. Most of the bushes had been chosen and planted by her mother, who'd been responsible for most of the hotel's garden layout. It always made her feel especially proud but sad whenever a guest complimented her on the gardens.

She saw the pastel colours blur in front of her eyes, and realized she was on the verge of tears. And for a while, she was able to convince herself that it was fear for her future and fear for the continued well-being of her beloved hotel that was the cause.

But then, slowly, inexorably but undeniably, she had to admit that there was more to it than that.

From the moment of their first explosive meeting, she'd been aware of the strong, intense, and, yes, sexual tension and interest that had sprung up between herself and Wendell James.

And over the last few days they'd been playing a subtle game of cat and mouse that could only mean one thing. She'd noticed that his eyes always sought her out. She heard his voice take on a slightly deeper, purring quality whenever he talked to her.

And she liked it.

Oh, she'd never intended to let it go anywhere of course — the man was far too potent and dangerous for her to even think of taking him for a lover. She knew she had neither the experience to enjoy it properly for what it was, nor the hard shell needed to cope once the affair ended.

But she wouldn't have been human — she wouldn't have been female — if she hadn't responded to it. It was a heady thing indeed to have a man like that look at her with such knowing, intense interest.

Which was probably why she now felt so betrayed. Oh, it was ridiculous to feel that way, and she knew it. But there it was.

And now she had to face facts. Wendell James was now her deadliest and most bitter business rival, and that had to take precedence over everything else.

She could no longer allow herself to feel those secret little thrills whenever she saw him. There could be no more restless nights fractured with brief, erotic and wonderful dreams of him. No more little lifts of anticipation whenever she thought she might encounter him again.

From now on, she was fighting for her survival — and the survival of the hotel, her father's legacy.

So far, she'd had things easy here at the Ray of Sunshine. Nothing much had blighted her days. But now she must toughen up. From now on, she'd do whatever it took to come out ahead. For once, the mighty, rich and devastating Wendell James was not going to come out on top.

Melisande smiled grimly, and told herself that she was going to enjoy the challenge. It was probably high time, anyway, that someone took him down a peg or two.

But even as she felt her backbone stiffen and her resolve harden, she felt her heart give a sad little throb.

CHAPTER SEVEN

Melisande stood before her wardrobe and ran a careful eye along the rack of evening dresses. As hostess for the hotel, she needed a wide range of good-quality clothes, and tonight especially she wanted to dazzle.

The impulse to shine was part defiance and part due to the need to bolster her confidence after a miserable afternoon.

After learning exactly who Wendell was, she'd popped into her bank to see her bank manager, who, although sympathetic to her concerns, was nevertheless very cautious about the possibility of a loan. The banks were still very wary about loaning money, even to well-established businesses such as her own, and since she'd spent the last of her liquid assets on acquiring the small fleet of canal boats, she only had the hotel itself to put up as collateral. And that was a move she was very reluctant to make.

She'd left the bank feeling both deflated and worried. The Ray of Sunshine had no land that it could easily sell off, and she was not going to reduce the size of the gardens by one inch.

Coming back to the hotel, she'd spotted Vin on the riverbank with a camera, taking photographs. Occasionally Melisande caught the turquoise flashes of kingfishers darting around, but at the moment her brother was photographing nothing more exotic than a pair of mallard ducks bathing. But the beating of their wings created a silver spray that, she guessed, when caught with the right shutter speed, would produce beautiful results, a supposition that her brother confirmed.

But when she told him about needing to buy the land, his face had fallen.

Although his income was a good one, and allowed him to live to a fairly high standard when he wasn't stuck in a tent in the outback of Australia or wherever, he had very little money saved. Knowing Vin as she did, she'd expected this live-for-the-moment philosophy, but it still came as a blow to have it confirmed.

So there was no help from that quarter.

Sick at heart, she'd returned to the kitchen to 'discuss' that evening's dinner menu with the sisters who ruled the dining room's cuisine, and now, at last, she'd come up to change.

And since she knew that Wendell James was dining in tonight, a fine trembling shook her frame.

She took a deep breath and forced herself to concentrate on her wardrobe. Her eyes went across the rainbow of colours and stalled on a sparkling silver evening dress. She pulled it out and smiled as it glittered like diamonds in the evening light. She laid it out on the bed, and took a quick shower, using the gardenia body scrub that had been a typically expensive and extravagant present from her twin last Christmas.

Towelling herself dry, she donned a pair of sheer, flesh-coloured panties and a clever strapless bra in the same colour. The silver dress had a plunging deep V on the spine, almost to the top of her buttocks, with only a slender set of criss-cross straps to contrast against her naked flesh. A gossamer-thin pair of straps glittered like slender ropes of diamonds on her shoulders, and when she slipped it over her head, her discreet underwear gave the cunning impression that she was naked underneath. The material was a shimmering satin shot through with metallic threads in a swirling, abstract design that sparkled in the light as she moved, and the whole thing clung to her body like a possessive lover.

With it she would wear a pair of silver sandals with the highest heels she possessed, but before slipping them on she spent a full hour on her hair, pulling it up into a classic and perfect chignon and weaving into it her mother's diamond and emerald hair clips. A matching single pear-drop emerald on the slenderest of silver chains completed her jewellery. The green stone nestled just at the top of her cleavage, drawing all eyes — especially male eyes — down towards her generous curves.

She dabbed a few spots of Chanel Allure behind her ears and at the base of her throat, and then — after a brief hesitation — on each wrist.

At last, she was ready.

* * *

Rupert Rice-Jones heard a brief hush in the conversation around him, and looked up. He was contemplating a glass of port, his third of the evening, and when he saw her walking through the door into the bar he felt his breath falter.

All around him, the hotel guests, after the momentary hush, began to talk animatedly again. Many of the women smiled and watched Melisande curiously, wondering what the occasion could be. Although she always looked good, tonight she looked absolutely stunning, and female intuition picked up at once on the fine, tight way in which she moved.

Speculation filled the air.

In one corner, sitting at the table with an untouched glass of cognac in front of him, Wendell James felt his heart begin to hammer.

She was a vision of silver with Titian hair — fire and ice, in one elegant, awe-inspiring vision. The very sight of her made him feel breathless, and a warning bell clanged hard and loud in his head.

This woman was getting to him, no two ways about it, he acknowledged fatalistically. First she'd been a maid, shy yet somehow bold. Then a siren, intent on seducing her way through the hotel's ruling family. Then she became the actual chatelaine, the lady of the castle, remote and yet vulnerable. And now here she was, a vision that had him on his feet without him even being aware of rising from his chair. He only knew that he had to go to her, to talk to her, to see those stormy grey eyes flash at him, to hear her voice and feel the rapier thrust of her wit. To play the age-old game invented by man and woman somewhere around the time of Eve.

And part of him couldn't help but wonder. Who was the real Melisande Ray?

But as he took a step towards her, he saw that another man was also on his feet and already approaching her, and Wendell gave an inner curse as he recognized the buffoon that she'd talked so fondly to before. Tonight, he didn't look so drunk, and when she saw him, she smiled that familiar comfortable smile that she seemed to reserve just for him.

And that smile made Wendell feel savage. True, it looked more affectionate than anything else, but still, it wasn't what he wanted to see. He wanted her to search the room for him, seeking him out and then smiling at *him.* And he wanted *that* smile to be a very different animal indeed. He wanted to see desire in it, and challenge, and maybe something else. Something more. Something he'd never really cared to see on any other woman's face before now.

Melisande, unaware of Wendell James's potent musings, saw Rupert and smiled. Of course! Rupert would lend her the money. Her smile widened into true radiance. Who knows, perhaps she could persuade him to buy the land for his property company and build on it himself? That would spike Wendell James's guns good and proper.

Wendell's steps faltered at the look on her face. She seemed really glad to see the other man. Had he misread the signs? Was this Rupert Rice-Jones character more of a threat than he'd previously thought?

'Rupert, darling, it's so good to see you,' she said, turning her cheek for the usual kiss.

Instead, to her surprise and horror, Rupert sank to the ground in front of her. For one awful moment she thought he'd become irredeemably drunk, and her eyes widened. She was about to turn to glance at the bar, seeking help from the strong young student who was working there this summer, but then Rupert spoke. His voice was loud and clear, and there was nothing inebriated about it.

'Melisande, you look ravishing,' he said, his eyes twinkling. And suddenly, Melisande knew what he was about. With a sense of dismay that she quickly hid, she saw his hand go to the inside breast pocket of his jacket and emerge with a small black case.

She knew what was inside, of course. It was his grandmother's engagement ring — a square-cut ruby and diamond ring that he'd proffered to her before. On that occasion, she'd just turned twenty-one, and had been touched but a shade embarrassed.

She'd turned him down, and then worried that they wouldn't be friends any more. But the next day, there he was back in the bar and cheerful as ever, as if nothing had happened. So the next time that he'd brought out the ring, one Christmas about three years ago, she'd teased him before turning him down.

Since then he'd proposed twice more — but never with the ring. She wondered with an inner groan why he'd decided on tonight, of all nights, to play this game. Just when she needed to have a serious financial discussion with him.

Then she heard the sudden susurration of human whispers, and her head shot up. And suddenly she realized that she was surrounded by her guests, most of whom were regular and valued customers. And they, of course, had no idea that they were watching a pantomime, a private joke that simply wasn't meant to be taken seriously. To them, this was a genuine marriage proposal, with a gallant, older but still attractive lover going down on one knee in public to propose to his beloved.

She felt her face flush. Oh, good grief! How was she going to get out of this? She glanced down at Rupert, who winked up at her, and bit back the urge to speak. She wanted to say something light and airy, like, 'Oh get up, you fool. You'll ruin your trousers,' but before she could open her mouth, he was already speaking.

'Melisande, darling, will you please, please, *please*, put me out of my misery and marry me?'

From a few feet away, Wendell James froze to the spot. He felt chilled to the bone and had to physically fight the urge to march across the room and grab the kneeling man by the scruff of his neck and drag him outside.

He took a ragged breath, realizing with a shock that hit him like a tidal wave that he was jealous. Mind-blowingly, coldly, insanely jealous.

Then he felt a low-level dread wash over him, and his eyes went to Melisande Ray. Surely she wasn't going to say yes? Surely she wasn't going to tie herself to this semi-pickled, ageing squire-of-the-manor Lothario?

His heart jumped as he saw that she was smiling tenderly. 'Oh, Rupert, what can I say? This is such a surprise,' she said sweetly, but her eyes, as they stared down into Rupert's twinkling gaze, warned him of repercussions to come.

All around the room, women began to make noises — some starting to clap, some giving a quiet sniff of emotion, others making approving sounds.

'I'll have to think about it,' Melisande added firmly, reaching down to help him up, careful not to touch the ring in its case.

A wave of groans swept the room, and Melisande laughed around at everyone. Belatedly, she wondered if they thought she'd dressed up so spectacularly because they thought she'd been expecting this proposal of marriage. It made her feel hideously embarrassed and somewhat ashamed to be turning

Rupert down so publicly. But the man had brought it on himself.

'Come on, let's go out into the garden,' she said, tucking her arm into Rupert's, then nodding and smiling as a genuine round of applause broke out.

Vin, who was standing in the doorway and had just caught the last part of the act, wasn't watching his sister lead Rupert away, however. No, his eyes were riveted on Wendell James.

And what he saw on that man's face caused his heart to fall in dread.

How had this happened? He was sure that Melisande had no idea how hard Wendell James had fallen for her. It was not in her nature to play games with people's emotions. And, he realized with a start, he had no idea how his twin really felt about James either. Once or twice in the last day or so, he'd thought he'd caught a look in her eyes whenever she saw him that made Vin's blood run cold.

But surely he was mistaken. Wasn't James the man who wanted to build a rival hotel not a mile away and run the Ray of Sunshine out of business? And Vin had a good idea, of course, of why that idea would appeal to him. In a way, Vin couldn't even blame him.

But now, here he was, looking like a man on a very different mission indeed.

Just what the hell was going on here?

* * *

As the night darkened and, in the rose gardens of the Ray of Sunshine Hotel, Melisande Ray gently berated Rupert Rice-Jones for his behaviour, miles away, moored up on the banks of the River Thames, Leonard Keating waited patiently.

There was a bare sliver of a crescent moon, which was perfect for his plans, since he didn't want a bright full moon glowing down on him and his planned activities for later on. Out in the middle of the countryside, the only faint light now came from the stars, and as the night slowly became older, only the occasional owl disturbed the growing silence.

He checked his watch, saw that it was only 11.30, and lay back down on his bunk to wait.

It wasn't until he heard a distant village church clock strike one that he got up and slipped into a pair of black sneakers. He was dressed in dark blue jeans with a brown leather jacket, with no patches of pale colour showing anywhere. When he slipped off *Skylark II* and on to the riverbank, he was all but invisible in the dark night air.

He checked his pockets, making sure that he had everything he needed, then set off quietly along the bank.

Once a startled moorhen in the reed bed splashed away from him, making him jump, but apart from that, the river was silent. There were very few boats moored up here, most of the other river craft having carried on into Henley-on-Thames itself, to find moorings there. Only the *Stillwater Swan* gleamed like a pale oblong further upstream.

Silently, carefully, he made his way towards her, his feet silent on the grassy towpath. When he was within just a few yards of her, he stopped, listening intently.

* * *

In his bunk on the narrowboat, Keefe Ashleigh abruptly opened his eyes. One moment he'd been asleep, and, as far as he was aware, not dreaming of anything in particular, and the next moment he was wide awake and alert.

And he knew what this sudden transition meant.

It was very different from waking up naturally in the morning, when he'd perhaps turn over and yawn, and muse vaguely about what he needed to get accomplished that day.

No, this sudden snapping from the state of deep sleep to one of utter awareness could only mean one thing.

Danger threatened.

This instinct for trouble was something he'd learned over time during his years as a soldier of course, but it was the first time his sixth sense had woken him since entering civvy street. He knew exactly where he was, and already his mind was processing his surroundings and options. The boat was silent and — as far as he could tell — inviolate. He couldn't hear Gisela, and didn't think the disturbance — whatever it was — had come from her.

He slowly sat up and swung his legs over the side of the bunk. He was wearing only boxer shorts, and he quickly reached for his slacks and pulled them on. His boots were right there by the bed and he slipped his feet into them and moved, bare-chested, towards the door. He slid it open and stood, waiting. Listening.

On the bank, Leonard Keating let out a long slow breath and moved forward.

He would have to be careful when he stepped on to the small stern deck of the boat not to displace the weight of the narrowboat too much. The last thing he wanted to do was make it rock, for that might wake the sleeping inhabitants inside.

So when he stepped on to the deck, he was very careful to step right into the middle, and his carefully considered choice of sneakers allowed him to make no sound at all on the metal floor.

Inside, Keefe tensed. Someone had just stepped on to the boat.

The movement was stealthy and noiseless, and when he glanced at the glowing luminous dials of the boat's only wall clock, and he saw that it was nearly a quarter past one in the morning, he knew that whoever it was could be up to no good.

This was no drunken fellow boater stumbling on to the wrong boat and trying to get in. Nor was it teenagers out for a spot of mindless vandalism. No — this was, at the very least, a burglar intent on theft. No wonder his inner alarm system had woken him.

He moved carefully to the front of the boat, stopping briefly outside Gisela's door as he did so. He put his ear to it, and thought he heard the soft sounds of someone deeply asleep. He smiled, and carried on through to the front of the boat. There, he carefully pulled a curtain aside and peered out.

It was almost pitch black outside, with only the tiniest sliver of moon in the sky and a scattering of stars. He patiently waited for his eyes to adjust to the darkness, but he could sense no movement.

He turned and began to walk to the rear of the boat.

On the stern deck, Leonard Keating withdrew a small pencil torch from his pocket and shone it on to the padlock. The boat had two steel doors with a hoop on each side, which could be secured by the padlock. This was for when the boat owners left the boat unattended and wanted to secure it. But on the inside, there would be bolts fixed on the inner door, which could be drawn across to ensure privacy and protection.

He saw that the padlock had been clasped shut on to one loop, and he swore softly under his breath. It would have been easier for him if the padlock had been left hanging loose. Then he could simply slip it off and manhandle it better. As it was, he would have to do what needed to be done in situ.

Inside the boat, Keefe reached the bottom of the three metal stairs that led to the rear exit and heard the unmistakable whisper of material against material.

Someone was out there all right.

Leonard, who'd just knelt down to get closer to the lock, withdrew a blank key from his pocket, one that had yet to be carved. This he inserted into the padlock and twisted firmly, before removing it and doing the same again. He would need to do this several times — quietly, so as not to cause a disturbance — allowing the mechanism of the lock to leave surface markings where it would need to be cut. He could then take it to a locksmith he knew, and within the hour, he'd have his own personal key to the *Stillwater Swan*.

Inside, Keefe put one foot on the bottom step and carefully levered himself up, his hand reaching out for the bolt.

Carefully, millimetre by millimetre, he pulled it back, careful to make not the slightest squeak.

On the deck, Leonard Keating impatiently inserted the key and twisted again, checking it each time with his torch to see if it had scored deeply enough. Come on, come on!

With the bolt now clear of the loop, Keefe felt himself become utterly calm. He reached for the small iron door handle and took a long, slow breath.

And thrust it open.

On the deck, Leonard Keating pulled the blank key out of the padlock, then jumped out of his skin as the door beside him suddenly shot open.

He leapt back instinctively, unaware that he still had the key in his hand, and then yelled as a hand reached out and grabbed his ankle. Immediately, he felt himself beginning to sprawl backward.

In the darkness he could just see the pale oval shape of a human face. In desperation he swivelled around on his one good foot and stamped down on the hand holding his ankle.

Sensing the downward movement, Keefe just managed to get his hand back in time. And then Leonard Keating got lucky.

If Keefe had not been crouched in a tiny stairwell with no room for manoeuvre, Leonard wouldn't have got away with what he did next. But his sneakered foot, which he sent whistling through the doorway, caught Keefe just on the side of his face. Even then, the ex-soldier was already rearing backwards out of harm's way, and the soft-soled shoe barely made contact. But it was enough to make him lose his balance and he staggered back, slipping off the bottom step and landing badly. He went down on one knee, barking it painfully on the metal step, but in the next instant he was up and charging up the steps.

Immediately Leonard took off, thrusting the blank key into his pocket as he did so.

In her bunk, Gisela, who'd been awakened by Leonard's cry of surprise, shot out of bed as she heard another muffled thud and Keefe's unmistakable voice giving a loud curse. Then she heard feet ringing out on the metal steps and she grabbed a robe, a white towelling beach robe. She slipped into it and cautiously pushed open the door. She peered out.

On the riverbank, Leonard Keating had already got a good head start. He'd also had the advantage of having studied the terrain before heading to the boat, and instead of running in a straight line along the bank, he immediately headed into a small line of trees that ringed a meadow.

By the time Keefe got off the boat, it was impossible to see Leonard in the near total darkness. Still swearing under his breath, he felt the adrenaline seep away, and he went back down into the boat, where he saw Gisela standing in the narrow corridor outside her berth, holding a knife for protection.

She wilted with relief when he flicked on the light switch and she could see that it was only Keefe. It made him wonder who else she'd been expecting. Soon, he'd have to sit her down and get the whole story out of her, but first he had other priorities.

'Are you all right?' she asked breathlessly, and he nodded.

'I need a torch — a big one. Have you got one?' he asked quietly.

Gisela hadn't — it wasn't something she'd thought to pack. Regretfully, she shook her head. 'Sorry, no. Why do you want one?'

'Someone was trying to get on to the boat,' he said flatly, and she felt her heart plummet. 'It's all right, I've chased him off. I nearly got a hold of the little hooligan, but he managed to give me the slip,' Keefe went on, and she realized, with yet more dismay, that he thought they were dealing with a burglar.

But she knew better. Now, without any doubt whatsoever, she knew that Ma Pride had meant her vicious threats.

'You don't want to go out after him!' she cried, moving towards him, reaching out and taking his arm in a white-knuckled grip.

He looked first at her face, then down at his arm, and she flushed and quickly let him go.

'No fear,' Keefe said cheerfully. 'The army taught me better than to go off half-cocked trying to chase an enemy I can't see, and without a weapon. No, I just need to check the outside of the boat to see if there's been any damage done.'

'Oh,' Gisela said with a sigh of relief. Then brightened. 'I've got a candle! It's only a scented thing — I like to light it when I'm in the bath. But of course, the *Swan* has only a shower, so . . .' she trailed off and flushed again as she saw him begin to smile slowly.

Keefe could see her in a bath now, surrounded by bubbles and candlelight, her cap of silvery hair damp from the steam, with the suds clinging to her pert little breasts. Abruptly, he thrust the image aside.

'A candle will be fine,' he said. When she came back with it he extracted a lighter from his pocket and lit it. The candle was a big, squat, lilac-coloured thing but it gave a steady flame.

'I didn't know you smoked,' she said, more for something to say than anything else.

'I don't,' he said. 'But as you can see, I'm always prepared, just like a good boy scout should be. Well, except for the torch.'

For a moment, the scent of lavender and carnations filled the air between them, then he turned and was gone.

On the rear deck he bent down and checked that the padlock was still in place, and was glad to see it still secure.

It didn't take him long to check the exterior of the boat. As far as he could see, no attempt had been made to open any of the windows, and when he came down inside the *Swan* a quarter of an hour later, it was to find Gisela sitting fully dressed and waiting for him in the parlour.

She looked up at him, a distinctly guilty expression on her face. Then she took a deep breath.

'Keefe, I think there's something you should know,' she said soberly. He slipped into the seat opposite her, relaxed but alert.

'Yes. I'm beginning to think so too,' he agreed with a kind of amused detachment.

He was still bare-chested, and Gisela found herself distracted by the impressive array of muscles on his chest and arms, and the washboard fitness of his stomach. His skin was also criss-crossed with scars, and she bit her lip, looking away, realizing he'd been wounded recently. How that must have hurt him. It made her want to weep to think about it.

Keefe saw her look away, and fought the urge to get up and put on a shirt. He knew she must find the scars distasteful, but there was little he could do about it now. But he made a mental note to keep himself covered up in future.

Gisela took a deep breath, and told him everything — from the moment she had walked to work one morning and had seen a robbery in progress, to the trial, and Ma Pride's chilling threats, which she hadn't taken seriously. Until now.

When she was finished she slumped back against the seat. 'Obviously, I'll leave first thing in the morning,' she said, her voice small. 'Unless you'd prefer to be the one to go back to the hotel?'

'And leave you alone?' exclaimed Keefe. 'No way.' What kind of man did she think he was? 'I'm not letting you out of my sight until this is all sorted. Whoever it was creeping around tonight meant business.'

Gisela felt her heart leap. He wasn't going to leave her! She felt like singing but then, as abruptly as her euphoria had come, it vanished. She was being selfish. The thought of having this man all to herself for the next few weeks was blinding her to the reality of the situation.

'But I've put you in danger,' she said. 'I can't expect you to look after me. It's not fair.'

Keefe smiled grimly. 'Don't worry,' he said. 'Whoever was trying to get on the boat tonight is bound to try again, but this time I'll be waiting for him.'

Gisela heard the steel in his voice, and couldn't help but shiver. Keefe saw it, and his face turned to stone. Abruptly, he got up. 'Well, we'd best get some sleep, I think. Don't worry, I'll wake up if anything happens.'

Gisela, somewhat bewildered by his sudden change in attitude, accepted the hand he held out to her and scrambled to her feet. He let go of her hand the moment she was upright.

And once she'd slipped forlornly back into her bed, she stared up at the ceiling, wondering why he'd suddenly shut her out. For a moment there, they'd seemed to be connecting. Did he not find her even a little bit attractive? Or was he just secretly angry with her for having involved him in her life's woes?

A few feet away, lying on his own bed with only some thin wooden walls between them, Keefe roundly cursed himself for being a fool. He was nearing forty, with a scarred body and nothing to offer a bright young thing like Gisela Ashley. Besides, any fool could see she was scared of him — and why not? What did an innocent girl like that know about soldiering?

Besides, the only thing she needed him for was to protect her and see her through this rough patch — nothing more.

He would be a fool to let himself fall for her, because when it was all over, and she turned and walked away from this wonderful boat and the enchanting river, she would leave him empty and aching and pining for what might have been.

And who needed that?

* * *

The next morning two men began to do some serious research, but their interest and intentions couldn't have been more different.

On board the *Skylark II* Leonard Keating began to get to know one retired Captain Keefe Ashleigh, and the more he learned, the more dismayed he became.

As he learned of the man's medals, his move from the Engineering Corps into Intelligence, and the long, long list of trouble spots around the globe where Keefe had been stationed, one thing became abundantly clear.

He would need a rifle.

After last night, the ex-soldier would be alerted to trouble, and the chances of him leaving the mark alone and exposed were practically zero. It was simply too much to expect the man to simply walk away, even though it wasn't his fight.

Leonard knew men like Keefe Ashleigh. They had a concept of loyalty and honour that was totally alien to his own way of thinking. No, he just knew that his job had become one hundred per cent more difficult.

And after last night, Leonard had no intention of ever getting close enough to the ex-soldier to allow any hand-to-hand fighting to occur. The man had been as fast as a striking cobra, and his instincts had been phenomenal. The strength in his hands too, as he'd almost thrown him off his feet, still made Leonard shudder.

No, he would need to get a rifle and put in some hours of practice. The only way to kill a man like the captain was from a safe distance!

Luckily for him, he knew quite a few lowlife arms dealers who could supply him with what he needed.

* * *

As Leonard Keating slowly made his plans, some miles away in his office in Windsor, Wendell James was also busy doing his own research.

And what he learned about Rupert Rice-Jones didn't make for pretty reading. Wendell had friends in all walks of business life, of course, and after a few hours, he was sure he had a full picture of Rice-Jones's company — which was on the verge of bankruptcy. His bank was making noises about calling in a loan, and he'd already sold off his major assets, unfortunately for Rice-Jones at a knock-down price. Unless he could come up with some major backers or find a private source of funding, the man would be out of business by the end of the year — if not sooner.

So what was he doing proposing to Melisande Ray? A man, a real man, made sure that he could support and look after a wife before even thinking about starting a family.

Unless.

Slowly, Wendell James leaned back in his chair, thinking things through. Then he nodded grimly, reached for his jacket and shrugged into it. Half an hour later he was pulling into the parking lot of the hotel.

* * *

It was nearly 10.30 in the morning. Melisande stepped out into the deserted garden and absently began to deadhead the roses and remove any unsightly leaves. It was a beautiful warm and sunny day, and she felt the need to do something soothing and mindless.

When she heard a step behind her and turned to see Wendell James watching her, she was not particularly surprised.

'Hello, Mr James,' she said politely. 'Is there something I can do for you?'

The silky professionalism of it jarred him, catching him on the raw. He felt himself tense.

'If you don't start calling me Wendell, I'm likely to do something we'll both regret,' he warned her gruffly.

She was wearing a simple white cotton dress with tiny sprigs of blue flowers on it, and her hair, for once, was loose and glorious, cascading around her shoulders. Her bare arms were taking on a golden honey tan, and he wanted so badly to take her in his arms and kiss her that he had to thrust his hands into his trouser pockets to keep from reaching for her.

'Oh well, we don't want that, do we, *Wendell*?' she said, allowing her voice to sound coolly amused.

He knew what she was doing, of course, and he was damned if he was going to let her keep him at arm's length like this, but first things first.

'Did you know Rice-Jones was all but bankrupt?' he demanded, and Melisande spun around to look at him properly, her eyes wide with surprise and disbelief. Whatever she'd expected him to say next, that hadn't been it.

'It's true. Construction jobs have been drying up everywhere, and Rice-Jones is in a particular fix after using up most of his capital in buying out his partner. The man's desperate for cash,' he continued brutally.

'Oh no,' Melisande gasped, genuinely dismayed. 'I had no idea. Oh, poor Rupert.' And to think she'd been about to ask him for a loan! She felt a spear of guilt pierce her, and shook her head.

'Unless he can get his hands on some collateral, he's likely to go under,' Wendell continued, watching her closely, making sure that she understood what he was saying. For it was vital that she did. He couldn't bear it if she fell for Rupert's tricks and got hurt in the process. He'd seen for himself how much this place meant to her. 'For instance, if he were to marry, and if his bride were to have substantial assets that could be liquidated, like a hotel . . .'

Melisande heard his words, but it took a moment for their full import to reach her. When it did, she felt the blood drain from her face, and a hot lance of humiliation and anger raged over her.

Of all the nerve! Here he was, defaming Rupert and hinting that he wanted to get his hands on her hotel, when all this time *he'd* been the spy in her camp, intent on undermining it!

What a hypocrite!

'Oh, don't worry, *Mr James*.' She used his surname coldly. 'I'm not about to let anyone destroy my hotel. Not even you.'

Wendell felt her words hit him like a punch in the stomach. So she knew. Well, of course she did, he thought a scant second later. He'd always known that eventually she'd learn who he was and what he was about. Planning permission for his new hotel was now there in the public records for anyone to see.

'That's just business,' he heard himself say defensively. 'Normal competition. I'm not trying to seduce this place away from you.'

Melisande caught her breath, and smiled grimly. 'As if you could,' she spat. She felt so hurt and humiliated she wanted only to strike out.

She saw his handsome face pale almost to white, and the line around his mouth tightened ominously as his blue eyes became the colour of steel.

'Why, you little . . .' he said. The next moment, she felt herself pulled towards him. Her breath left her in a whoosh, and her hair flew around her head, distracting him for an instant.

Then her mouth parted in a sound of surprise and his eyes fixed on her lips. All protest died as she saw his eyes darken even further, and all the strength abruptly left her knees.

She felt herself being pulled closer into his arms, and the warmth of him, the pine scent of his aftershave, the sound of his harsh breathing, all combined to fill her senses.

And she knew in that instant that this was the moment she'd been waiting for all her life; and certainly ever since she'd first looked up and seen him that very first day, when she'd been pushing that ridiculous floor-polishing machine. And for every moment in between since then, this was what she had been longing for. Even when she'd found out who he was, and what he was up to, it had made no difference.

And now his mouth was moving to hers, and she felt herself melting into him, her heartbeat thundering in her ears.

Then his lips were on hers and her eyes feathered closed and she felt herself clutching him closer, her hands on his shoulders, her fingertips sensitized to the material of his jacket. Her breasts tingled, mashed as they were against his hard chest, and when his mouth parted under hers, forcing her lips open, she moaned softly, deep in her throat.

Wendell James sighed, surrendering to the inevitable. When at last he lifted his head to look down at her, he wondered how he could ever have imagined life without this woman.

Melisande's eyes opened, and she blinked up at him. For a moment she wanted to stay there for ever — locked in his arms, her mouth warm from his kiss, her eyes swimming in his.

Then reality intruded like a wave of cold water.

Did he really think he could seduce the Ray of Sunshine away from her after all? Did he really think she was such a pushover?

She took a step back and smiled coldly.

'Well that was . . . *interesting*,' she forced herself to say, trying for casually amused and surprised to hear herself succeeding.

Wendell winced and reached out for her, but she skipped back skittishly. 'And I'll give you nine out of ten for artistic merit,' she said. 'But I don't think you'll be seducing my hotel from me any time soon, Mr James.'

And with that, she managed to turn and walk away without breaking into tears and making a complete fool of herself.

Wendell James watched her go with bleak eyes, then drew a deep, ragged breath. It only added to the sense of hollowness in his heart to know that he had no one to blame for this mess but himself.

CHAPTER EIGHT

Leonard Keating was the kind of man who always liked to have more than one plan if possible. And since he knew that it would take him time and some trouble to procure a rifle, not to mention getting in enough practice to make it a viable option, it was not surprising that he'd spent some quality time thinking of a plan B. One that wouldn't be too expensive or, naturally, involve too much risk.

Besides, he would prefer to leave the option of using a rifle as a last resort. After all, the police were known to keep an eye on arms dealers, especially the more downmarket and illicit kind that he was forced to use, and purchasing a speciality piece wasn't something to undertake lightly anyway. Not only were there inherent risks in meeting such men, but it also gave them more information than he wanted them to have. Many a man in his line of work had been put behind bars when fences and gun-runners had turned over Queen's evidence in exchange for lighter sentences for themselves.

So when he saw the *Stillwater Swan* pull into the riverbank not far from the Willow Marina in Wargrave, he smiled, mentally crossed his fingers and cruised casually past. If his quarry would co-operate enough to leave the boat unattended for just a short while, he'd be in business.

He pulled his own cabin cruiser into the riverbank just beyond Wargrave itself and walked back into town, keeping an eagle eye out for a pharmacy, which was crucial to the plan he'd eventually decided upon.

Most laypeople's knowledge of poison was extremely limited, and the average member of the public's thoughts tended to run to the obvious when it came to murder by toxin. But the simple truth was, you didn't need cyanide or strychnine or anything remotely that exotic and hard to come by if you wanted to see someone dead. The means of killing someone could be found under the average person's kitchen sink.

And a diabetic, for instance, could quite legitimately order insulin with a prescription, too much of which would kill anyone. Likewise someone on certain kinds of heart medication. Then there was the average garden, where such poisonous plants as foxgloves, oleander and yew grew in profusion. And these were only some examples. A man like Leonard knew of many, many more.

But what he had in mind was a cocktail of his own devising, which had a proven record as being hard to detect by your average pathologist. As he entered the pharmacy he picked up a basket and began to make his carefully selected choices.

* * *

Walking away from their locked boat, Keefe and Gisela headed towards a pair of iron gates, allowing the sound of the traffic flow to lead them into the town centre. As they stepped off the kerb to cross a road, without a word Keefe reached out and took her hand. Gisela felt her face flush with pleasure.

Keefe had been keeping a careful watch on anything and everything since the events of last night. He'd noted all the other river traffic as they'd made their steady progress past Henley and further into the countryside. Unfortunately

Henley was on a busy part of the river, since it was a Mecca for rowers from all over the country, but he'd still noticed the small white cabin cruiser that had been behind them until it had overtaken them just before coming into Wargrave itself. It had been hard to see the boatman, for he'd been wearing a cap and sunglasses and was tucked well behind the wheel in the wheelhouse, but at least he'd know the boat if he saw it again. He had made a mental note of its name.

Not that Keefe was particularly suspicious about it. Whoever the vindictive Ma Pride had sent to menace Gisela could just as easily be following their progress by road. The River Thames, after all, was not exactly the Limpopo, out in the wilds. It was easily accessible day and night, which only made his job harder.

This morning, before Gisela had risen, he'd checked the boat for bugs or hidden devices, but had been unable to find any. He hadn't really expected to, but he was a man who liked to be thorough and prepare for all contingencies.

Now, as they walked hand in hand through the picturesque riverside town, he kept watch for any idling cars or motorbike riders who might seem to take any undue interest in them. But there was nothing out of the ordinary.

His practical side said that he should look on this as a dry run for his new business. He'd been thinking of offering bodyguarding as part of his services, and now he was getting some unexpected first-hand practice. But another part of him knew that this had nothing to do with business. He wanted to keep this lovely young woman safe, and was damned well going to do so.

It was another pleasant late spring day in England, and Gisela window-shopped and chatted, trying to get to know this enigmatic man who was by her side better. But it wasn't easy. He seemed reluctant to talk about himself, and it was making her feel more and more despondent as the morning wore on.

Keefe sighed deeply, sensing her frustration and the reason for it. He stopped beside a plate-glass window and looked down at her with a wry smile. 'I'm sorry to be so monosyllabic. I just don't like talking about the army,' he said abruptly, startling her from her morose contemplation of the display of lamps in the shop window.

'What?' she blinked up at him, puzzled.

'It's why I can't make small talk,' he explained. 'All my adult life I've lived a certain kind of life, doing things that aren't always pleasant to talk about. And I'm just no good at flirting or even simply just chatting about this and that. Do you understand?' he asked softly, squeezing her fingers in his.

And Gisela felt her heart lift. Of course he wasn't like all the men she'd known before. He didn't have anything 'small' to talk about. He was a man who'd seen the world, and the best it had to offer. And the worst. He was a hero.

And she felt her sudden relief ebb.

'You must find me very boring,' she said quietly, and looked back at the lamps in the shop window.

Beside her, Keefe laughed suddenly. 'My darling girl,' he drawled with genuine amusement, 'let me make it quite clear here and now that there's nothing boring about you!'

Gisela, after another startled hesitation, began to smile. Was he trying to flirt with her, even though he professed to be no good at it? If so, that was progress indeed.

* * *

Wargrave was not a large place, and it didn't take Leonard long to spot them. On the other side of the road, he watched them from beneath the cover of a greengrocer's awning, and saw Gisela Ashley rest her silvery gold head briefly against the ex-soldier's arm, her face turning up to look at him. She was laughing, and looking very much like a woman in love.

Which was a bit of a shame, Leonard thought vaguely. Still, at least she'd die happy. When he got back to the *Stillwater Swan* another boat had moored up just behind her, but after ten minutes of careful observation, he was satisfied that that boat too was empty. He approached the *Swan* cautiously, as if he was half-expecting it to be booby-trapped, then stepped casually on board, reaching into his pocket for his replica key. He'd had to get up early for a quick trip into London to get it made, but he didn't resent the dawn start.

Now he looked like the legitimate boat owner to anyone who might be watching, as he inserted the key into the padlock, opened it, opened the metal doors and walked down inside, careful to duck his head as he went, so as not to bump it on the low aperture.

Once inside, he looked carefully around, whistling quietly at the beautiful decor. He'd made sure not to step in anything damp, so he knew that his sneakers would leave no trace on the thick carpet, and after donning a pair of gloves and taking a quick look around the sumptuous interior, he made straight for the galley.

There he put the kettle on to boil, and put his morning's purchases on the counter top. He found a pestle and mortar in one of the well-stocked cupboards, and began to mix up and pound his ingredients. Trial and error had taught him just how to make the stuff soluble in liquid, and within ten minutes he was ready.

He searched the kitchen shelves for something to put his mixture in, but nothing really leapt out at him until he opened the refrigerator and saw a bottle of white wine chilling in the door. It was a good, strong-tasting brand, and would hide the very slight bitterness of his creation. Perfect! They were obviously going to drink it with either lunch or dinner, either of which would be fine with him.

Carefully, Leonard Keating extracted the hypodermic syringe he'd bought and very carefully filled it with the lethal mixture he'd just ground up. Next, he very carefully injected it into the wine, and even wet his finger and soothed over the tiny hole in the cork, so that not even an eagle-eyed ex-soldier would notice that anything was amiss.

He put the wine back in the fridge, in exactly the same spot from which he'd extracted it, then carefully cleaned up after himself in the galley, and left quickly.

Although he'd been calm and careful throughout, he'd also been keeping a constant lookout in case the lovebirds should return early, so he felt a distinct feeling of relief when he locked the padlock behind him and stepped back out on to the riverbank.

Now all he had to do was find a good place from which to watch them — perhaps from the opposite side of the river, where there was a stand of trees for cover — and with a bit of luck it would all be over before dark.

The stuff he'd used would induce unconsciousness within an hour and death within six.

* * *

Walter Jenks sighed heavily as he reached across and accepted the cheque Wendell James held out to him.

They were sitting in the kitchen of his farmhouse, a mug of strong tea in front of each of them, although his own was left largely untouched.

Melisande Ray had told him last night that she was unlikely to be able to raise the money, so when Wendell James had called him that morning with a very impressive offer indeed, he'd been unable to come up with any excuse to ward him off.

Now the old farmer sat staring at the cheque in his hands, looking at all those noughts, and feeling about as low as a snake in the grass.

Wendell James watched him, then smiled briefly as the old man sighed heavily, folded the cheque and put it into his shirt pocket. Having got the measure of the man during their first meeting, Wendell held out his hand firmly. He knew that a handshake with a man like this was as good as a signature on a contract — although he had that ready as well.

Walter Jenks shook the man's hand reluctantly, then signed the documents, after reading them carefully.

'You know, I've been friends with the Ray family for nearly forty years,' the old man said, looking up across the paperwork. 'Little Mel has done a right good job of looking after her father's legacy, but she's still naught but a slip of a thing. Her father, now, he was different. I can tell you straight, if Gareth Ray was still alive I wouldn't be signing this now. He'd have found some way to buy the land instead.'

Wendell felt his stomach clench. He wasn't going to sit here and listen to someone praise Gareth Ray. He had been about to tell the old man that he had no reason to feel guilty over selling the land to him. That Melisande Ray and her precious hotel were no longer in any danger from him.

But now he felt the urge wither. If people around here wanted to treat the memory of a man like Gareth Ray as if he'd been some sort of saint, let them.

Wendell knew better. Much better.

* * *

At the Ray of Sunshine, Melisande was overseeing the first of the early lunch guests. Most of the hotel's residents tended to stay out for the whole day, but some of them, and also quite a few locals, liked to have their midday meal at the hotel, since it had an enviable reputation for food.

So the dining room was beginning to fill, even at midday. She recognized one couple immediately.

They lunched at least once a month at the hotel, and as she approached their table she smiled brightly.

'Dr Thorndyke, Mrs Thorndyke, how lovely to see you again. Have you been out rambling?'

Dr Thorndyke was an emeritus fellow in something arcane at St Cross College in Oxford. His wife, a keen amateur botanist, was also a watercolourist of no mean talent, and often took along a sketchbook with her on their countryside rambles. They'd discovered the Ray of Sunshine on one such trek many, many moons ago now, and both of them smiled fondly at her as she reached them.

'Yes we have, and now we're famished,' Matilda Thorndyke said with a grin. 'Please, won't you join us for a while, Melisande?' She was a tall, thin woman with iron-grey hair and an eagle's beak of a nose. Her husband, by contrast, was one of those small, white, fluffy-haired men who reminded Melisande of a Munchkin.

'All right, but only until your meal is served,' she said, pulling out a chair and sitting down. 'Mustn't do anything to spoil your concentration for that!'

Both of the Thorndykes, she remembered, were dedicated foodies.

'Indeed not,' Matilda said with mock severity. 'We've ordered the grilled trout with cashews and the hazelnut torte for afters.'

'We're in a nutty mood today,' her husband quipped, and his wife laughed, rather as a matter of habit, Melisande thought, but then, after fifty years of marriage who was in a position to judge them?

'Have you been sketching?' she asked, spotting Matilda's sketchbook, and being more than polite. Several of Matilda's framed watercolours hung on various walls throughout the hotel, and her eyes twinkled with genuine curiosity.

'Of course, but I don't think there's anything in there yet that you'd be interested in,' Matilda said. 'We've been up through Benhams Wood and down to the water meadows by the river. Oh yes, that reminds me, look at this,' she went on, skipping through the pages until she found what she wanted. 'What do you think of this?'

She turned the pad round and presented it to Melisande, who gazed down at a beautiful pen-and-wash sketch of a delicate, bell-shaped flower.

'Oh, Matilda, it's gorgeous. Is it some sort of fritillary?'

'I think so, yes. I found it in the water meadow — and this too.' She rapidly turned another few pages, and tapped one.

Melisande smiled and nodded. 'Even I recognize that. Orchids,' she said reverently. 'You can't mistake them, can you? Even a novice like me can spot them.'

Matilda nodded wisely. 'Ah, but not many like this,' she added, tapping her own drawing thoughtfully. 'At least, I don't think so. I know most of the usual variety of orchids and I've never come across this. The fritillary, too, I think is rare.'

Melisande felt the sketchbook in her hands begin to tremble.

'Really?' she heard herself ask, and cleared her throat. 'They're both rare, you think? And you found them in the meadows just past Benhams Wood?' she persisted, wanting to make quite sure of her ground.

Matilda nodded, and Melisande swallowed hard. The only meadows up there were the ones owned by Walter Jenks.

If these flowers were growing on Walter's land, land that he was going to sell to Wendell for his new hotel, and if the flowers were rare enough, could she, after all her worrying and fretting and furious thinking, just have stumbled on a way to spike Wendell's guns?

'Matilda,' she said softly, 'tell me what you know about sites of scientific interest.'

'Eh?' It was her husband who spoke, looking suddenly interested. The professor, as Melisande knew, had a habit of appearing to be nodding off, only to come to sudden life when something caught his attention.

'I mean, if these flowers are really rare, maybe they're also endangered?' Melisande asked, holding her breath. 'And if they are, shouldn't they be protected?' She looked from the husband to the wife hopefully, and Matilda Thorndyke's eyes sharpened. She was not only a keen amateur botanist but something of a conservationist too.

'Well, naturally. But I thought the land up there was farmland?' the old woman said.

'Walter Jenks is selling that particular plot of land to a developer,' Melisande rejoined flatly.

'Oh no!' Matilda wailed. 'That's one of our favourite walking spots!'

'It's not easy to protect land, you know,' her husband said mildly, but Melisande, relieved, could already see the light of battle in Matilda's eyes.

'But it can be done, Ronnie, you know it can,' she said firmly, and her husband at once agreed. It had always been obvious who wore the trousers in the Thorndyke marriage.

Melisande smiled at them both fondly.

'First things first,' Matilda said firmly. 'I'll show these sketches to one of Ronnie's friends at college. What's that botanist fellow called?' Matilda asked, somewhat scathingly, Melisande thought.

Melisande supposed that, as an amateur, Matilda wasn't regarded all that seriously by the high-flying academics at her husband's place of work, and probably smarted about it accordingly.

'Oh, Professor Wouk. But he's on sabbatical,' Dr Thorndyke mumbled. 'He's got a junior research fellow on his team though. Er, an ex-Cambridge chap I'm afraid,' he apologized. 'I can always show them to him for you, dear.'

Matilda nodded. 'Then we can get him to come out and take a proper look for himself,' she said. 'I've made a note and a small map in the sketchbook showing their position. I always do, you know, if I come across something unusual,' she added.

Melisande hid a smile. If it had ever occurred to Matilda that a junior research fellow from Oxford might not want to come out and look at her 'finds' it certainly didn't show on her steely determined face.

Just then, Melisande spotted one of the waitresses approaching the table with two plates of steaming, perfectly presented trout, and quickly got to her feet.

'You leave it to me, Melisande,' Matilda said firmly. 'I'll phone you as soon as I've set something up.'

And Melisande, with a smile of genuine appreciation, murmured her heartfelt thanks and left the old couple to enjoy their lunch in peace.

But she felt like singing as she made her way back to her office. At last, she might have some genuine ammunition in her fight against the giant that was James Leisure.

And she couldn't wait to see the look on his handsome arrogant face when he realized it.

* * *

Gisela and Keefe returned to the boat, laden with goodies from the delicatessen. She took the purchases into the galley, and began arranging them on plates. There was a crumbly blue cheese, the name of which she hadn't recognized, delicious Parma ham, couscous and a spinach and rocket salad with a tangy dressing.

Behind her, Keefe reached into the fridge and withdrew the bottle of chilled white wine. He reached for the corkscrew. Gisela cut a crusty cottage loaf in half and brought out the pat of butter.

Keefe set the table and sat down, smiling across at her as she laid the feast upon it. Purple grapes and nectarines sat in a glass bowl, and would serve as dessert.

Still standing, Gisela reached for the bottle of wine and poured some into the fluted glass at his place setting. When it was full, she turned to do the same for her own, vaguely aware of a roaring sound that was gradually getting closer.

It wasn't until a large speedboat raced past, however, steered by a grinning teenage boy showing off to the teenage girl sitting beside him, that she realized what it was. A moment later, the heavy wash from the passing boat hit the *Swan* and made her bob up and down quite vigorously at her moorings. The wine bottle at the lip of the glass jerked upwards, then downwards, spilling some of the wine on to the glossy surface of the small dining table.

'Oh damn!' Gisela laughed. 'I'll get a cloth. Please, get stuck in.' She waved a hand over the table and took a few steps back to the galley, where she searched for a dishcloth.

In his seat, Keefe watched her with hooded, troubled eyes. Despite all his warnings to himself last night, he was becoming very attached to this little blonde who seemed to take death threats in her stride.

After admitting that there was little to tell her about himself, he'd turned the tables and quizzed her about her life story, which she'd been more than happy to divulge. It had ended with him being given a half-serious invitation to meet her family one day soon for Sunday lunch.

She'd been as open and transparent as a piece of glass, and he could sense that here was a girl who longed for a family of her own. It made him wonder about the lucky man who would scoop her up.

The thought made his throat ache.

He turned away from his perusal of her. He noticed a wasp settle on the table and crawl towards the spilled wine, no doubt attracted to the sugar in its content. He was about to swat it, then remembered that Gisela wouldn't approve. No doubt she'd rescue this creature as well and set it free.

He reached for a hunk of bread, spread on some butter and bit into it thoughtfully, eyeing the Parma ham.

Gisela returned to the table with the dishcloth, but sat down with it still in her hand. She simply sat and watched him eat for a few moments, and wondered why such a simple thing as watching him chew and swallow could make her feel so good.

Keefe glanced up at her, one eyebrow raised in query, and she blushed. She put down the cloth, reached for a spoon and began to ladle couscous on to her plate. She helped herself to the salad and a small wedge of cheese, then reached for her wineglass.

She raised it to her mouth and felt the coolness of the glass connect against her bottom lip, then gasped and gave a little cry as Keefe's hand shot out and grabbed her wrist. Again, wine spilled on to the table top.

'What?' she said, wide-eyed, as she saw how tight and grim his face had become. 'What is it?' she asked again, breathlessly.

Keefe nodded down at the table. 'Look at the wasp,' he said.

Gisela blinked, puzzled, and looked down, and for the first time noticed the insect sprawled in the previous wine spill, lurching about as if it couldn't stand upright.

She laughed. 'Is it drunk?'

But Keefe's grim expression didn't fade. 'No. I don't think so,' he said. He still had a firm hold on her wrist, but neither of them realized it.

Instead, they stared at the yellow-and-black insect as it lurched on to its side, then began to convulse, legs flailing the air.

Gisela, upset to see any living creature in distress, stared at it appalled. 'But what's wrong with it? Is it drowning?'

'No, there's not enough liquid for that,' Keefe said, his voice curiously emotionless now. No sooner had he finished speaking than the wasp went suddenly, ominously still.

Keefe stood. While Gisela watched him numbly, he reached for her glass and took it very carefully from her hand. He then reached for his own glass and carried them into the galley. 'Don't touch the wine bottle,' he said over his shoulder, and Gisela began to shiver as she suddenly realized what had just happened.

Or what Keefe *suspected* had just happened.

Her mouth went bone dry and she began to feel just a bit sick.

As she watched, he found a half-empty jar of mint sauce in the cupboard. Carefully he emptied it out and washed it in hot soapy water, before rinsing it thoroughly. Then he poured the contents of the two wineglasses into it. He attached the lid and screwed it on tightly, reached into a drawer and put the whole thing into a plastic bag. This he knotted tightly.

When he returned to the table with another plastic bag, Gisela watched him wordlessly as he pushed the cork back into the bottle with agile, strong fingers, and then put the bottle into the second bag.

'I've got a friend who works in a proper forensics lab,' he told her. 'He's based in London. I'm going to give him a ring, ask him to come up and fetch this and put a rush job through on it.'

Gisela swallowed hard. 'All right,' she agreed, her voice little more than a whisper.

'Once we've got some hard evidence that someone is out to hurt you, we can take it to the police,' he added. 'Until then, there would be little they could do anyway, which is why we haven't reported last night to them yet.'

'OK,' Gisela said, only then realizing that she hadn't even given the police a single thought. Although she'd only known him for a few days, she was already entrusting her life to this man without a qualm.

Keefe looked across at her. He saw the dark shadows in her eyes and before he could stop to think he reached down and kissed her.

It was meant to be a kiss of reassurance and comfort. It was meant to drive away her fear and remove the shadows from her eyes.

But from the moment their lips met, Keefe knew that it was more, much more than that. He felt her arms loop around his neck, and felt her lips soften under his. Her little tongue snaked out into his mouth, making his loins harden so fast that he actually stiffened in her arms.

She felt it and instantly pulled away, her face flaming with embarrassment. Why was she always pawing him? He must think her a proper sex-pot.

'I'm sorry,' she said shakily.

Keefe stood upright, and took a careful deep breath. 'For what?' he managed to ask jauntily.

Gisela folded her hands primly in her lap and looked away, out of the window. She supposed a man like this was used to casual affairs. And the kiss had probably meant as little to him as the attempt to poison them both had seemingly done.

As she watched him get to work clearing away the table, rightly guessing that all her appetite had fled, she was amazed at how cool and calm he was.

And it was good, of course, that he was like that. A cold-headed, cold-hearted man was just what she needed to protect her.

So why did she wish with all her heart that he could bend just a little? Show just a little human weakness. The kind of weakness that a man felt for a woman who had just kissed him, while wearing her heart on her sleeve.

* * *

Leonard Keating, watching from the stand of trees on the riverbank opposite, could see very little of what was going on inside the boat, even with the help of the binoculars.

He thought he could see movement against the windows from time to time, and he glanced at his watch. It was nearly 1.30 now, and he wondered impatiently how long it would be before they finished lunch. Of course, they could be leaving the wine for their evening meal. But that would be no problem.

If they dined on the riverbank as they had the previous evenings, he'd be able to see them actually pour and drink the wine with his own two eyes. After that, he could simply get in his boat and head back to the capital. He wouldn't even need to stay and watch the results of his handiwork, so confident was he of his formula.

With a reluctant sense of patience, he settled down in the shade of the trees, and prepared to wait.

But when, an hour later, a motorbike pulled up on the road opposite the boat, and the rider, still wearing his helmet, walked to the boat, he felt deeply uneasy. And when the rider emerged barely ten minutes later, he felt even more agitated. What had he wanted? Who was he? A courier of some kind? If so, what kind of message had he been delivering, and who to? He'd been carrying no obvious package, although he did have a backpack so a delivery wasn't out of the question.

He didn't think a switch had been made — the motorbike rider was a heavy, squat man, and it was a man with the same build who climbed back on to the Kawasaki and roared away. So he was sure both the ex-soldier and his mark were still on board.

But he didn't like surprises. And Leonard would have felt even more uneasy if he'd known that the man on the motorbike was a fully trained forensic lab technician who now had a sample of his poisonous brew packed away in a phial in the pocket of his leather jacket, and the bottle of wine in his backpack.

* * *

Back on board the boat, Gisela went to her bunk and lay down, and when she heard the boat's engines start up a few minutes later, she closed her eyes and let the *Stillwater Swan* carry her sedately out into the middle of the river. There they would ride the current together, to wherever it would take them. Keefe, herself and the *Swan.*

But where would that be?

CHAPTER NINE

Rupert Rice-Jones read the letter a third time, but still couldn't take it in. Thrusting it into the unlit fireplace, he left his house with a sick feeling in his stomach and walked slowly down the lane, railing silently at the beautiful spring evening that tried to welcome him.

He didn't even have a dog to walk at his heels.

Suddenly he snorted with laughter, realizing just how self-pitying he was in danger of becoming, and headed straight for the Ray of Sunshine Hotel.

He needed to see Melisande. He wasn't sure how his proposals of marriage to her had come to be a joke. When he'd first proposed, he'd been in deadly earnest. She was young, beautiful, local and independently wealthy. What more could a man ask? So when she'd turned him down, he'd pretended it didn't matter, just to preserve his dignity, but unfortunately she'd taken his airy attitude at face value. And he'd somehow become stuck with his role as the court jester to her queen.

So when he'd plucked up the nerve to ask again, and she'd turned him down again — this time with a carefree laugh that told him in no uncertain terms that she didn't take him seriously — he'd begun to appreciate exactly what kind of a hole he'd dug for himself.

It had been annoying, then faintly entertaining, but now it was very far from being funny. Because if he didn't do something soon, losing face would be the least of his worries — he'd lose the business, the house, the car, and the lifestyle that went with it.

It had caused him to do some furious thinking, and he'd thought he'd been so clever, proposing that last time, getting down on one knee in public the way he had, right in the middle of her precious hotel. He knew how much Melisande valued the respect and goodwill of her clientele, and he thought the psychology of it had been spot on. She'd simply have to agree to marry him with everyone watching her, all dewy-eyed and wanting to witness a fairy-tale ending!

Of course, he'd expected her to try and wangle out of it later, but by then, who knew. Perhaps he could have persuaded her into a trial engagement, to see how it went? With time, he was sure, he could have persuaded her to go through with it. After all, the hotel was her life, so it wasn't as if she had another man just waiting in the wings, was it? And with thirty beginning to loom on the horizon for her — wasn't that a time when women's thoughts became more focused on home and starting a family life?

But somehow she'd managed to turn him down graciously in front of all those people, and he'd found himself manoeuvred into the garden, where even he had heard the displeasure and touch of steel that lay behind her laughing scolding.

So now, Rupert thought with renewed determination as he pulled down the waistcoat of his blue silk suit and straightened his regimental tie, now was the time to show some steel of his own.

He needed the Ray of Sunshine for collateral, or he'd be ruined. And the only way he could get his hands on such a sizeable asset was to marry the owner.

As he approached the hotel he heard the sound of fiddles wafting across the garden. He realized with a sigh that it was Folk Night. Once a month, Melisande had a local, but very good, English folk band in to provide entertainment — something the Americans especially seemed to appreciate. It always attracted a lively crowd, and in spite of everything he felt his spirits lift a little as he walked across the hall and made for the bar, for Rupert was nothing if not a social animal.

Inside it was, as ever, packed. Some large French windows were open, and outside he could see couples dancing on the patio. Others sat around tables that had been lined up against the wall, leaving another small dance floor in the middle of the room.

And it was there that he saw Melisande. She looked wonderful, once again in that long, amber velvet dress, this time with a silver and amber pendant hung around her neck, and long dangling matching earrings catching the light from the setting sun. She was wearing her gold sandals again, and was looking up at her dancing partner with a curiously intense look.

Rupert recognized the tall, black-haired man only vaguely. He was obviously a hotel guest and Melisande was in full hostess mode, but something about the sight of them together made Rupert uneasy.

For a start, she was not smiling. Always before, whenever she'd been 'stroking the guests' as he'd always thought of it, she'd been smiling, charming, witty and careful to please without giving anything of herself. But now she looked utterly absorbed, and even from a distance he could feel the tension in the air that surrounded the two of them, as if they were responsible for creating an electrical storm centred only on themselves.

He worked his way grimly to the bar and ordered a double whisky, frowning across the room. He didn't like the way her partner was holding her, either. Nor, when they turned in time to the music, and he could see the other man's face, did he like the look in his eyes.

His gaze seemed to scream possessiveness.

Rupert took his drink and downed it quickly in just three gulps.

* * *

Melisande felt the strong arms around her waist guide her into another turn, and twirled obligingly. The song the 'Throstles' were playing was a poignant, more modern rendition of an eighteenth-century love ballad, something to do with a maiden loved and abandoned, watching the sea for the return of a lover who would never come back.

It had always made her throat ache, and now, looking up into Wendell's dark blue eyes, she felt her heart ache as well.

When he'd walked up to her and asked her to dance, her first instinct was to say no. But, of course, other eyes were on her, and she was obliged to smile and take his hand.

When he'd led her to the centre of the floor and pulled her into his arms, her breath had left her in a whoosh, leaving her feeling weak and vulnerable. And the moment the ballad started, and they began to move together, she'd felt a tingle play up and down her spine.

During all the years she'd danced with men, nothing had prepared her for this. It was as if the room around them receded into a darkening cavern, and only she and Wendell existed. She could feel his hand burning in the middle of her back, and felt every individual touch of his fingertips and the gentle guiding pressure of his hard masculine thighs as they stepped out and around. She could feel the cool touch of his breath on the top of her head when they dipped, and smell the clean tangy scent of the soap he'd used as they moved closely together. His hair was slightly damp from the shower, and it was all she could do to keep her fingers from running through the ebony strands.

At last the ballad ended, and a lively jig filled the room. To the merriment of the others, a large party of silver-haired ladies tried their own rendition of a cancan. Clapping hands suddenly filled the air, and Melisande took the opportunity to get out of the giddy orbit that surrounded this man.

'Well, I think a long, cold drink is in order,' she said, her voice sounding shaken even to her own ears, but when she spotted Rupert sitting at the bar, she thought better of it. She was in no mood to deal with Rupert tonight. She didn't realize, however, that she had made her change of mind quite so obvious when she visibly hesitated, then headed for the French windows instead. Wendell's gaze shot to where she'd been looking, his eyes narrowing ominously as they spotted Rice-Jones.

At the bar, Rupert too saw and understood her gesture. He dragged in his breath with a hiss as he realized that he'd been taken for a fool. And right in front of his rival too. He flushed with shame. How could he have been so stupid as to think that there wasn't another man in Melisande's life? Wasn't there *always* another man? Even his fifteen-year-old nephew could have told him as much.

He watched the handsome couple step through into the garden, then ordered another drink, a dark, ugly colour suffusing his face. Then he thought better of it. He bought a whole bottle instead, and took it back to his empty house, where he commenced to get very drunk indeed.

He stared blankly around the library, knowing he wouldn't own it for very much longer, thanks to Melisande Ray, and felt the maudlin desire to weep.

But the more he drank the more his desire for revenge and the need to strike out and make someone pay for his misery formed and hardened.

* * *

As the sun set on the gardens of the Ray of Sunshine Hotel, and Wendell James and Melisande Ray sat beneath a weeping willow and watched it in a strange, almost ethereal silence, some miles away Leonard Keating swore silently to himself.

He was still watching the *Swan* and, in the darkening evening, the couple sitting on deckchairs on the riverbank, enjoying the last of their barbecued meal — a meal that they had washed down with fruit juice from long, ice-filled glasses. It was the first thing he'd checked on through his binoculars when he'd seen them setting up the trestle table.

He cursed and lowered the binoculars, then walked back along the riverbank to where he could cross over a bridge. He then faced a bit more of a walk to where he'd moored his own boat. With nothing to show for it he was in no mood to enjoy the sight of the first stars appearing in the sky.

Damn it, why hadn't they drunk the wine yet?

Back on the *Skylark II*, he allowed himself a single vodka and lime, then settled down for the night.

He was feeling restless and uneasy. He didn't like it when his plans failed. He didn't like the unexplained presence of their motorbike visitor earlier in the day either. In fact, he didn't like the way this job was shaping up altogether.

He wanted it over and done with, so he could be on his way. Never really a superstitious man, Leonard was, nevertheless, beginning to get a very bad feeling about all this. It was almost as if this particular job had been cursed.

* * *

Dr Ian Patterson stared down at the orchids with a smile of pleasure. When that stalwart flower-finder Matilda Thorndyke had called him last evening, enthusing over her finds near the River Thames and begging him to take a look, he hadn't been reluctant. Apparently, nobody at her husband's college had been that keen to do so, but Ian, now retired and always willing to find ways to get out of his pleasant but lonely house, had been her next port of call.

Of course he'd been an ex-Durham man, but any botanist in a storm, as Matilda had so delightfully put it, would do.

He'd already found her fritillaries, which were beauties, but not, alas, yet endangered. And now here were her orchids — but again, they were not yet considered quite rare enough to be added to the all-important list needed to make them officially protected.

He sighed down at the beautiful spotted caramel-and-gold-coloured flowers and shook his head. Matilda would be disappointed. She'd told him something about the background of these flowers, and the danger they faced of eradication, and as he looked around at the peaceful, somewhat swampy meadow, it pained him to think of it being built upon. Cows grazed just beyond the hedgerow, and a pair of brown birds flitted about, busy building a nest in the sedges at the water's edge. No bird expert, he supposed they might be sedge warblers, or maybe willow warblers. All little brown birds seemed alike to him. The lime yellow butterflies flitting about him, he knew, were yellow brimstones, but the names of the brown spotted butterflies and small powder-blue ones that also abounded were mysteries to him.

He sighed and walked back to his car, and, after asking the way of a man walking a Yorkie dog, he found his way to the Ray of Sunshine Hotel. It was, as Matilda had promised him, a gem of a place. The original house hadn't been mucked about with, and the architecture was simple and pleasing to the eye. The gardens were extensive and gorgeous, and the views to the river were nothing short of breathtaking.

Knowing that Matilda could also be trusted on all matters relating to food, he decided to stay for lunch before seeking out the owner, and was glad that he did so. The venison was superb, and the wild-strawberry mousse served with white chocolate-chip biscuits was little short of heavenly.

He was sitting, replete and happy, over coffee, when he eventually got the chance to talk to the owner. If he'd been forty years younger, he'd have been quite smitten with the young lady. As it was, he still felt a flush of pleasure as the beautiful woman took her seat opposite him.

He'd introduced himself simply as Matilda's flower expert; now she listened pensively as he gave her the bad news.

'Of course, it doesn't have to end here,' he finished gently. 'Just because the flowers themselves aren't rare enough to save the site, I can still put you in touch with the local green societies hereabouts. They often consult me about various things, and I know they'd want to save the meadows. I saw all sorts of birds and insects there; it would make a perfect little nature reserve.'

Melisande smiled distractedly. She was still thinking about last night, and how it felt to dance in Wendell's arms. And then about their silent vigil as the sun went down. It was if they'd said more without a single word than if they'd spent hours talking.

Now she only felt more confused than ever. What was he doing, still staying on at the hotel? Now that she knew who he was and what he was about, why hadn't he left? The man must have a neck made of brass! And yet, in his arms, she'd sensed that there was something else going on behind that dark, mysterious handsome facade that he presented to the world. She felt as if he had things to tell her, but was deliberately holding back.

Or was she just fooling herself?

'You know, well-organized conservationists can work wonders,' Dr Patterson was going on, distracting her. 'I'll have a word with the Reverend Michaels. He's a big mover and shaker around these parts, and he commands a veritable army. They have solicitors and all sorts in their group. They can sometimes make such a nuisance of themselves, filing petition after petition with the courts, that construction companies have been known to give up and simply abandon a project as not being cost effective anymore.'

For some reason, instead of feeling her heart swell with hope and glee at his words, she felt instead only flat and despondent, as if she was somehow being cheated of something. Which was ridiculous. She'd asked Matilda for help, and now this man, her emissary, was here offering her just that. She forced herself to smile at him warmly. 'I'd be really obliged if you'd do that. I don't think the river needs another development on it, do you?'

Ian Patterson smiled, patted her hand, and reached for his mobile phone. And as she heard him talking to the militant reverend, organizing a meeting to alert the forces to the danger facing yet another water meadow, Melisande Ray felt like a traitor.

So much so that, after Dr Patterson had left, she got up from the table and went to Wendell's room.

Not surprisingly he wasn't in.

She paced for a while, debating the wisdom of trying to track him down to his office, which she assumed must be in Windsor. Eventually, however, she decided to take the coward's way out instead.

She walked to her office, thankful that it was one of Gina's afternoons off, and wrote him a letter, advising him not to buy the land from Walter Jenks. She didn't want him to pay out thousands and thousands and then be left with land that was useless to him.

But after reading it, she shook her head in despair and tore it up. She tried writing another letter, warning him that the land wasn't suitable for development; trying, without betraying Dr Patterson's plans, to warn him about unforeseen difficulties. Then she tore that up also.

No matter how she phrased it, it always came out sounding like a desperate woman's last attempt to stave off the competition. And she couldn't bear the thought of him sneering at it in contempt as he read it.

She had to keep some of her pride intact, or what would she have left?

Plus, she would be doing a disservice to Walter, who she knew needed the money and had done her a good turn in offering the land to her first.

Perhaps she'd be better off thinking of ways in which to improve the Ray of Sunshine's services and facilities. After all, if the worst came to the worst, and Wendell did get his latest hotel built on her doorstep, it didn't necessarily mean that it would be the one to come out on top. Who could know? Perhaps the Ray would be able to drive *it* out of business!

She wandered out into the gardens and went to the river. But for once, even the reliable Father Thames was unable to soothe her.

* * *

Leonard Keating saw the *Stillwater Swan* pass his moored boat at nearly eleven the next morning, but he was very careful not to set off himself until nearly an hour later.

It was not, after all, as if he could 'lose' them. The Thames didn't have that many tributaries, and his boat was much faster than the sedate narrowboat. Besides, he knew that Keefe Ashleigh, like the good soldier he was, was almost certain to have made a note of all the boats he spotted on a regular basis, and he didn't want the *Skylark II* to stand out on that list.

So, as he slowly headed towards Reading and saw the stretch ahead known as Sonning Eye appear on the horizon, he took the decision to moor up not far from St Patrick's bridge. From there he decided to take a small hike up into the fields to see if he could spot the narrowboat ahead, without them also spotting him.

He was glad that he did. In fact, when he lifted the binoculars to his eyes and saw what lay ahead, he could hardly believe his luck.

He ran back towards his boat but, instead of climbing on board, reached instead for the long pole that lay almost the full length of the boat. With some difficulty, he managed to gauge its centre of gravity and set off with it along the deserted stretch of green countryside.

The pole was an eight-foot, stout and fairly rigid length of fibreglass or something similar, and would no doubt prove handy in many circumstances. Most commonly, he suspected, to push off with if you got your boat stuck in the mud or needed, for some reason, to push away from the riverbank without the use of the engines.

But right now, Leonard Keating had a very different task in mind for it.

* * *

Keefe saw the lock up ahead, first alerted to its presence by the now familiar black-and-white paint on the far edge of the large wooden lock gates.

For once, there was no queue to get through, since the majority of river traffic hereabouts was still congregated around Henley and the regatta being held there. As he approached the lock he could see that it was full and open, which would save him from having to empty it before he could nudge the *Swan* into position. He began to pull into the bank, cutting the engine altogether to allow the *Swan* to idle into position using only the forward momentum she'd already created.

On top of the roof of the *Swan*, Gisela, who'd been sunbathing lying on her stomach, lifted her face from the towel and glanced across just in time to see Keefe jump across nearly three feet of open river and land nimbly on the bank.

'One of these days you're going to misjudge that and fall in,' she warned him teasingly, knowing he'd do no such thing.

He grinned at her as he walked past, and Gisela raised herself up on to her elbows, cupping her chin in her hands. She was wearing a skimpy halter top in bright scarlet, with very short white shorts to complete the outfit. Her feet, of course, were bare.

'Are you sure you don't need me to do anything? Open the lock or drive the boat or something?' she offered.

Keefe smiled at her and waved the big heavy iron 'key' which he was holding. 'No need. I'll empty it, then open the gates, and then climb down the ladder set in the wall to get back on board and get the old girl through. You just relax.'

He doubted whether someone as slight and petite as Gisela would be able to push open the heavy lock doors anyway, even when the water had been emptied on this side.

'Who are you calling an old girl?' Gisela laughed back, giving the *Stillwater Swan*'s pristine white paintwork a gentle pat. 'She's a brand-new girl, and sparkling. Apologize at once.'

Keefe grinned and set to with the key, cranking on the black metal rivets, which steadily opened to let the water flood out. And slowly, inch by inch, the *Stillwater Swan* began to sink. It was a deep lock, this one, Keefe mused, nearly twenty feet, he thought, once emptied.

He peered down into the waters foaming out at the other side of the lock, noting the green algae that thrived on the slippery-looking walls.

And his distraction was just the chance that Leonard Keating had been waiting for. From his position, crouched behind a thick but low hawthorn hedge, he stood up, manoeuvred the pole over the narrow towpath, and aimed it towards Gisela Ashley.

She was still lying on top of the boat, but was looking away to her left, watching as the walls of the lock slowly loomed over her on that side as the boat descended. A few moments more, and he wouldn't be able to touch her as she was lowered out of sight and out of reach.

Like a pole-vaulter, Leonard aimed the tip of the pole just below her waist, and thrust forward with all his upper-body strength.

Gisela felt a sudden hard, painful thump against her side. She cried out in pain and surprise. With a sickening lurch of her stomach she felt herself slithering off the *Swan*'s roof. She made a desperate scrabbling with her fingertips for something to hold on to, but there was nothing. Then she felt another push against her thigh, the force of it propelling her over the edge.

The lock, of course, was narrow, for like all locks, it was designed to take just a single boat — with very little spare room. She felt herself going over head first, and knew she wasn't going to be able to stop herself. She screamed Keefe's name. As she did so Leonard Keating ducked back behind the hedge and started to run, crouched over, the other way. It was hard to do so while dragging the cumbersome pole with him, but he needed to put some distance between them — and fast. Not that he was all that worried. He was sure that Keefe Ashleigh would be more concerned with trying to save the girl than in giving chase to him, even if the ex-soldier did spot him fleeing.

Gisela saw a strange kaleidoscope of colours for the briefest of moments — the pure white, sparkling side of the *Swan*, with the gay touches of orange and the deep glossy black as her trim; the dun-and-green colour of the river water that rushed up to meet her; and the darker brown, algae-dotted pattern that was the wall beside her.

If she'd tried to straighten up, or put out a foot, or do anything in order to try and get herself upright, she would almost certainly have broken some bones. The wall of the lock was unremitting brick, and the *Swan* herself was made of some hard stuff. And if she'd been bigger, too, she would have been in serious trouble indeed.

As it was, she simply slipped down the side of the boat like an eel and had just enough sense to stop screaming and close her mouth and eyes as she hit the water.

The water felt cold and alien, and she had felt herself begin to panic the moment she hit it. For although she could swim, she was in no position to do so. She had mere inches between herself and the wall, and herself and the boat. She couldn't move her arms or her feet in a swimming stroke, and for a few seconds, she had the horrific notion that she would simply embed herself head first into the grungy muddy bottom of the river and drown not in water but in silt.

But she never hit bottom, simply because the lock was still half-full, and by reaching out and touching the side of the *Swan*, she was able to pull herself forward, gradually going from upside down to horizontal, and then to face up. Her hands felt a ridge below the waterline of the boat, and she held on to it, just managing to get enough purchase on it to heave herself upright. As she did so, she had the absurd feeling that the boat had just saved her, and was lovingly urging her on. Then, the next moment, suddenly she felt the air on her face again. She opened her eyes, winced as some dirty water ran into them, then she closed them again and shook her head, like a dog might after having a swim.

She took a deep gulp of air, and heard herself whimper. She was beginning to shake, as much with shock as with the cold, but when she felt the *Swan* sway gently towards her, all but pushing her up against the wall, she realized that she'd been fearing the wrong thing.

It was not drowning that was the real danger. It was the likelihood of being crushed!

'Keefe!' she screamed again, knowing that with the sound of the water gushing out of the lock ahead, he probably couldn't hear her.

And nor could he.

But, after watching to see that the water was flowing well, Keefe had turned to look down at the boat — and frowned.

Gisela was no longer on top of the roof. Of course, she could have climbed down and gone below, but he didn't think she'd have had the time to do it.

'Gisela?' he called down, trying to duck and see inside the boat, but it was now so far below him that he couldn't see into the windows. Quickly, he walked across the lip of the lock, and saw a touch of scarlet down below in the water. The next instant he could see her clearly, pressed against the wall, the *Swan* swaying towards her.

He didn't panic; he simply thought furiously, then leaned over the edge and shouted down.

Try and bring your knees up!' he instructed her. He saw her pale face turn up to look at him. Her eyes lit up, but she didn't seem to understand his words.

'Try and bring your knees up against your chest!' he yelled again. 'The boat won't crush you if you can get some purchase against it. Do you understand?'

With a wave of relief he saw her blink, then nod. She stretched her arms out along the wall and tried to bring her knees up, as she'd been told. But it was hard. She was still floating in the water, for one thing, and her chin began to sink beneath the surface as she tried to do as she was told. Keefe cursed. He ran back across the lock and raced to the lock entrance, all but flinging himself down the slippery iron ladder and on to the aft deck of the boat.

There he grabbed the iron rings set in the stone wall nearest him and, planting his feet like a stubborn mule on the deck for purchase, he began to heave.

At first nothing seemed to happen but then the *Swan* began slowly to edge closer to the right-hand wall. Keefe gritted his teeth and heaved again, feeling every muscle and sinew in his arms and upper body begin to strain. Sweat popped out on his forehead and face as he continued to strain. At last he felt the *Swan* nudge the wall.

Over his shoulder, and not daring to let go of the metal ring, he shouted, 'Make your way to the back of the boat. It's all right, I'm holding her fast, she can't pin you to the wall, and the engine's off — you needn't worry about the propeller. But you've got to hurry!'

He felt his biceps begin to burn with the pain and effort of holding the boat still. He wasn't even sure that she'd heard him. And then, what felt like an eternity later, he heard her splashing about, and over his shoulder he saw the tips of her pale fingers edging along the side of the boat.

Seeing that, he let go of the ring and ran to the side, reaching down with both hands to grab her strongly by the upper arms. Then he pulled her up.

She came up easily, shaking, streaked with algae and smelling not at all sweet, but she was the loveliest sight he'd ever seen.

Without thinking he took her into his arms and held her tight.

Pressed against his strong chest, Gisela began to sob with reaction. 'Something p-pushed me in,' she said. 'I f-felt som-something hard against me, here.' She pulled away to show him, and Keefe looked down, clearly seeing the two bruises that were forming at her waist and thigh.

He cursed softly. 'It looks as if someone used a pole on you to push you off. Did you see who it was?'

Gisela shook her head. 'I was looking over the other side of the boat.'

Keefe nodded, and took charge. 'Right, a hot shower for you first. Come on.'

He picked her up and carried her carefully down the cramped stairs into the boat and towards the bathroom. There he ran the shower until it was warm and turned to look at her. 'Do you need help?' he asked softly, and she blushed and shook her head. 'OK. I'll go and finish getting the boat through the lock, then I'll moor up and be back. We've got some brandy in the drinks cupboard; I'll mix it up with some hot water and sugar and lemon.'

Gisela smiled and nodded, then gave a cry of alarm as she realized she was leaking muddy, smelly water on to the pristine carpet. Keefe followed her eyes down, then smiled and shook his head. 'Don't worry, I'll clean that up. You just get yourself warm again.' He turned, then looked back at her and added softly, 'I won't be far, and I won't leave you on your own. OK?'

She nodded again. When he was gone she managed with badly shaking hands to get out of her ruined clothes and step into the shower. The hot water was lovely, as was the scent of her shampoo. She washed her hair twice, then used conditioner, and soaped herself all over. Slowly, as she washed away the smell of the river, so she seemed to wash away most of the fear.

She felt the boat moving. Quickly she wrapped a towel around her wet hair and reached for a voluminous white terry robe. She tied it around her slender waist.

Then she gathered her dirty clothes together and put them into the hamper. She was still towelling her hair dry when she heard the murmur of the engines become still. She looked out of the window to see Keefe hammering in the stakes and tying off the ropes.

She looked up when he came down the stairs, and swallowed hard. 'You saved my life,' she said simply. 'Again.'

Keefe stopped dead in the centre of the room and looked at her. She looked amazing, with her hair wet and standing in little golden tufts across her delicate skull, her body bundled up shapelessly in what looked like a white tent. Her face was free of make-up and her eyes looked huge. She was no longer shivering, and she looked so damned brave, he wanted to go up to her and kiss it all better.

Something in his eyes must have given him away, for he saw her gaze darken, and something in the air between them shifted and began to pulsate. She took a step towards him.

His throat went dry.

'You're very young,' Keefe heard himself say. 'And I'm practically middle-aged.'

Gisela laughed softly and took another step towards him.

'I'm just a beat-up ex-soldier,' he warned her, but still she kept coming. 'I'm not even sure where I'll be living in a month from now,' he tried again. But each sentence was getting harder to say, and a voice was clamouring in the back of his head, screaming at him to be quiet.

He'd never wanted a woman as he wanted this one. Right now, in this moment.

Gisela was now close enough to him to lift her hand and trace her fingertips along the line of his jaw. He swallowed hard and made one last effort. 'You've had a shock. It can affect the way you think. I can't just take advan—'

Her finger moved along to his lips, and then silenced them. With her other hand, she reached down and untied the belt of her robe, letting it fall away, revealing her pale, slender body. Her breasts were small but perfectly shaped, Keefe noted, her nipples large rose-coloured buds that were beginning to stiffen. The golden triangle at her thighs was still moist with dewdrops from the shower and he felt his own loins harden.

Keefe groaned aloud. 'I'm not made out of stone, child,' he said gruffly, and Gisela scowled.

'I'm not a child. Can't you see that for yourself?' she said huskily and with a shrug of her shoulders, cast the robe on to the floor. 'Now stop being so damned chivalrous and take me to bed,' she demanded.

So Keefe did.

CHAPTER TEN

Keefe laid her down gently on the double bed, and would have stood upright again but, perhaps sensing that he was having second thoughts, Gisela quickly looped her arms around his neck to prevent his escape.

Their eyes sparking at each other, he smiled wryly. 'Are you sure you know what you're doing?' he rasped, and for reply, she let one of her hands drift down then back up again to roam underneath his T-shirt. Relishing the feel of his bare, warm, firm flesh against her palm, she sent her thumb and index finger to seek out and tweak one hard male nipple.

Keefe drew in his breath sharply, and in wordless demand, she tugged the bottom of his shirt upwards, and after a moment's hesitation, he obligingly put his arms up so that she could pull it off his head. His chest was lightly muscled with just a sprinkling of dark, curly hair; but her eyes darkened as they took in once more the criss-cross tracery of white scars on his skin.

'Do they hurt?' she whispered, running a fingertip along one large line.

'No. It hurt when I got them,' he admitted ruefully, 'but not now.' He wished, suddenly, that it was dark outside. At least then he'd be able to turn off a lamp so that she wouldn't have to see them.

'I'm glad,' she said softly, and he felt his breath catch as she leaned forward and kissed him where her fingertip had just been. He felt his eyes become hot, and he swallowed hoarsely, looking down tenderly at her bent head.

'You don't have to do that,' he said thickly. 'I know they're ugly.'

Slowly, Gisela withdrew her damp, golden head from his chest and looked him carefully in the eye. 'You really think that, don't you?' she asked softly.

Keefe looked at her, confused.

'Keefe Ashleigh,' she said softly, 'there's not an ugly mark on your body — or your soul. I know. I can tell. Now come here,' she said and pulled him down on top of her. For a moment, he rested his head against her breast, and his eyes feathered closed. Then he turned his head slightly and sucked one rosy nipple deep into his hot mouth. Gisela moaned slightly, her back arching off the bed.

She felt his hands, hard and capable, slide under her waist and suddenly she was half-sitting up in the bed, and his lips were on her throat, the column of her neck, nibbling on her ears, then tracing the delicate lines and sinews of her shoulders.

She closed her eyes in ecstasy and sighed deeply. When he laid her back on the bed, his hands went down to her ankles pulling them apart, and he kissed the soles of her feet, making her squirm and then giggle in delicious tickling eroticism. Then his lips began to move upwards, slowly and tormentingly tracing a path along her calves up to the tender, sensitive skin behind her knees. She felt her legs jerk in helpless response. And when she felt his tongue on her inner thighs, she tensed on the bed, her hands gripping the sheets on either side of her as his hot, seeking tongue at last found her centre and began mercilessly to tease her.

Her crashing cries echoed off the low ceiling and narrow walls of the *Stillwater Swan*, which bobbed gently at her anchor, as if in approval. When he stood, she felt suddenly cold and bereft, and she opened her eyes in protest, only to smile when she saw him shucking off his trousers and deck shoes.

He moved over her again, his dark eyes watching her every move for signs of withdrawal. Understanding what he was doing, and wanting to let him know in no uncertain terms that she was not going to change her mind, she slowly and languorously scissored her legs over his thighs. Then, holding his eyes in thrall to her own, she pulled him into her in one hard, sure thrust. She moaned and thrashed underneath him.

He began to stroke her with the hard core of himself, slowly at first, deep and easy, almost driving her wild. She heard herself begging him, almost cursing him, but then he was moving faster, pushing her higher, taking them both over the edge as their mouths fused, and their combined moans and breaths intermingled like a single feral animal.

When, at last, it was over, and he lay once more with his face on her breast, she absently stroked his back, her sensitive fingertips finding yet more ragged scars there.

But this time he didn't even think of them. Gisela smiled a slow, satisfied smile in the rays of the warm afternoon sun that slipped in through the *Swan*'s wide windows.

* * *

Rupert Rice-Jones drove into Marlow, and parked up at the first pub he came to. He needed to put the Ray family and that damned hotel far from his mind, so he was surprised and disgruntled to find that the first man he saw, when walking into the largely deserted bar, was Vin Ray.

He was about to back out and find another pub when Melisande's twin brother spotted him. Vin gave him a rather grim, bleary-eyed smile, followed by a half-hearted wave to encourage him over.

Rupert sighed and went. Vin's first words confirmed what he'd already suspected: he was well on the way to becoming drunk.

‘Rupe, old man, sit yerself down and I’ll get you anozzer.’

Rupert slid in beside the photographer, and eyed the glasses set up in front of him. It looked as if he’d been drinking vodka martinis for some time and, somewhat amused, Rupert ordered the same.

‘Not drinking at the Sunshine this ev’nin’ then?’ Vin slurred. ‘Thought it would take a pack of wild horses and all that to keep you away from my sister.’ If there was just a touch of unkindness in his words, Rupert chose to ignore it. He’d known Vin for years, and he wasn’t churlish by nature. Then again, Rupert had never known him the worse for drink either.

‘I don’t think I’m all that popular there at the moment,’ Rupert said, forcing himself to sound cheerful about it. ‘Your sister not only turned me down — yet again — but she seems to have found herself another admirer.’

As he spoke, he saw Vin Ray’s face darken. ‘Oh, don’t talk to me about Wendell bloody James,’ Vin said savagely. ‘I wish the bu’stard would just push-sh off and leave ush alone. Us Rays don’t need him in our lives again.’

He tossed off another vodka martini and slammed his glass down on the bar.

Intrigued now, and sensing that he might just have stumbled on a way to make trouble, Rupert smiled and ordered him another drink. ‘Really, Vin?’ he said glibly. ‘I didn’t realize you knew one another.’ He took the drinks from the barman and firmly steered Vin to a corner table. ‘Why don’t we sit down and console one another properly, huh?’ he said, pushing the vodka towards the younger man. ‘And you can tell Uncle Rupert all about it.’

* * *

The sun wasn’t quite setting yet, but was turning a more mellow shade of tangerine as a motorbike pulled up beside the *Swan*’s latest mooring spot just past the Caversham Lock in Reading. With a view of Fry’s Island, Keefe and Gisela were about to dine on board.

They'd done their shopping and restocked the cupboards, and had agreed that they didn't really want to spend any time in Reading. They would leave first thing in the morning to head towards the Oxford canal.

Little more than an hour previously, however, Keefe had heard from his friend, who now knocked on the door and peered inside. Keefe invited him on board.

Don Walton was a large man with a greying beard. Dressed in his black leathers, he often got mistaken for a Hell's Angel, much to the amusement of his fellow PhDs at Reading Laboratories.

He nodded shyly at Gisela, and when Keefe ushered him to one of the large padded sofas that lined the salon, he sank down gratefully. 'Beer?' Keefe offered.

'Better not. I don't want to lose my licence. I'm fine for a drink, anyway, mate.'

'Fair enough. So what have you got for us?' Keefe asked, moving to sit opposite him. He saw his friend cast Gisela a quick, worried look. He sighed gently. 'It's all right, Don. We're in this together.'

As if in emphasis, Gisela moved to sit beside Keefe and the two held hands. Their new intimacy and closeness shone out of them both like a beacon, and Don grinned widely. He was glad Keefe had found a lady at last. He'd sensed loneliness and aimlessness in his old friend whenever he'd visited him in hospital, but now all that was gone. In gratitude, he gave Gisela another wide, but still shy smile.

'Well, it was poisoned, as you thought, but with a concoction of easily available, non-prescription drugs,' he began, more confident now that he was on his home ground. 'It was very clever, really, since whoever did it wouldn't have had to sign any drugs register, or get on the radar at all. And the mixture was lethal all right. One glass of wine would have killed you both. The whole bottle — well, overkill really.'

Beside him, Keefe felt Gisela shiver, and he tightened his grip on her hand in encouragement.

'I've got all the info here.' He held out an official-looking envelope, embossed with the laboratory's name and postal and email addresses. 'Just give this to the Old Bill and they'll know what to do with it.'

Keefe smiled grimly. 'Don't worry, that'll be our next stop now that we have something concrete to show them. I can't thank you enough, Don, for this.'

Don Walton flushed and waved a meaty paw. 'Oh, that was nothing. If you need me for anything else, just let me know.'

Keefe rose and the two men shook hands. But this time, when Don left, there was no one on the riverbank to watch him go.

For when Keefe and Gisela took his evidence and walked to the nearest police station, Leonard Keating was back in the capital, buying a rifle.

* * *

Wendell James was used to working out of office hours, and when he pulled into the lane nearest his latest parcel of land, he was glad to see a dirty Range Rover already parked there.

It meant that his expert, who could only get away from a busy life perhaps one or two evenings a week, had already arrived.

He climbed out of his car, pausing to listen to a blackbird singing gloriously from a nearby rowan tree. On the five-barred country gate, a new PRIVATE PROPERTY — STRICTLY NO TRESPASSING sign had been attached, as per his instructions.

As he walked across the lush meadow the drone of insects was like an early lullaby and the sight of an imperial-looking curious emerald-green dragonfly, which dogged his walk across the grass, made him smile.

He spotted the lone figure near the river, and headed towards him at once. As he did so, out of the corner of his eye, he saw someone else emerge through a gap in the hedge on the far side of the field. He hadn't realized there was access from there, and supposed it was a rambler or someone from the nearby village taking a shortcut. He'd have to find out where the public footpaths went, and make sure to signpost them properly. Until he was ready, he didn't want any visitors on his land. Not until his expert had had a chance to give the site a good look-over and tell him whether or not his proposition for the site would be viable.

'Hey, Quinn,' Wendell said, holding out a hand in greeting as he approached the figure who was still staring into the river. The man who turned to face him was dressed in a rather dirty pair of grey-green shorts, with bare mosquito-bitten legs and old leather sandals. He wore an old Rolling Stones T-shirt, but his face was lean and lively with intelligence and his eyes were alert. Regardless of all the learned letters that he was entitled to use after his name, everyone knew him simply as Quinn. Wendell, in fact, didn't even know whether that was his first or his last name.

He'd known him for a long time, though, but had never really thought he'd have need to hire Quinn in a professional capacity, since his speciality was so far removed from Wendell's usual working world. A sentiment that his old friend obviously shared, as his opening words confirmed.

'Well, well, well, the concrete giant,' Quinn said, using his rather unkind nickname for Wendell, but without any real bite. 'You could have knocked me down with the proverbial feather when I got your call. Who'd have thunk it?'

Wendell smiled and nodded. 'Yes, yes, mock all you want. But what do you think?' He turned and held out his arms, encompassing the land all around him. 'Is it ideal, or what?'

Quinn nodded. 'From the quick scout around I've done, more ideal than "or what", I'd say. And have you noticed how spongy it is underneath?' he added, stamping down with his sandaled feet.

'A problem?' Wendell asked with a frown. Quinn grinned. 'For a hotelier, maybe,' he drawled. 'But for our purposes, ideal. We could even help it along a bit and have part of the site as marshland. Think elevated wooden walkways, with marshland species proliferating.'

'And the building itself?'

'Oh, over there in that far corner,' Quinn said, pointing to the other end of the field, not far from where the trespassing rambler was now stooping down and peering closely at something. 'It's the driest site, and the glass will have some natural screening from the tall hedges on two sides.'

'You don't want full sunlight then?' Wendell mused, somewhat surprised. Quinn shook his head. 'Too harsh.'

Wendell nodded, then frowned. 'What's that chap doing, can you tell?' he asked, still looking at the only other occupant of the meadow.

Quinn shrugged. 'Looks to me like he's taking a picture of something.'

Wendell sighed. 'Well, let's go and see what he's found so fascinating. And as we go, you can tell me what else has occurred to you that hasn't to me. And how much it's likely to cost me!'

Quinn grinned and obliged. By the time they'd reached the trespasser, Wendell was glad he'd decided to pay Quinn's rather large consulting fees. The man knew what he was doing, without any shadow of a doubt. The finished project should be spectacular.

As they approached him the trespasser heard them and straightened up, turning to watch them. He was indeed holding a camera, but both men noticed the eye-catching dog collar first. He had a thatch of white hair and twinkling, welcoming blue eyes. The reverend greeted them amiably. 'Hello there. Lovely evening.'

Wendell smiled. 'Yes. I see you're into photography?'

The churchman looked down at the camera in his hand and smiled ruefully. 'Well, not really. But I did want to take some pictures of these wonderful orchids just to give the troops something as a visual aid that they can rally around. I've already got some snaps of the fritillaries.'

'Yes, I noticed them earlier on,' Quinn said with enthusiasm. 'This meadow is particularly lush in native species. I don't think it's been extensively farmed in generations.'

Wendell coughed a warning. He didn't want any hint of his plans to leak out before he was ready. Quinn gave him an amused smile, but fell silent.

'You mentioned troops?' Wendell said softly, then listened with growing dismay mixed with humour as the reverend gentleman introduced himself, and amiably told the new owner of the meadow that he, and his Friends of Nature Society, would be making sure that he wasn't allowed to 'rape' the land.

Quinn began to laugh uproariously.

* * *

Inspector Paul Dane listened carefully as Keefe Ashleigh outlined the problem.

When they'd arrived at the station, the sergeant at the desk had steered them to an interview room, where they'd first talked to a young officer who introduced himself as Sergeant Mike Connell. He was a short man, not much over five feet seven, Keefe guessed, and had a mop of blond hair and rather large eyes. But for all that, there was an air of competent wariness about him of which Keefe had approved. And once the seriousness of their business became clear, Connell had quickly called in a superior officer.

Now they went over it all again for the tall, dark man who'd joined them. Although Keefe would have put him at around the forty-five mark, his eyes looked ages older.

When he mentioned Gisela's recent court appearance, Dane nodded to the blond sergeant, who left and returned a short while later with a note, which he handed over. Keefe knew that Connell had been checking up on that part of their story from their colleagues in High Wycombe, who had obviously confirmed it.

When Keefe told them about Don, and handed over the findings from the lab, Paul Dane read them carefully, his face becoming extremely grave.

'Well, I wish you'd come to us sooner, sir,' Paul Dane said, eyeing Keefe carefully. 'Perhaps then Miss Ashley could have been spared the ordeal in the lock.'

Gisela, who'd been mostly silent throughout, immediately leapt to Keefe's defence.

'That's not fair, Inspector,' she said firmly. 'Until then, we had nothing but suspicions to go on. The wasp could have died for any number of reasons, and Mrs Pride could have been speaking in the heat of the moment. Besides, if we had come to you sooner, with what little we had then, what could you have done?' Her chin lifted in challenge. 'You'd hardly have been able to offer us round-the-clock protection, would you?'

Mike Connell hid a smile and avoided looking his superior in the face. The feisty little blonde had obviously hit the nail right on the head, and Inspector Dane, knowing it, sighed heavily.

'Unfortunately no. We couldn't have spared the manpower needed on such little evidence. But now it's obvious that you've been seriously targeted. And I doubt, after two attempts, that this man is going to give up any time soon.'

Keefe nodded. 'I agree. Since I'm about to set up my own private security company, I'll carry on acting as Miss Ashley's bodyguard — that means you won't have to waste manpower watching over her safety, but can concentrate it on finding the man shadowing us. I think you'll agree that staying on the river, and the boat, is the best plan.'

Dane eyed Keefe with an amused smile. 'Yes. It means he'll either have to try to keep track of you by road — which will eventually trip him up — or follow you on the water, which will make him easier to spot. If he's following you by land, we'll soon have a list of car registration numbers that keep on showing up suspiciously wherever you are.'

'So you'll put two officers on a boat to follow us and try and spot any other boat doing the same?' Keefe guessed. Dane sighed heavily. He didn't like being second-guessed by the public — even one as well-qualified and heroic as this man Ashleigh.

'Yes, sir,' he agreed. He couldn't, after all, look a gift horse in the mouth. The budget was tight this quarter, and he knew his superiors wouldn't be able to give him all the manpower he really needed to see this new case through.

So they spent nearly an hour at the station, thrashing out the arrangements until both parties were satisfied. When the pretty blonde and her ex-soldier were gone, the two policemen remained in the interview room, making notes.

'What do you think, guv?' Connell asked. He'd worked on the inspector's team for nearly three years now. He liked him and trusted his judgement.

'Those two are an item,' Dane said. Connell grinned.

'No prizes for guessing that, guv. The young lady was fairly glowing.'

'Yes. It's obvious she trusts him, and he's just as obviously determined to look out for her. And he's eminently well-qualified to, according to his file.' He leaned back in his chair and shook his head. 'Let's just hope being up close and personal doesn't affect his cool head and judgement when the time comes,' Dane said darkly. 'The joker who dreamt up this poisonous concoction is no amateur.'

Connell nodded. 'It'll be good to get him behind bars then, won't it?' he said with grim cheerfulness. 'I bet once we get our hands on him, we'll be clearing up several unsolved murders and suspicious accidents.'

Dane smiled briefly. 'Then we'd better not slip up, Sergeant, had we?'

* * *

Wendell James pulled into the hotel car park and walked through the garden. He spotted her at once, sitting in a shady, rose-covered arbour, for once alone and not chatting to guests.

He walked over to her, and watched the way her eyes lit up on first seeing him, then the way her face closed down, hiding all that treasure behind shutters of polite interest.

The pain of it hit him. His fists clenched by his sides and he had to deliberately loosen them before he reached her. 'Melisande.' He said her name softly, his eyes running over her like a man in a desert spotting an oasis.

She was wearing a pale lilac sleeveless summer dress, with a delicate scoop neckline and a scalloped hem edged in silver. The slender straps on her shoulders were made of silver too, and small dangling silver earrings glinted like white fire among the more blazing colour of her hair.

'You look stunning, as ever,' he said, sitting beside her on the padded bench.

'Thank you,' she said quietly. 'Have you had a good day?'

Wendell, thinking of Quinn and his report, smiled widely. 'As a matter of fact, I have. Which reminds me — I ran into your pet Rottweiler today.'

Melisande blinked, not sure that she'd heard him correctly. Neither of them saw or heard Rupert Rice-Jones, who'd just taken up a position at a table and chair a few yards away. Hidden from view by a riotously flowering pink-and-yellow rose, which climbed the lattice walls of the arbour, he eavesdropped shamelessly.

'My what?' Melisande asked.

Wendell grinned. 'The rebellious reverend. He was at the meadow site today. Taking pictures, and informing me that he and his merry band of fellow greensters were going to picket me into submission. Or something along those lines.'

'Oh,' Melisande said. So Martha's green friends had already swung into action. That was faster than she'd imagined.

She shifted restlessly on the seat. 'I did try and warn you not to buy the land,' she said, casting a quick glance at him.

'Really I did. I kept trying to write you a note, but in the end, nothing I wrote sounded sincere, and I gave up.'

Wendell quirked up one dark eyebrow at her. 'Sounded like sour grapes did it?' he asked, understanding, and she smiled in relief.

'Yes. Just like it,' she agreed.

At his table, Rupert sneered to himself. How very civilized they were being. In fact, they were getting to sound downright cosy. He'd learned from Vin that afternoon just who Wendell James was, and that he was planning to build a hotel less than two miles away. So it didn't take a genius to guess what they were talking about. But for a man who'd just had a seriously effective pressure group sicced on to him by the object of his passion, he wasn't sounding particularly angry.

'It doesn't matter,' Wendell said softly.

Melisande half-turned in the seat and looked at him warily. 'Oh? You're so sure you can bulldoze all over them, are you? As well as a delightful meadow?' she asked, a touch of asperity in her voice now.

'No, that's not what I meant,' Wendell said quickly, then sighed. 'Look, let's not argue, shall we?'

Melisande bit her lip and looked away. He'd looked almost pleading there for a moment. 'Yes, you're right. I'm sorry. It's too beautiful an evening to spoil it,' she agreed. She wondered why she was so eager to meet him halfway, but suspected she already knew the answer to that. In spite of everything, she was falling for him.

She simply didn't know how to stop it from happening. Hell, she didn't even know how to make herself *want* to stop it from happening.

'Good. Then will you join me for dinner this evening?' he asked.

'I don't usually dine with guests,' Melisande said at once. Then she stiffened as she felt his finger on her chin. Slowly, she let him turn her face towards him, and her heart rate stuttered as his eyes met hers.

'But I'm not just a guest, am I, Melisande?' His eyes went to the slender column of her throat as she swallowed compulsively.

'No,' she felt herself being forced to admit, her voice both reluctant and breathless.

Wendell smiled a heartbreaking smile. Well, at least the admission was better than he could have hoped for. Now all he had to do was build on it, carefully and slowly. After having mishandled it all so badly in the beginning, he was now desperate to do things right.

'In an hour then?' he said. He reached for her hand and raised it to his mouth. He turned her hand over, palm upwards, and planted a kiss square in the middle, his lips warm and provocative against her sensitive skin.

Melisande caught her breath, and swallowed again.

At his table, Rupert felt his gorge rise. He needed to put a spoke in this wheel once and for all, and now, thanks to a drunk and very indiscreet Vin, he knew just how to do it.

Melisande watched as Wendell got up and walked away, then she jumped as another male figure loomed in the doorway of the arbour.

'Hello, darling girl,' Rupert said.

'Oh, Rupert,' Melisande said, her voice still shaky. 'Hello. Look, I have to go . . .' She needed breathing space badly and simply couldn't cope with Rupert now. She got up, but to her surprise, Rupert didn't step aside to let her pass.

Instead his voice sounded unusually grave as he said, almost diffidently, 'Look, Mel, old thing, I think there's something I need to tell you.'

She felt herself sitting back down in her seat with a bump, trying not to look as dismayed as she felt. If Rupert was about to tell her that he was going broke, or ask her for a loan, or maybe even put it to her that she put the hotel up as collateral in a joint business venture of theirs, she was going to have to let him down lightly.

But his first words took her totally by surprise.

'It's about that chap you were just, erm, talking to.'

Melisande felt her face flame. Surely he wasn't jealous? She didn't think she could bear it if Rupert tried to warn her off Wendell James. She didn't think her nerves could take it.

'Rupert,' she began warningly, but he was already sitting beside her. And again, his next words totally unbalanced her.

'I may be wrong, but from the way you're acting, I don't think you fully understand about the family history. You know — the bad blood that exists between the Rays and the Jameses.'

Melisande blinked and looked at him nonplussed. 'Rupert, what on earth are you talking about?'

Rupert hid a gleeful smile behind a sorrowful shake of his head and sighed deeply. Oh, this was going to be delicious. Such sweet, sweet revenge.

'No, I didn't think so,' he said sadly. 'It all happened while you were at uni. Somehow, I didn't think your father would tell you about it. But I thought Vin might have.'

Melisande felt herself go cold. 'Vin?' she said sharply. And all at once she remembered her twin's rather ambivalent reaction to Wendell James. All along, she'd felt that there was something her brother had been hiding from her. She'd even made a mental note to herself to find out what it was.

But now, when it seemed she *was* about to find out, she suddenly wasn't sure that she wanted to know. She felt sick, almost scared, as Rupert sighed once more. She almost opened her mouth to tell him to stop.

'I'm afraid it'll come as a bit of a shock, Mel,' Rupert warned her softly. 'But if you're, well, thinking of Wendell James the way you seem to be,' he shrugged helplessly, 'I think you should know the whole story. Especially as Wendell might have ulterior motives that have nothing to do with business. Oh yes, I know about his plans to build a hotel nearby. But it's nothing to do with that.'

Melisande took a long, slow breath and told herself not to be so feeble. If there was something going on, she needed to know about it. She couldn't become an ostrich and stick her head in the sand just because she was afraid of being hurt.

'What do you mean, an ulterior motive?' she forced herself to ask calmly. 'Really, Rupert,' she tried to make herself sound amused, and wasn't sure she quite succeeded, 'you make him sound like some sort of villain from a Victorian novel.'

'Oh no, my dear,' Rupert said, with oily, sweet, false pity. 'I'm afraid it's not Wendell who's the villain of *this* piece.'

And he went on to tell her all that Vin had told him earlier on, spilling the bile in careful, devastating drops.

When he'd finished, and oh-so-solicitously and tactfully left her alone, Melisande Ray was white and trembling and on the verge of tears.

It explained so much about Wendell, about the sudden anger she'd sometimes sensed in him. It even explained his determination to see the Ray of Sunshine ruined. It also explained why he seemed so determined to seduce her.

Oh yes, it explained so much.

And it hurt, oh so much more.

CHAPTER ELEVEN

Melisande, after what felt like hours, eventually roused herself from the arbour. She felt cold and curiously remote, and as she made her way to the kitchens to tell the sisters that she wasn't well and wouldn't be overseeing dinner that night, she realized that she was suffering all the symptoms of shock.

The cooks were duly sympathetic, commented on her pallor and told her to get herself to bed. Melisande didn't argue but, on her way through the hall, waylaid one of the waitresses and told her to deliver a message to Wendell James that she wouldn't be able to join him for dinner that night after all.

The maid, who knew that Melisande never dined with individual guests, looked surprised. When Melisande told her to further inform Mr James that she'd been called out of the hotel on business, she looked even more startled. Sensing romance, or at least intrigue, she went into the dining room to discuss matters with her friends.

Upstairs, in her room, Melisande locked the door and, still in a daze, undressed and climbed naked under the summer duvet. There she lay shivering and sometimes weeping into the early hours of the night, when an exhausted sleep overtook her at last.

* * *

It was nearly dawn when Leonard Keating returned to the *Skylark II* and carefully unpacked the lightweight aluminium case he'd just purchased for rather more money than he'd wanted to pay for it. Ma Pride had given him a flat — albeit generous — rate for the job, and he fretted grimly that the rifle inside the case had better be worth the expense.

It took an hour or so to familiarize himself with the weapon, clean, check and test it. He supposed he could consider it an investment, if he could find a good enough place to hide it between assignments. So long as he left no fingerprints or any residue of himself on it, it shouldn't be that risky — even in the unlikely event that it was found and the police got hold of it.

Sighing, he disassembled the rifle and repacked it into its case. He now needed a quiet place somewhere where he could practise with it.

Luckily, there were lots of quiet woods in this area of Berkshire and south Oxfordshire that would fit the bill.

* * *

Detective Constable Will Proctor was not yet twenty-five, but had already passed his sergeant boards, and was only waiting for a spot to open up in order to be promoted. He was a tall, lean man with dark hair and was something of an amateur long-distance runner. His ambition was to someday win the London marathon. A local lad, he'd been as pleased as punch when the sergeant he worked with, a grey-haired, twenty-year veteran of the Berkshire police called Charlie Bolton, had been chosen for the job of babysitting the couple whose lives were thought to be in danger.

Will liked the river, and at school had even been on the rowing team. Unlike Charlie, who wasn't happy with water, he now piloted the small cabin cruiser with a bright smile.

It was barely eight o'clock in the morning, and the merest traces of a lingering mist still clung to the water, although the morning sun was quickly chasing it away.

Sitting in the back of the boat and trying to look like a tourist, Charlie stared around gloomily. It had been decided very early on that Will would do whatever needed doing with the boat, while Charlie used his eyes and ears to see if they could spot 'Chummy', as Charlie insisted on calling him.

Inspector Dane had briefed them thoroughly on their assignment yesterday, and when Will spotted the long, elegant form of the white barge moored just up ahead, he turned from his position at the wheel, and nodded at Charlie. 'The ex-soldier told the guv he'd be heading towards Whitchurch-on-Thames this morning, but they've not started off yet.'

Charlie nodded back. 'Just pass 'em by and then moor up just around the next bend. I'll double back and keep an eye on them with the binoculars. You stay on board this floating palace and make a note of all the boats you see. Take pictures too — plenty of 'em. The brass like that,' he advised with a slightly cynical smile.

Will, who'd been given a rather smart digital camera just before setting out, nodded happily. After years walking the beat and dealing with the often grisly aftermath of RTAs, this assignment to catch an underworld hired killer in the act was a touch of the real thing at last. And he was determined not to screw it up.

* * *

On board the *Stillwater Swan*, Keefe Ashleigh saw the small cruiser go by. He checked the name of it — *Lucy Lou* — and gave a mental nod. He'd been told by Inspector Dane last night the name of the boat the police had hired for the duration, and now he eyed the two men on board as it passed.

The man piloting it was young and fit-looking, while the man in the back was older and obviously experienced. It was, he thought, a good combination, and he was glad the police were taking the threat seriously.

He only hoped it wouldn't take long to find the thug who'd been hired to kill Gisela, and — more important — before he had the chance to try another hit.

Although she'd slept deeply and well last night, curled up in his arms like a contented kitten, Keefe felt restless and edgy. He had good instincts, and something told him that things were coming to a head.

He watched the undercover police cruiser head a little further upriver, and then turned and smiled easily as he heard her moving behind him.

'Up at last then, lazybones?' he asked lightly, turning to smile at her. 'And what would madam like for breakfast?'

Gisela laughed, and shrugged. 'Whatever sir is cooking,' she said cheekily.

She watched him set about making an herb omelette, wondering what would happen once Ma Pride's hired killer was caught and put away.

Would she see Keefe again?

She knew she'd aroused all his protective instincts, and while right now she knew nothing would prise him from her side, would he still want her once she was no longer the maiden in distress?

It was a chilling thought, but it brought home to her how little she knew about this man. He was currently rootless, looking for a new home, a new job and a new life. And for the last few glorious days, their time aboard the *Stillwater Swan* had been like something from a fairy tale — a life of enchantment on a magical river, complete with a Prince Charming and even a villain. But had she been foolishly optimistic to think that, once the journey was over, she and Keefe Ashleigh would build that brand-new future of his together?

Was she taking too much for granted?

As he turned, frying pan in hand to slip her omelette on to a warm plate, she forced the thought aside, and smiled at him in thanks. But Keefe caught the wistful, worried look in her eyes, and felt himself tensing all over again.

He'd be glad once she was safe. But then, of course, she'd no longer need him.

He turned and, blank-faced, began to whip up his own eggs.

Gisela stared at his tense back, and forced herself to eat her breakfast.

* * *

Melisande awoke with a headache, and with the raging certainty that she needed to see Wendell's mother. She was the only one who could answer all her questions and either confirm or deny what Rupert had told her last evening.

She got out of bed, relieved to find that her curious feeling of detachment had passed. Instead she felt a low-level hum of dread, which made her feel wooden and clumsy.

She showered and put her hair up in a loose chignon, then dressed in a pair of cream slacks with a horizontally striped top in deep red, orange and cream. She put on a little make-up and a pair of red canvas shoes.

She sneaked out through the back entrance of the hotel, avoiding her office, where she could hear Gina busily typing at her keyboard, and also the kitchens, where the sisters were amiably arguing over the best recipe for kedgeree.

She breathed a sigh of relief when she made it to the car park unnoticed, and slipped behind the wheel of her nippy, maroon-coloured Mazda. It wasn't until she was on the open road and heading towards Windsor that she realized she hadn't the faintest idea where she might find Wendell's mother.

She might not even be alive, or she might be living in Kathmandu, for all Melisande knew.

* * *

Leonard Keating walked through the small copse and spent a good hour simply looking and watching. After ten minutes, he saw a tractor trundle through a field down below, and then disappear over the rise into the next field. A herd of cows in the field opposite shifted about in search of the best grazing, but there was no road visible, and nobody came walking a dog.

Satisfied at last, he got out the rifle, assembled it, and set up his target — a plain piece of old blackboard with a rough round target, consisting of an inner and outer ring.

It took him nearly an hour to get the rifle sighting the way he wanted it. It always annoyed and amused him, in equal measure, whenever he went to the cinema and saw the black-clad, cool-as-a-cucumber assassin get out a rifle, bolt it into place, and with one perfectly executed shot, kill the president of the United States or the Russian spy or whatever.

It simply didn't work like that.

But after a few hours, he was sure he had the rifle working to his satisfaction, and therefore he would not disassemble it again. He'd missed the target more than hit it to begin with, but by the time he'd finished, he was satisfied that his hand and eye were in working conjunction.

He would not, after all, be shooting Gisela Ashley from any great distance, and with the high-penetration bullets he'd purchased, a kill was assured with almost any body shot. He was not stupid enough to try for a head shot. After all, dead was dead. Leonard did not, and never had, thought of himself as any kind of an artist. A messy but fatal bullet to the chest was good enough to get the job done, and that was all that concerned him.

* * *

Melisande smiled at the receptionist at the Windsor branch of James Leisure and gave a sigh. 'Hello, I was hoping you could help me.'

The receptionist, a middle-aged, well-preserved woman with a neat cut of black hair, smiled back with a professional, non-committal smile. 'I'm sure I'll do my best. But if you want an appointment to see any of the senior staff today, I'm afraid you're out of luck. They'll be in meetings all day.'

Melisande laughed. 'Oh nothing so ambitious as that, I promise. I'm a freelance journalist specializing in the leisure industry and I was wondering if it would be possible to set up an interview with Mr Wendell's mother.'

The receptionist blinked. 'His mother? Not with Mr James himself?'

Melisande grinned. 'Oh no. I'm sure Mr James has given many interviews, and I'm not sure I could sell another one to the upmarket magazines I prefer to deal with. No, I was looking for a different angle — a mother's pride, that sort of thing. There isn't a problem, is there?' She tried to look suddenly concerned and interested. 'Mother and son aren't estranged or anything, are they?'

The receptionist, mindful of the need to avoid any kind of negative publicity, was quick to rebut such a thought. Obviously, she was not going to give out Janet James's address or personal details, but she did agree to give her a call to see if she would be willing to talk to a journalist.

Melisande smiled gratefully, and sauntered around the impressive lobby of the office building, giving the receptionist time to do her magic.

Although what she'd do next if Janet James refused to be 'interviewed' she didn't know.

* * *

Sergeant Charlie Bolton put the binoculars down and walked quickly back towards the boat. The *Stillwater Swan*'s engines had just come on, and it was obvious that the couple were on the move.

He was careful not to run or draw any attention to himself, because he knew that, just as they were looking out to try and spot the assassin, the assassin was probably keeping a wary lookout as well. He must know that Keefe and Gisela were on to him, and might reasonably have expected them to have gone to the police by now.

In fact, there was nothing to say that he hadn't been scared off permanently, in which case they were all wasting their time. But Charlie didn't think so. In his experience, hired killers were nothing if not persistent. After all, they needed to maintain an excellent reputation for getting the job done, or the commissions would pretty soon dry up.

Besides, he was banking on the assassin not being aware of just how much evidence they already had on him. He could, Charlie mused, be reasonably sure that the bottle of wine he'd poisoned was still on board, and had simply not been opened yet. And he'd made sure that Gisela hadn't seen him when he'd pushed her off the boat. No, he reckoned that the killer would be fairly confident that, even if the couple *had* gone to the police, they wouldn't have had enough to go on to justify an operation such as the one that was now in place.

Or so Charlie hoped.

On board the *Lucy Lou*, Will saw the sergeant coming back, and quickly started up the engines.

* * *

Melisande had to stop to ask for directions twice before she eventually found the leafy suburb where Janet James lived.

After the receptionist had succeeded in getting in touch with her, she had passed the telephone over to Melisande, who, feeling each lie sticking to her tongue like glue, had nevertheless managed to get out her spiel. Perhaps because she'd been feeling guilty about her deception, she'd written down Janet James's directions to her house wrongly.

So it was that she was nearly twenty minutes late when she pulled up in front of a smart, detached Victorian villa in a street lined with flowering cherry trees. But now that she'd arrived, Melisande felt the heavy weight on her press down even further. She had no idea what to expect from now on.

In her dream scenario, Janet James would rebut everything Rupert had told her, and she'd leave here not feeling as though her world had come crashing down around her after all. A slightly more realistic scenario had Mrs James confirming Rupert's words, but in a more gentle, less devastating way.

But what if Janet James did neither of those things? What would she do then?

But first things first. Melisande took a deep breath and opened the charming wrought-iron gate, went through, walking up a front garden full of early spring blooms, and pressed her finger on the doorbell.

Before she did anything else, she'd have to explain to Janet James about her subterfuge in posing as a journalist. And that couldn't help matters much either.

* * *

Leonard wrapped the rifle in a large bath towel and walked with it back to his parked car, where he was careful to lay it flat in the back of the boot.

Once back at his mooring spot, he was a little annoyed to see that the *Stillwater Swan* had already left, but he supposed it didn't really matter. He knew where they were headed, and he'd soon catch them up.

He carefully checked all the river traffic — both the moored boats and those passing — as he got under way. But nothing looked suspicious and nobody took any notice of him. Furthermore nobody followed him, either by river or on land, and he was sure he'd be able to spot any sign of the Old Bill, should they be around.

He'd decided he was going to make his hit that evening, if Keefe and the girl followed their usual habit of dining on the towpath — providing they were in an isolated spot of course, which they seemed to prefer. He was going to make the hit from right here, on board the *Skylark II*, then simply motor past and turn the boat in at the prearranged marina and disappear back to the smoke.

He'd be glad to finally get it over with.

* * *

Melisande tensed as the door opened in front of her. A slender woman in her late sixties with pure white hair and a striking, handsome face looked back at her.

'Miss Johnson?' Janet James asked, and Melisande, after a momentary hesitation, nodded. It was the name she'd given to the receptionist, knowing that Janet James would probably have had good reason to pause if given the name of 'Ray'. She bit her lip with shame as the other woman smiled brightly and stood aside to let her pass.

'Please, go on through into the sunroom. I practically live in there during the summer months. Can I get you some lemonade? I made it fresh this morning.'

Melisande nodded miserably, and followed her hostess through to a large orangery, which was decked out with comfortably padded patio furniture, an old sideboard and a large iron table.

'I must say, I was rather intrigued by your idea,' Janet James said, darting into the kitchen and then coming back with a tray. She sat down opposite Melisande.

'Yes, about that,' Melisande said, anxious to confess her sins and get them out of the way. 'I'm afraid that was a . . . a bit of a fib.'

Janet James's clear eyes sharpened on her quickly, and a small frown tugged her silver brows into a V-shaped furrow. 'Oh?'

'Yes,' Melisande said, swallowing hard. 'I'm afraid I'm not a journalist. And my name isn't Johnson either. But I needed, quite desperately, to see you, and I didn't know of any way of finding you, let alone getting you to talk to me.'

Janet James looked at the younger woman thoughtfully. Being what most people would describe as 'elderly', and having a stranger in her house who had just admitted to gaining admittance by false pretences, she supposed she should be feeling more alarmed than she actually was. After all, the woman might, for instance, be creating a distraction for a partner to slip in and attempt a burglary.

But Janet didn't think so.

The beautiful young lady opposite her looked strained and pale, and Janet instinctively knew that she was suffering. And she'd never been able to see people in pain without wanting to help.

'Perhaps you'd better just tell me about it,' she advised softly.

Melisande took a slow, deep breath, and said, 'My name's Melisande Ray.'

Janet James stared back at her in dismay, and said simply, 'Oh!'

* * *

Sergeant Bolton glanced back over his shoulder and saw, nearly a quarter of a mile away, the prow of the *Stillwater Swan* come into view.

'OK, Will, there they are. Now remember, you've got to keep this distance between us. Think you can do it?'

It had been decided last night, in the meeting with Inspector Dane, that he and Proctor would shadow the *Stillwater Swan* not from behind, but from the front. This unusual situation wouldn't have been possible on the road of course, because of the speeds involved, and all the possible side roads and other variations. But on a river, which only flowed between two banks, and with the four miles per hour speed limit of the canal barge, it should be a snip.

Furthermore, Inspector Dane and Charlie agreed that the assassin was more likely to follow from behind, and would thus be less likely to spot the *Lucy Lou* as a potential threat.

'Oh, I can keep the distance all right,' Will Bolton said now, 'but it's gonna look kinda funny, Sarge.'

'Funny?' Charlie Bolton said, looking back at the youngster. He might have known there'd be a problem of some kind. The moment he'd been given the assignment and realized that a boat was involved, he'd felt his heart plunge. He'd never understood the fascination some people had with messing about on the river.

'What kind of problem?' he asked ominously.

'Well, this is a faster boat, Sarge. It's gonna look kind of odd, us keeping up the same slow speed as the *Swan,*' Will pointed out.

Charlie cursed under his breath. Damn it, they should have thought of that before. If the assassin wasn't keeping watch on his quarry from the river, but was checking in on them from wherever the river was in sight of the road or other public-access areas, then the *Lucy Lou*, dawdling along like a tortoise, was going to stand out like a sore thumb.

'I've got an idea though, Sarge,' Will said, demonstrating one of the reasons why he'd just won his promotion. With a grin, the younger man reached into the cabin and came out with a fishing rod. 'I brought it along in case we needed a cover for hanging around. Just dangle that over the side. Fish expect a worm to be caught in the current, so we can tow it along with us, so long as we don't go too fast. That way, if anyone sees us, they'll just assume we're going so slow in order not to give the game away to the fish.'

Charlie Bolton picked the rod up gingerly and blinked at it. He'd never gone fishing in his life. Will Proctor hid a grin. 'The maggots are in the tin, Sarge,' he said helpfully. 'Of course, it would help our cover if you could actually catch a roach or two. Maybe a dace, or even a chub.'

Charlie shot the youngster a savage scowl.

* * *

'I'm sorry to just spring it on you like this,' Melisande said, leaning forward a little in her chair. 'But, like I said, I needed to speak to you.'

Janet James sighed heavily. 'This is something to do with my son booking in to your hotel, isn't it?' she questioned. 'I knew that nothing good could come of that.'

Melisande shrugged. 'Well, I daresay that'll come into it somewhere,' she agreed wearily. 'I mean, I know he's bought some land just a few miles away, and means to build a hotel there,' she added. 'But that's not what I want to talk to you about.'

Janet James sighed again. 'No. I don't suppose it is. It's about your father, yes?'

Melisande felt a giant fist clench inside her, and, unknowingly, her already tense pale face went an even whiter shade. 'Yes. Just last night I heard something that . . . well, I didn't know what to make of it. You see, I now own the hotel — my father left it to me when he died.' She paused, then shook her head. 'I don't know why I mentioned that. This has nothing to do with the hotel. This is something someone told me about my father. Something I find so hard to believe.' Her voice cracked a little, and she cleared her throat, horrified to feel hot tears seep into her eyes. She forced them back ruthlessly. 'And if it's true, I need to know about it.'

Janet shifted abruptly on her seat. The young woman sitting in her orangery looked on the edge of tears, and her distress was palpable. It had been many years now since Janet had wept her own hot and bitter tears of regret and recrimination, and she hated to see it all being dragged back into the here and now.

It was all so futile.

And this young woman, who was so totally innocent of it all, should surely have been spared.

'Did Wendell talk to you?' Janet James asked grimly. 'Because if he has, I'll scalp that young man when I see him.'

Melisande blinked. 'Oh no. It wasn't Wendell who told me. Actually my brother Vin is back in town — he's a wildlife photographer, and is usually away globetrotting. But when he came to visit me, and saw Wendell, I realized from his behaviour that something was, well, off.'

Janet relaxed slightly. 'Oh. So it was he who told you?'

Melisande opened her mouth to say that no, that wasn't exactly how it was, but then left the words unsaid. After all, what did it really matter who had told her or why?

Melisande was not naive, and she knew that Rupert probably hadn't been feeling quite so benign and solicitous as he'd been making out. It was her one ray of hope that he'd been out-and-out lying as well, but the more she talked to this woman, the more she doubted that that was the case.

'Is it true?' Melisande at last plucked up the courage to ask, watching the older woman with big, wide, hurting eyes.

Janet leaned forward, playing for time, and poured them both a glass of lemonade. 'I suppose that depends on what, exactly, you were told.'

Melisande licked her lips that had gone suddenly dry. 'Did my father have an affair with your daughter?' she asked flatly.

'Judith?' Janet said her daughter's name softly. 'Yes.' She glanced across to the sideboard, and, following her glance, Melisande saw an array of framed family photographs arranged there.

She spotted Wendell easily, both as a uniformed schoolboy of about fifteen or so, then one of him in his early twenties. Then she looked along to the most recent. Sharing space with him was the photograph of a man in his fifties, a handsome man, with the same dark Irish looks as Wendell, whom she took to be his father. There were several of a lovely girl with long black hair and blue eyes, who she knew must be Judith.

'Judith was just twenty when she met your father,' Janet said softly.

'This was back in the mid-nineties, when I was away at university?' Melisande croaked.

'Yes, it must have been,' Janet confirmed.

'My mother had been dead for a few years then,' Melisande said.

Janet James sighed and took a sip of lemonade. 'I lost my husband nearly ten years ago now,' she said. 'And I know how lonely it can be. The first few years are just a daze. Nothing is the same, and you think it never will be. Then the raw pain begins to abate a bit, and you begin to feel simply lost. Rudderless. Suddenly the future's spread out before you, and your mate is gone, and what are you supposed to do with the rest of your life? I can understand how your father must have felt when Judith came into his life. They were both adults, after all.'

Nervously, Melisande took a sip of lemonade and let her eyes wander back to the photographs. She realized that there wasn't one there of Judith as an older adult.

She understood that they weren't over the worst of it yet. Not by a long shot.

'Did Judith fall pregnant by my father, Mrs James?' she whispered, and Janet turned her face quickly away. Even now, after all these years, the pain of it could still catch her unawares.

'Yes. Well, let's be honest,' Janet said, forcing herself to meet Melisande Ray's unhappy eyes. 'Nobody has any need to become pregnant nowadays unless they want to. And I think Judith did want to.'

Melisande swallowed hard. 'I was told that my father . . . my father tried to force her to have an abortion,' she got out painfully, and almost sobbed with relief as Janet sat bolt upright, looking angry.

'No, that's not true,' she said forcefully. 'Gareth offered to pay for an abortion, yes, if Judith wanted one. But she didn't. That was never an option for her, although . . .' Janet suddenly slumped back in her chair, and ran a hand over her face. 'Although I wish now that Judy *had* done so.'

Again Melisande's eyes darted to the photograph of Judith James.

'They died, didn't they?' she said softly, and Janet nodded.

'Yes. Judith died in childbirth, and the baby — a boy — lived for just three hours after that.'

At last Melisande felt the hot tears spill over her face. Wordlessly, she reached into her bag for a Kleenex.

Janet James took a deep breath and sighed. 'Judith, well, Judy had problems. With drugs, I mean, as a teenager. We, her father and I, had no idea.' Janet laughed grimly. 'Well, aren't parents always the last to know?' she asked bitterly.

Melisande blinked, then said softly, 'I'm sorry. I had no idea.'

Janet shrugged helplessly. 'I daresay it began with her taking something at the teenage parties she went to. Ecstasy or whatever. That's how it usually happens, isn't it? And then the drugs got progressively harder, and she took them more often, until, well, she was an addict. It was Wendell, funnily enough, who first realized the danger. He came to us and we confronted her, and got her to admit it. This was just after her eighteenth birthday. We got her into rehab, but it didn't take, and she had something of a breakdown. Then she went back on drugs and nearly died, and I think that was a bit of a wake-up call for her. We got her into rehab for a second time, and that time it seemed to work.'

Janet James's sad voice faltered for a moment, and then carried wearily on. 'The doctors tried to warn us that the drugs had taken their toll on her — both physically as well as emotionally and mentally. But when she seemed to rally and get her life back together, I suppose none of us wanted to face any more bad news. She went back to college to study fine art, and then she met your father. To be honest, I think we were a bit worried that he was so much older, and Wendell really didn't like it, but after talking it over, Francis and I — that's my late husband — decided that perhaps it wasn't such a bad thing after all. I mean, your father was a respectable widower, and we thought that perhaps Judith needed someone older and wiser to give her life more stability.'

Janet sighed. 'But then she became pregnant.'

Melisande closed her eyes briefly. 'My father must have realized how vulnerable she was,' she said painfully. 'He must have known that she couldn't be expected to cope like other women.'

'Oh, I don't think he knew,' Janet James said, with devastating simplicity. 'I was sure Judith never mentioned it to him, and, well, we didn't either. I'm not saying we were ashamed of her or anything like that,' she added hastily, turning to look at the photograph of her late daughter. 'I think we just didn't want to jinx her and her new chance of happiness by talking about her past. And you have to understand, it wasn't as if Judith looked or acted like the walking wounded or anything. She was young and vibrant and full of life. She had mood swings, of course, and I think your father came to be worried about them, but it wasn't as if she wore a sign around her neck carrying a warning sign that she was delicate or vulnerable. And she could be very wayward when she wanted her own way. I think she decided that she wanted to be a mother, and wanted to have a normal life, and in your father she saw a way of getting it.'

Janet shook her head. 'But she wasn't strong enough. The pregnancy was hard, and she had to spend a lot of her time in the hospital. That depressed her. Plus they had to be wary of what drugs they gave her, and she sometimes got hysterical and refused to take any medication at all. And that didn't help. It wasn't . . .' Janet braced her shoulders, then carried on. 'I think it wasn't really a surprise to us when the worst happened. The doctors had been hinting at trouble ahead for some time, but . . . well, you don't think of tragedy on that scale actually happening to you, do you?'

Melisande swallowed hard and shook her head. 'No,' she said gruffly. 'You don't.'

'I know Gareth was devastated when she died,' Janet continued. 'We were all at the hospital that afternoon, waiting for news of her. The doctors wouldn't allow any of us in the delivery room. Francis and I, Wendell, who'd been called back from some important meeting in the United States, and your father; we were all there, pacing around. But we knew, as soon as we saw the doctor's face, that it was dreadful news. But for a little while, at least, the baby was alive, and we all crowded around that tiny bundle of life, in that little glass incubator, willing him to live but . . . it was just no use.'

Janet's voice faded with defeat and Melisande felt more tears falling down her cheeks.

'So I had another brother,' she said softly. 'At least for a few hours.'

'Your father named him Thomas David,' Janet whispered. And then added kindly, 'We had him buried with his mother. Do you want to see their grave?'

Melisande nodded her head wordlessly.

CHAPTER TWELVE

Leonard Keating overtook the *Stillwater Swan* at just gone 2.30 in the afternoon. He was relieved to see Gisela Ashley at the wheel, and he was careful to avoid her eye as he went past, looking over the side of his boat furthest from her, as if checking for entanglements or obstacles.

When he pulled ahead around the next bend he put on a little more speed. He knew at which distances he felt comfortable using the rifle, and after a while, he cut the engine back again.

Up ahead, he noticed a little cruiser, a few years older and a bit more battered than his own boat. As he got closer, he could read the name of the boat on the stern. The *Lucy Lou.* On board her were what looked to be a father and son team, for a young man was steering while an older geezer sat on the back, dangling a fishing rod into the water.

On board the *Lucy Lou,* Charlie Bolton stared at the top of the gently bobbing orange float malevolently. Will had had to put the maggot on the hook for him several times now, as river weed kept pulling it off. He'd been pretending to fish for nearly two solid hours and was bored out of his mind. How people did this for pleasure, he didn't know.

When he noticed the nice-looking cabin cruiser coming up behind them, his eyes sharpened at once. He could only see one male on board, but of course, that didn't mean he didn't have someone down below. He was careful not to give it more than a passing interested glance. After all, if it *was* the man they were after, he didn't want him getting cold feet.

He returned his eyes to the float and saw it beginning to waggle. 'Huh, you don't fool me, you stupid piece of plastic,' he muttered. When he'd first seen the float do that same dance, he'd felt a little shaft of excitement, only for it to turn to disgust when he rapidly and clumsily reeled in the line to find nothing more than lime-green river weed on the hook.

Will Proctor had nearly laughed himself sick. Now Charlie hauled on the reel as Will had shown him, and nearly fell off his deckchair in shock when he felt a definite hard tug of resistance.

Instantly, the boredom of the assignment left him. 'Will! Will!' he yelled with genuine surprise and delight. 'I've got a bugger! At long last. It feels like a big 'un too.'

His happy voice floated clearly across the still, quiet air, and Leonard Keating gave a scornful grin. From the fuss the old man was making, you'd have thought he'd hooked a marlin. As he overtook them, the son powered the boat down and went to help his old man by reaching out for a landing net.

'Keep the line tight,' he heard the younger man say loudly as he passed. 'Or you'll lose it. Look, there it is. Looks like a dace.'

Leonard, no fisherman, wondered idly if dace were edible. On the back of the *Lucy Lou*, Will Proctor said quietly, 'Did you see him?'

And cunning Charlie Bolton whispered back, 'Yes, I did. And I couldn't see anyone else below decks either.'

Will caught on at once. 'From what I've seen of all the other boats about, it's been mostly couples or families. I can't remember many single males.'

Charlie made a big show of landing the fish, using the opportunity to bend over the catch to slew his glance forward to the rear of the passing boat.

'*Skylark II*,' he muttered. 'There have been the odd one or two boats handled by lone men, but I reckon most of them live on the river. You can tell by their boats; they've got a lived-in look. But that one looks like a rental to me. No homey touches or obvious knick-knacks in the windows.'

'You think he could be our man?' Will asked, sounding young and excited now.

Charlie smiled grimly. 'Could be. We'll see how far ahead of us he gets.'

'Right, Sarge. Now, shall I show you how to unhook a fish?' Will asked, and Charlie said something unprintable.

* * *

Melisande drove slowly and carefully back to the hotel. After parking in a shady spot, she walked off across the gardens to a spot beneath a stand of weeping willows set in a little dip back from the river. She had to push her way through the trailing fronds of lush greenery, which reminded her of those beaded curtains you sometimes saw, and she stood with her back against the trunk, taking slow, deep breaths.

The afternoon was hot, and damselflies flew in and out of the reeds at the river edge. A slow lapping sound from the river a few yards away complemented the tune of a song thrush in a holly bush, and a light breeze sounded in the leaves around her.

Somehow, having felt the curtain of greenery behind her move, she wasn't surprised when he was suddenly standing beside her.

'I noticed your car, and saw you come down this way,' Wendell said simply. 'I hope you don't mind if I join you. I've got something to tell you, something I think you'll be pleased to hear.'

Melisande turned to look at him, seeing him as if for the first time. 'Oh?' she said softly.

'It's about the hotel site,' he said, and he saw her gaze flicker. 'Except it's not,' he added confusingly. 'A hotel site,

I mean. I've decided not to build a James Leisure hotel there. Instead, I'm going to build a butterfly house, and turn the land into a mini nature reserve.' Melisande gazed at him, frowning slightly, but saying nothing.

'I've had an eco-expert look at it, a friend of mine called Quinn. He reckons, properly managed, it can be a haven for wetland and wildfowl species. I hope to use the revenue from the butterfly house to keep it self-sufficient. It'll also provide another attraction for your customers. It should help the Ray of Sunshine, not hinder it.'

Still Melisande said nothing, and Wendell shifted restlessly beside her.

'I hoped you'd be pleased,' he said at last, sounding deflated. It was his big gesture, his last hope at apology and reconciliation, but it seemed to be falling flat. 'Look, I know I got this all wrong,' he ploughed on. 'Us, I mean. At first, I was determined to treat you as if you were nothing special. I think,' he took a deep breath, determined to be strictly honest with her, 'I think that you scared me a bit. My attraction to you was so strong and instant, I needed to convince myself that I was mistaken. I was determined to think of you as just . . .' he trailed off and shrugged helplessly.

'Just another one of your women?' Melisande said, sounding faintly amused rather than scandalized or hurt.

Wendell looked at her sharply. He was wearing a pair of black slacks with white deck shoes and a plain white shirt, open at the neck, with the sleeves rolled back to his elbows. Dark hairs matted his powerful forearms, and Melisande felt the usual tug of desire as she felt his blue eyes looking down at her.

'Yes,' he agreed wryly. 'But of course, that didn't last long. It was obvious from the start that I was falling for you. And then I realized who you were.'

'Yes,' Melisande said. And that had changed everything. 'You realized I was Melisande Ray. Daughter of your enemy.' She heard him draw his breath in harshly, and carried on determinedly, 'That is how you think of my father, isn't it? After what happened to Judith?'

Wendell went very still. 'I didn't think you knew about that,' he said at last, sounding puzzled. 'In fact, I was sure you didn't. I knew your brother knew, but from your total lack of reaction around me, right from the beginning, I was sure you weren't aware of our family's joint history.'

'I wasn't,' she said simply. 'I was away at university when your sister and my father were . . . together. I'm so sorry about Judith, Wendell,' she said. 'I learned about it only last night. And I went to see your mother today.'

Wendell blinked at that news, then said, 'I see. Who told you?'

'It doesn't matter. Your mother took me to their grave. Today I found and lost a brother all in the space of a few minutes.'

Wendell moved restlessly.

'You blame my father for what happened, don't you?' Melisande said, turning to face him, feeling her heart begin to ache. What happened in the next few minutes would determine her fate for the rest of her life. And it scared her. 'Please be honest. It's important.'

Wendell nodded. 'I did blame him, yes,' he agreed. 'I suppose, looking back on it, I *wanted* someone to blame. Judy was young and so fragile. I felt as if I'd let her down, failed as a big brother to look out for her. And your father was a convenient scapegoat. An older man who seduced her and then let her down.'

'He couldn't have stopped her from dying,' Melisande said sadly. 'Nobody could. Not you, or your mother, or my father.'

'No. I know. Deep down, I've always known that. Even so, I resented the Rays. I resented your father still having his grown-up children, and his precious hotel, and his life intact, while my sister was dead at twenty-one.' Melisande winced at the raw hurt and anger still clearly audible in his voice.

'So when you saw a chance to hurt the Ray family, you took it,' she said simply.

Wendell grimaced. 'Doesn't sound very noble does it? But yes, I think I did. Oh, I didn't go out of my way to do so. All these years, I'd almost forgotten about Gareth Ray. But then that land came up for sale, and I just couldn't resist it.'

'So you came here, booked into the Sunshine, and started to make your plans.'

Wendell suddenly laughed. 'And got my comeuppance in no uncertain terms,' he added ironically. 'While you were still a gorgeous maid, or a rather naughty hostess, I could still make believe that I could have my cake and eat it too. But once I realized who you were, the whole house of cards I'd built up came crashing down around me. I saw how much your customers valued this place. I saw how genuinely warm and welcoming the atmosphere was here. More than that, I saw how much you loved it and what you did. It wasn't just a hotel, it was your home. Your life. And the more I watched you, the more I understood how wonderful you are. And I realized that no man could raise such a daughter and still be the villain I needed him to be.'

Melisande swallowed hard. So she was in with a chance. Her heart thundered in her breast, and she felt herself teetering on the brink.

'So you decided not to go ahead with the rival hotel because you had a guilty conscience?' she asked quietly.

Wendell smiled grimly. 'Not quite. I'm still a businessman, and there are some people who'd tell you that I have no conscience to be troubled. No,' he shrugged and moved to stand right in front of her, his hands hanging loosely by his side, looking and feeling vulnerable for probably the first time since he'd been a boy, 'I decided I couldn't build the hotel because it would hurt you. And hurting you had become unthinkable.'

He took a slow, shaky breath. 'You see, I love you, Melisande Ray,' he said softly.

And with a cry that was part sob, part joy, Melisande stepped into his waiting open arms.

* * *

On the river, Charlie Bolton reached for his mobile phone and keyed in Keefe Ashleigh's mobile number.

'Ashleigh.' On board the *Swan*, Keefe flicked open his phone and spoke briskly.

'Sir, this is Sergeant Bolton. I'd like you to moor up for the day, if you would. Can you find a convenient spot?'

Keefe, who was sitting in the salon, glanced up the stairs through the open doorway, to where he could see Gisela's beautiful legs as she stood at the tiller. 'I daresay we can. It's a bit early though. You have something?'

'Maybe,' Bolton said cautiously. 'It'd help us to be sure if you moor up.'

Keefe's eyes narrowed. It didn't take him long to figure it out. The two coppers in the boat ahead had spotted something suspicious, either a craft or a person, and they wanted to see what effect the change in the *Swan's* apparent routine had on them.

'In which case, we'll moor up the next good spot we see. You're in visual range?'

'Just about,' Charlie Bolton said, and after a few more words, hung up.

Keefe went up the stairs and joined Gisela on the rear deck, glancing around. They were in deep countryside, with a large field off to their left full of growing barley. Cattle grazed in a field lined by a thick hawthorn hedge to their right.

'Let's moor up here, shall we?' Keefe said, and Gisela, who'd been enjoying her spell at the helm, looked at him in surprise, then glanced at her watch. 'It's not four yet. It's a bit early, isn't it?'

Keefe shrugged. 'We're in no hurry, right?' He wasn't going to tell her why he wanted them to stop so soon. 'Why don't you go below for a bit? It's getting really hot anyway, and you don't want to burn.'

Gisela shot him a quick, questioning look and bit her lip. 'All right.' She powered back the engine and turned the *Swan* towards the bank. Keefe leapt lithely off, hammered in the mooring stakes and tied her up.

About 150 yards away, Charlie and Will watched the white narrowboat pull into the side, and looked upstream. The cabin cruiser was out of sight.

'Think it'll come back?' Will asked tightly.

'Maybe,' Charlie said cautiously. 'More likely Chummy, if it *is* Chummy, will tie her up and walk back on foot to see what's happening. Which means we can't be caught moored up so close. We might as well hang a big sign around our necks saying 'Guardian Cops'. So just motor along at a very steady rate and see if we can spot the *Skylark*.'

'And if we do?'

Charlie smiled. 'Just go right on past her. Then we'll call for backup.'

'And if the *Skylark's* not in sight?'

Charlie sighed glumly. 'Then he's not our man and I'll have to do some more bloody fishing.'

* * *

Wendell reached up and carefully pulled out the pins in Melisande's tresses, letting them fall around her like a shimmering curtain.

Slowly and with one accord, they sank down, lying on the cool, sweet-scented grass. The weeping-willow fronds around them shielded them from the view of the outside world. He looked down into her luminous grey eyes, his breath catching at their stunning, gentle beauty. 'Do you think we can start again?' he murmured.

For answer, Melisande ran her fingers through the raven locks at his temples before pulling his head down to hers. At long last their lips met. She pushed her hands through the opening in his shirt and let her fingertips explore the smooth hard planes of his back, the hard-ribbed expanse of his stomach, and the warm firm muscles of his shoulders. Wendell's body leapt in response to her handling and, against her lips, she felt him gasp.

Wendell lifted his head to look down at her, her Titian hair spread around her like fire against the cool green grass.

Her striped top had ridden up from her slacks, and he bent his head to dip his tongue hard into her navel, as if prospecting for gold. Melisande cried out in response. Instead liquid heat flooded into the centre of her, and her legs fell apart, feeling weak and heavy.

Slipping the top up her body, he watched her raise her arms to help it slide off, and then his dark blue eyes deepened to sapphire as he looked down at the revealed beauty. Slowly, his dark head lowered and Melisande's eyes feathered closed as his lips began to explore her pale, tender breasts.

The first touch of his hot seeking mouth made her tremble beneath him, and a moan sounded low in her throat.

* * *

On the river, Leonard Keating sat on the back of his boat, which he'd moored just in front of a bridge, and stared through his binoculars. He glanced at his watch. Damn it, it was nearly a quarter past four. Where were they? He'd been keeping meticulous notes on their routine, and always before they'd ridden the boat until between 5.30 and 6, before mooring and starting on their barbecue dinner. He couldn't have got that far ahead of them.

Sighing, he set off back on foot to see where they'd got to.

After walking for about ten minutes, he saw the father and son team aboard the *Lucy Lou* gently chugging their way towards him. The old man was still on the back of the boat and still fishing. The son was wearing a pair of headphones, and his head was bobbing up and down in time to some unheard music.

Leonard barely cast them a glance as they passed.

Will, whose earphones had no music pumping through them, steered on casually. Then, once he was sure they were out of earshot, and still facing forward, he said softly, 'I think that was him.'

'Yeah, me too,' Charlie Bolton agreed. 'Can you see his boat?'

'I think it's just up ahead. There's a white cabin cruiser tied up just before the next bridge.'

'Perfect. Steer us under the bridge, then see if you can tuck this tub up just the other side, so that it can't be seen by Chummy when he comes back. Think you can do that?'

With his hands tensing on the wheel, and a mixture of dread and excitement coursing through him, Will said softly, 'I'll do my best, Sarge.'

* * *

Melisande gasped, her back arching as Wendell's hands slipped around her waist, his knuckles grazing the grass beneath her as his hands tugged on the waistband of her slacks. She lifted her rounded derriere further off the ground and felt the dappled mix of warm sunshine and shadow caress her bare legs as he pulled her feet free of the garment.

She was now lying naked, not far from the river or her hotel, with a man who'd said he loved her. She had no idea whether or not he meant it. She had no idea what the future held. For once, she was not in control of her life, or the moment, or her emotions, or even her body.

And it felt wonderful.

Wendell James stared down at the beautiful woman he knew he didn't deserve, and ran a hand along one long, slender, pale leg. His eyes went to the fiery red triangle at the meeting of her thighs and his sapphire eyes turned almost black. He growled low in his throat, and Melisande heard her heartbeat roar in her ears. When she felt his naked body move across hers, his hard, slightly hirsute legs pushing hers aside, her eyes flew open.

'Wendell,' she said, his name a sigh and maybe a curse, a question and a plea.

And then he was inside her, hot and strong and hard, and her fiery femininity was engulfing him, pulling him in further, clenching and claiming her territory. He gave a harsh, compulsive cry, and their lips met and fused.

Melisande's bare feet ached into the grass, her toes digging into the soft, slightly cool ground. The rest of her felt on fire, as they plunged and drew apart, only to plunge together again. She felt her fingernails raking his back and heard herself cry out his name, which spurred him on to stroke faster and harder, deeper and faster, until Melisande cried out again, flinging her head back, her throat taut and exposed to his ravishing lips.

* * *

Keefe's phone rang again. They were in the galley, preparing the vegetables for their evening meal — carrots that would be glazed in honey and roasted in the oven, and mangetout, which he'd steam for just ten minutes after the steaks were nearly done. He reached for the phone casually, his eyes on Gisela's blonde head, which was bent over the carrots she was scraping.

'Ashleigh.'

'I think it may be on,' Charlie Bolton said grimly. 'You know the procedure.'

Keefe did.

* * *

Leonard Keating swore as he saw that the *Stillwater Swan* was moored up ahead. He quickly turned and began to walk back the other way when he saw the ex-soldier emerge from the back with a couple of deckchairs. For some reason they were eating early. Perhaps they wanted to eat first, then head for either Streatley or Goring for a late night out.

If so, their plans were going to be rudely interrupted. He moved quickly back to his boat, which it didn't take him long to turn round and head back.

From behind the grey walls of the bridge, Charlie and Will watched this procedure.

'It really is him, isn't it?' Will said, his voice tight with tension.

'Looks like it,' Charlie said, with a bit more caution. But in his bones, he knew they'd found Chummy. And that he was about to make his move. And Charlie didn't think backup would arrive in time. He swore softly underneath his breath, then reached for his phone and pressed redial.

On the towpath, Gisela looked up from the trestle table she was setting up as Keefe's mobile rang yet again. She heard him answer, listen, and say absolutely nothing. He hung up a few moments later.

She felt slightly sick and her heart rate began to soar. So this was it, then. Her hands began to shake as she tried to lay the knives and forks in place, but a moment later she felt his comforting presence beside her and his hands moved over hers, helping her set the table.

'I won't let anything happen to you,' Keefe said softly. 'Just promise me you'll do as I say, when I say it.'

Gisela swallowed hard and nodded.

She wasn't sure she could have spoken, even if her life depended on it. Then, realizing what she'd just thought, she had to bite back the hysterical desire to laugh.

* * *

Leonard Keating turned the boat yet again, the better to make a getaway once the deed was done. The *Skylark II* was now lying just off the turning in a slight bend, providing him with ample cover. The gleaming white barge that was the *Stillwater Swan* lay more than 200 yards behind him, on the opposite side of the river. He thought it unlikely that anyone on board would have noticed him or the fact that he'd turned his boat. And even if they had, so what?

It was nearly over now. Leonard was anxious to get the job done and be gone. There wasn't another boat in sight, the nearest road could just be heard but definitely not seen, and there was not a farm worker or dog-walker in sight. It was now or never.

He went below and removed the rifle from the towel. Then he opened the window on the side of the boat facing the far bank, and carefully knelt on the padded seat beneath it, looking back towards the *Swan*.

The angle was a little bit acute, but it was manageable.

Behind the hedge on the other side of the river, Will and Charlie crouched as they heard the scraping of the window. Charlie found a gap in the hedge and looked through. And swore viciously.

'What?' Will whispered.

'The bastard's got a rifle and he's moored on the other side of the river. The nearest bridge is back where we left the boat. Forget it. He's already sighting them up. We're out of time. Will, son, I hope you can swim,' he said grimly. 'Come on, back this way as fast as you can.'

So saying, he began to backtrack until he found a thin patch of the hedge. Chancing a quick look over the top, he realized that if Chummy looked back down this way, he'd spot them the instant they broke cover. But he was sure that the man with the rifle would be looking the other way, watching the *Stillwater Swan* and the young couple, whom he could just make out setting up their dinner camp on the towpath.

'All right. We need to get in the water without any splashing, and get across to the other side as fast as we can,' Charlie said urgently. 'So it's the breaststroke for us. Once there, you go to the back and get on board — try not to rock the boat if you can help it. After that, it's up to you. Play it by ear.'

Will, his face tense, nodded. 'What about you?'

'Me? I'm going to swim up alongside the boat until I'm right under that window. Unless I miss my guess, he's going to take a shot from where he is.'

Will swallowed hard. 'Right, Sarge.'

'OK. Take off your shoes.' The two men bent and kicked off their footwear.

'Right. On the count of three then. Crouch down, and slip in as quiet as you can. And remember, no splashing.'

Charlie looked at the young man beside him, a mixture of pride and anger warring inside him. He knew that if Inspector Dane had known that firearms were likely to be involved, they'd have had specialist manpower on hand to help. But there was no use wishing an armed response unit would magically appear. It was up to them.

'OK. One.' He reached into his pocket and pulled out his phone, hitting the send button as he did so. 'Two.' He left his phone in the grass by the hedge, confident that the warning message had winged its way to the ex-soldier. He took a deep breath. 'Three.'

The two men pushed their way through the hedge, hunched down and slipped feet first into the River Thames.

Will's breath rasped in shock. Even for a hot May day, the water felt cold. But he didn't hesitate. With a strong, smooth breaststroke, the fit and brave young man headed across the water at an angle, his gaze fixed resolutely on the stern of the *Skylark II.*

Beside him, not quite so fit, but also pulling away strongly, Charlie Bolton headed for the window of the boat. Even as he did so, he saw the long black barrel poke out even further from the window, seeking a comfortable resting place on the top of the frame.

Abruptly, the adrenalin flooded through him. Now he could only pray that he or Will would be in time. And that Keefe Ashleigh's soldiering instincts didn't let him down.

* * *

Lying in his arms, her heated body slowly cooling under the dappled green curtain of the surrounding trees, Melisande turned and looked at her lover's profile. With one fingertip she traced it, as if learning Braille. The smooth curve of his forehead, the hard straight sweep of his nose, that funny little tender dip, then the padded firmness of his lips. Last of all her fingers traced the uncompromising line of his jaw.

Obeying her wordless command, he too rolled on to his side and now they were face to face, cheeks pressed into the grass, grey eyes meeting blue.

'So what happens now?' she asked.

Wendell James smiled gently. 'Whatever you want, my darling,' he said softly. 'Whatever you want.'

* * *

Keefe glanced down as his phone vibrated in his pocket. He surreptitiously eased it out and opened it up. He glanced down at the text message, and took in the single word in a flash.

NOW.

He took the two or three steps that brought him right next to Gisela, and said quietly, 'Lie down in front of me. Curl up in a ball, knees tucked as tight to your chin as you can, arms over your head.' Whatever happened next, it was the safest position for her to be in.

Gisela cast a single, frightened blue-eyed gaze his way then dropped to the ground, curling up into a tight ball of misery. In front of her, Keefe dropped on to his haunches, tucking his head down. And as he did so, he felt a familiar feeling creep up his spine. It was a feeling he'd only ever felt a few times before, but he knew it instantly from the patrols and the reconnaissance missions he'd done during his time in the army. Someone, somewhere, was watching him. And that someone had a gun, almost certainly a sniper's rifle, trained on his back.

On the ground in front of him, Gisela looked up at him, her eyes widening. She couldn't lose this man. She simply couldn't.

Their eyes locked, and, incredibly, Keefe Ashleigh smiled.

To the man in the boat moored up the river, it looked as if the ex-soldier was hunching down in front of the barbecue to light it, and Leonard Keating cursed softly. He had him in his sights now, but would have preferred it if he'd been standing upright. It would have given him a bigger target of body mass to go for.

He hesitated, wondering whether or not to wait. How long would it take to light the barbecue? On the other hand, he had the man's bent back firmly in the middle of his cross-hairs. Leonard didn't think he would miss if he pulled the trigger now.

But what if he did?

Again he hesitated, knowing it was both stupid and incredibly amateur to dither like this.

He didn't know it, but it was especially stupid in this case, since it gave a certain Sergeant Charlie Bolton time to finish his swim and come up beneath him, unseen in the khaki water.

Even as Leonard made up his mind and decided to pull the trigger, Charlie Bolton reached up with his right hand. As he did so, he felt the boat move sharply to the left, and realized that young Will had just pulled himself on board.

He realized that Chummy must have felt it too, for from the boat, he heard a brief exclamation, and the barrel of the rifle started to move and withdraw.

Oh no you don't, Charlie thought. Quickly he reached up and snatched the barrel of the rifle in his hand.

As he did so, Leonard Keating heard a rushing sound of feet behind him. His finger tightened compulsively on the trigger.

The rifle gave a single, deadly *crack* of sound.

As it did so, several things happened at once.

Charlie Bolton swore and quickly let go of the rifle barrel, which was now hot, and had recoiled against the top of the window, giving his hand a painful smash.

Will Proctor gave a yell of triumph and launched himself on Leonard Keating, who, totally unprepared, found himself thrown to the floor beneath the fit young rugby player. He felt his arms being twisted behind his back and the cold feel of steel handcuffs being slipped over his wrists.

On the towpath, Keefe Ashleigh threw himself bodily over Gisela's trembling form, tucking his arms around her, totally concealing every bit of her underneath himself. There he lay for several seconds, seconds which felt like hours, as he assimilated what was happening.

He knew he wasn't hit. There was no pain, no shock, no punch of stunning contact.

Beneath him, Gisela whimpered, then cried out, the sound unmistakably that of a heart breaking. Understanding it at once, Keefe began to stroke her hair.

'It's all right, sweetheart. Everything's all right. I'm not hurt. Neither are you. Just stay still and wait. Do you understand?'

He felt her head nod beneath his hands, and he risked a quick glance over his shoulder. But there was little to see. Then, what seemed like hours later, he felt the phone vibrate in his pocket. He flipped it out and gave a shout of triumph as he read the three words printed there.

WE GOT HIM!

* * *

It was the next day before Gisela and Keefe were eventually able to leave the police station and return to the *Stillwater Swan*. In that time a lot had happened.

A white-faced Inspector Dane had arrested and charged Leonard Keating with two counts of attempted murder. He'd recommended both Charlie Bolton and a pleased-as-punch Will Proctor for gallantry awards. In London Ma Pride had been arrested after Leonard Keating had grassed her up in the vain hope of receiving a lesser sentence. And Gisela had spent hours on the phone with a hoarse-voiced but fast recovering Andrea Gormley, bringing her incredulous, flu-ridden friend up to date on her 'relaxing' holiday. She had promised that when she returned to High Wycombe she'd introduce her to Keefe Ashleigh.

But now, as Gisela stood inside the *Stillwater Swan,* gazing out at the peaceful scene of grazing cattle, she wondered whether she was going to be able to keep that promise, after all. For behind her, Keefe Ashleigh was packing his bags.

'So you're leaving,' she said softly.

Keefe nodded. 'I've still got a house to find and buy, and a business to set up,' he said matter-of-factly. But leaving her was agony.

Gisela nodded, still staring out the window. 'Will you marry me?' she asked.

And all movement behind her suddenly ceased.

She turned and looked at him, crossing her arms somewhat defensively over her breasts. She was wearing a buttercup-yellow summer dress, and she appeared small and wary as she looked across at him.

'Feel free to say no,' she said, looking at his startled face, 'but for some time now, I've had the feeling that you want me, but that you've been holding back. Probably out of some chivalrous notion that you're too old for me, or those damned scars of yours make a difference, or worse, that you think what I feel for you is gratitude and not love at all.'

She took a deep breath, and Keefe blinked, still frozen in place.

'Oh, I daresay you've got your reasons for doing so,' Gisela swept on. 'I mean, let's face it, the past few days have been pretty fraught, and I know you've had far more experience of this sort of thing than I have. And I imagine it *would* be easy for someone in my position to think of you as her hero, and get all caught up in the moment and mistake relief and desire and so on for something that it isn't.' She paused to take another much-needed breath.

Standing a few steps away from her, Keefe Ashleigh felt his heart began to pound.

'But I know myself pretty well, Keefe, and I know what I feel. And I know I love you, and I want to marry you, and I'd like to pick out a house with you, and in time fill it with children. Four at least. Well, maybe not four. Three. Two girls and a boy, although of course we've got to take what comes and . . .'

Keefe strode across to her and picked her up and kissed her, ending her flow of nervous words.

With a little sigh Gisela snuggled against him and kissed him back. When they were finished, he gently set her back down on the floor.

'Are you sure?' he said, looking down into her wide, brimming, beaming blue eyes. 'I mean, really sure? Perhaps we should take it nice and slow. Have a long engagement. Give you plenty of time to back out.'

In his voice still lingered a last vestige of doubt, and it made her heart ache.

Gisela forced herself to shrug nonchalantly. 'We can be engaged for twenty years if you like,' she said simply. And let her eyes promise it all. *You won't be getting rid of me, even then,* they sparkled up at him.

And he felt the last of the weight float free of his shoulders, leaving him looking almost boyish with delight.

'Well, perhaps not twenty,' he said mischievously, mimicking her earlier rush of words. 'Maybe ten. Or five, or perhaps . . .'

And Gisela stretched up to kiss him.

* * *

Later, the *Stillwater Swan* rocked gently at her mooring, her hull resounding to the murmur of muffled cries of human happiness and desire and she seemed to almost sigh with approval. Her maiden voyage had come to an end.

THE END

AUTHOR'S NOTE

While every effort has been made to be accurate in the descriptions of the River Thames and its environs during the writing of this novel, in the interests of dramatic narration certain liberties have been taken! Therefore any reader familiar with the country covered in *An Oxford Trial* might be surprised to find themselves going through a non-existent lock, or suddenly thrust into deserted countryside where they might reasonably expect to find at least a semblance of human activity.

ALSO BY FAITH MARTIN

DI HILLARY GREENE SERIES

Book 1: MURDER ON THE OXFORD CANAL
Book 2: MURDER AT THE UNIVERSITY
Book 3: MURDER OF THE BRIDE
Book 4: MURDER IN THE VILLAGE
Book 5: MURDER IN THE FAMILY
Book 6: MURDER AT HOME
Book 7: MURDER IN THE MEADOW
Book 8: MURDER IN THE MANSION
Book 9: MURDER IN THE GARDEN
Book 10: MURDER BY FIRE
Book 11: MURDER AT WORK
Book 12: MURDER NEVER RETIRES
Book 13: MURDER OF A LOVER
Book 14: MURDER NEVER MISSES
Book 15: MURDER AT MIDNIGHT
Book 16: MURDER IN MIND
Book 17: HILLARY'S FINAL CASE
Book 18: HILLARY'S BACK

JENNY STARLING MYSTERIES

Book 1: THE BIRTHDAY MYSTERY
Book 2: THE WINTER MYSTERY
Book 3: THE RIVERBOAT MYSTERY
Book 4: THE CASTLE MYSTERY
Book 5: THE OXFORD MYSTERY
Book 6: THE TEATIME MYSTERY
Book 7: THE COUNTRY INN MYSTERY

MONICA NOBLE MYSTERIES

Book 1: THE VICARAGE MURDER
Book 2: THE FLOWER SHOW MURDER
Book 3: THE MANOR HOUSE MURDER

GREAT READS
THE LYING GAME
AN OXFORD REVENGE
AN OXFORD SCANDAL
AN OXFORD ENEMY
AN OXFORD SECRET
AN OXFORD FRAUD
AN OXFORD TRIAL

More coming soon!

FREE KINDLE BOOKS

Do you love mysteries, historical fiction and romance? Join 1,000s of readers enjoying great books through our mailing list. You'll get new releases and great deals every week from one of the UK's leading independent publishers.

Join today, and you'll get your first bargain book this month!

www.joffebooks.com

Follow us on Facebook, Twitter and Instagram

@joffebooks

Thank you for reading this book. If you enjoyed it please leave feedback on Amazon or Goodreads, and if there is anything we missed or you have a question about, then please get in touch. The author and publishing team appreciate your feedback and time reading this book.

We're very grateful to eagle-eyed readers who take the time to contact us. Please send any errors you find to corrections@joffebooks.com. We'll get them fixed ASAP.

Printed in Great Britain
by Amazon

82560967R00130